Sing A New Song

a novel

ANN PURDY

© Copyright 2005 Ann Purdy.
All rights reserved. No part of this publication may be reproduced, stored in a retrieval system, or transmitted, in any form or by any means, electronic, mechanical, photocopying, recording, or otherwise, without the written prior permission of the author.

Cover Art and Sketches by Angela Dow
Bayside Brushtrokes – Ellsworth, Maine

Note for Librarians: A cataloguing record for this book is available from Library and Archives Canada at www.collectionscanada.ca/amicus/index-e.html
ISBN 1-4120-5692-6

Printed in Victoria, BC, Canada. Printed on paper with minimum 30% recycled fibre. Trafford's print shop runs on "green energy" from solar, wind and other environmentally-friendly power sources.

TRAFFORD
PUBLISHING

Offices in Canada, USA, Ireland and UK
This book was published *on-demand* in cooperation with Trafford Publishing. On-demand publishing is a unique process and service of making a book available for retail sale to the public taking advantage of on-demand manufacturing and Internet marketing. On-demand publishing includes promotions, retail sales, manufacturing, order fulfilment, accounting and collecting royalties on behalf of the author.

Book sales for North America and international:
Trafford Publishing, 6E–2333 Government St.,
Victoria, BC v8t 4p4 CANADA
phone 250 383 6864 (toll-free 1 888 232 4444)
fax 250 383 6804; email to orders@trafford.com
Book sales in Europe:
Trafford Publishing (UK) Limited, 9 Park End Street, 2nd Floor
Oxford, UK ox1 1hh UNITED KINGDOM
phone 44 (0)1865 722 113 (local rate 0845 230 9601)
facsimile 44 (0)1865 722 868; info.uk@trafford.com
Order online at:
trafford.com/05-0590

10 9 8 7 6 5 4

Acknowledgments

These are the people to whom I am grateful for their kindness, love, patience and encouragement.

David Richardson, friend, teacher, editor. His expertise has made this novel better.

Angela Dow for her insightful interpretation in designing and creating the art for the cover.

Those who listened and encouraged when I spoke of the writing process: my college English professor, my therapist, members of the church, friends, relatives, and neighbors.

Gord Bain who read a first draft out loud to his wife, Vi.

Tricia, Jill, Phoebe, Nancy, Linda, Trudy, Susan and Angela who read subsequent drafts.

All the children who bring joy into my world especially Denny, Kelsey, Cameron, Ethan and Brian.

Our many friends who live and work on Prince Edward Island.

My family: Charlie, my stepfather, a generous and kind man who has loved me as though I were his own; Vida, my mother, in whom I saw the leprechaun; and Buzz, my husband, whose support has been consistent and genuine.

While this novel is a work of fiction, all place names are real as are a few of the characters. However, their role in this novel is purely a figment of my imagination. To them I am deeply grateful for their inspiration and guidance: Ernest MacDonald who turned 102 in the year 2005; Susan, my best friend, who continues to write about the wildlife communities in the salt marsh behind her home; Casey and Katie, both beloved pets of friends. Cedar Dunes Provincial Park, The West Point Lighthouse, the Seaweed Pie Café and the North Cape Wind Farm are worth a visit or two.

Dedicated to Vida, my mother,
the one who loved me,
unconditionally.

and to

Ernest MacDonald, a man of 102 years,
who, back in the day, paid for his lobster boat
with one day's catch.

♪♪♪

I waited patiently for the Lord;
he inclined to me and heard
my cry.
He drew me up from the
desolate pit,
out of the miry bog,
and set my feet upon a rock,
making my steps secure.
He put a new song in my mouth,
a song of praise to our God.
Many will see and fear,
and put their trust in the
Lord.

Psalm 40:1-3

Prologue

Life had changed suddenly that cold October morning. All the busyness of the previous few years halted abruptly with the heart attack, as though there had been no other life than that one of uncertainty and dread. As my husband slipped into unconsciousness, so did I, unable to remember anyone's name or what happened. I could think only of him and pray and get angry with God who had been so good to both of us...up until that moment. Why? Why now? Why any time?

My younger brother Tom arrived just a few moments after I was told that my husband would not regain consciousness. He stayed with me in the Coronary Care Unit that painfully long night as we listened to the sounds of life ebbing from the man I had loved for twenty years. When the morning sun woke us, confusion, then death, entered the room.

The funeral was difficult. The church pews were crowded with people that I was supposed to recognize but couldn't remember. Friends and relatives hugged me and cried over me, pulled at my arms, pushed cards into my hands, and said a lot of words that didn't make much sense. I tried so very hard to listen to everyone and to acknowledge them, mindlessly shaking hands with some and hugging others, as my thoughts wandered back to the early days of our marriage. Mercifully, the consummate love we had shared for twenty years sustained the strength and courage it took to smile pleasantly at each one who wanted to tell me, "It will be all right." How on earth did they know that? I was so tired, and so angry.

Tom, and his two daughters, walked with me down the aisle and out of the church into the afternoon sun, where we slid into the back seat of the black limousine waiting there to carry us to the cemetery. "This is a universal sight," I thought. "Those driving by us in cars and those watching from behind their draperies all know where we're going and why. We have just celebrated my husband's life and who he was for all of us. Now we must give him back to God; but that is so hard to do."

The service at the cemetery was brief. I stood at the edge of the grave, shaking with emotion, until Tom indicated with a slight pressure on my arm that the time had come to depart. I do not remember the solemn ride to the home my husband and I had designed and built. When I stepped through the front door, I swallowed the familiar words of greeting he and I had exchanged each evening as we returned from work.

Susan, who had taken care of every detail for the after-funeral reception, rushed from the kitchen when she heard my voice. Plates of sandwiches and desserts had been set out on the dining room table. The aroma of brewing coffee drifted throughout the house, settling around my shoulders like a comfortable sweater.

Suggesting I take a moment for myself, Susan put her arm through mine as we walked down the hall to the bedroom. She hugged me and returned to the task of greeting those arriving from the church. I watched her go, then turned and opened the bedroom door. My heart stopped. The warmth of the afternoon sun had enhanced the aroma of the aftershave my husband had placed on his dresser. The smell of it lingered in the room, as though he were standing there somewhere, waiting to welcome me into his arms. Trembling, I crossed the room to our bed, sat down and wept. Nothing was ever going to be the same. My life and my heart were broken.

The comfort of our big bed was inviting, but there were too many people in the house who expected me to smile at them, assure them that I would be all right, and answer all their well-meaning but probing questions. "What in the world will I say to them?" I wondered.

I don't remember what I did say, but somehow with Tom and Susan and my two nieces for support, I withstood the rest of the day. Susan stayed with me for a week after that and then returned to her home. I went back to work a week later.

The months that followed were dreadful. Family and friends insisted that I join them for the Thanksgiving and Christmas holidays, but the festivities held none of the joy and wonder of the past. My job no longer meant anything to me. Nothing meant anything to me. I applied for a leave of absence, retreating to my bedroom sanctuary, where I slept through the days that followed, only padding down the hall to the kitchen once a day. Losing weight and all interest in life, I just wanted to die. My nieces were away at school, my brother was busy with his job, and everyone else, tired of my moods, was leaving me alone. Only Susan called every day believing the lies that I was eating and caring for myself. Something I said one afternoon alarmed her so much that she drove the hundred miles to my home to investigate.

She found me asleep in my bed, a cold cup of tea perched on the bedside table, and quietly closed the bedroom door thinking I was merely taking an afternoon nap. She told me later that while she waited for me to wake, she wandered through the house, instantly realizing the truth. The shades and drapes were drawn shut. The house was cold, damp and musty. When she looked in the refrigerator, she discovered the rotting remains of the food she had cooked for me weeks before. She returned to the bedroom. When she couldn't wake me, she called 911.

She moved in with me then, cooking nutritious breakfasts and insisting that I get out of bed and get dressed every day. When the afternoon sun had warmed the air, we left the sanctuary of the house for long rides to the coast. Over suppers of nourishing homemade soups and hot biscuits, we shared joyous memories and our philosophies of life, sometimes laughing hysterically, sometimes crying uncontrollably. She saved my life.

Further recovery from the depressive illness took another two months. My employer granted an extension of the leave of absence, but I knew I would never return there.

In May, on my birthday, Susan announced that she had made arrangements for the two of us to go to Prince Edward Island for the summer. True to her word, we left for the Island on June twenty-first, the first day of summer and the longest day of the year, eager to embrace the promise of peace.

Part One

The Old Song

Old Morris Chair

Chapter 1

West Point, Prince Edward Island　　　　　　　　　　　　　　*July – 1993*

The Island has been a refuge these past weeks, a peaceful sanctuary where fear and anger can do no business. Breathing is easier here…until I remember…and it is then that the heaviness of grief overwhelms me. I wonder if the vacationers in nearby cottages hear my distress in the early morning hours when I awake already sobbing, fighting to breathe. I have learned to release the night's sorrow, nevertheless, by turning onto my stomach and burying my face into the sweet smell of the line-dried sheets. With two pillows covering my head to muffle the noise, I wail until I am dry and silent once more…dead to the pain.

Mercifully, the cycle between life and death is longer here. My mind, heart and soul, have been encouraged by the beauty of the Island and the generosity of its people to embrace that which is outside. Every sense within has been stimulated in some wondrous fashion so that each smell, each sight, and each sound are new and fresh. The grief rests, so I can rest. Life has a chance.

Just now, the sun has slipped below the horizon, taking with it the warmth of the afternoon. A soft, cool breeze playfully lifts the corner of a magazine that slid from my lap onto the deck. Seagulls, soaring effortlessly over the silvery blue waters of Northumberland Straight, suddenly stop in flight and dive straight down into the top of the waves, crying out their shrill evensong as they fish for their last meal of the day. The pungent scent of the salt air and the tranquil voice of the sea are smells and sounds that are as haunting as they are peaceful, recalling memories of other times near the ocean…memories that are a catalyst for both pain and joy.

Once brilliant, the hot pink horizon has faded into the next time zone leaving a cold grey sky. Only a hint of the sun's fiery passion lingers, barely visible now along the undersides of the clouds, as though a giant bellows on the other side of the world were fanning the dying embers of the solar fire. But in the blink of an eye, that, too, is gone.

Gone. He's gone. And unlike the sun, he will not come back tomorrow. Never. Always gone. Gone too quickly. Gone before the words could be said…before expressions of compassion and forgiveness could be formed…before our passion could be rekindled from the ash-grey dust of all that remained.

The sky continues its evening transformation. The pink-seared clouds have evaporated into long, white fingers of light beckoning to me, calling me to another world.

♪♪♪

"Annie!" Susan's call from inside the cottage startled me. In an instant, the peace of the moment was gone, lost in the swift and jerky reaction to surprise. My journal flipped shut, swallowing the memories of the day; the pen flew out of my hand disappearing through a crack in the wooden deck, forever lost to the cool, damp sand below. In the same motion, my elbow knocked over a glass of wine sitting on the arm of the bulky old Morris chair. I watched with an odd fascination as tiny pieces of broken crystal shimmered in the rainbow mist settling to the deck's surface.

Unaware of the chaos outside, Susan continued to speak to me from within the cottage, her soft, comforting voice floating through the open door. I was on my hands and knees picking up the broken pieces of my life when she stepped out onto the deck, leaving the first half of her sentence behind the wall.

"…but I've just got to get back home. Are you sure….oh, honey, what happened?" she asked.

"The sunset lured me to another time and place, as it usually does this time of day, and your call back to reality startled me," I laughed, as I reached for a sharp fragment that was inexplicably wedged under the leg of the chair. With the swiftness of a snake striking suddenly from beneath a rock, the little piece of glass cut a deep red line across my thumb.

"Ouch," I cried, instinctively pulling my hand away from the source of the pain. The blood oozing out of the cut dripped a pattern of rough-edged polka dots into the spilled wine. I stared at the bright red liquid falling from my thumb and in slow motion fell back onto the deck. "What's wrong with me?" I whined, staring up at her as she bent over to assess the damage.

"There's nothing wrong with you, Annie. Your life has been turned upside down, and now you need some time to heal. That's why we came up here, remember?" The words of support flowed out of her, spilling down over me like a warm water bath. She cupped her hand under my elbow and guided me to the battered old chair. "Here, sit down," she directed, "and I'll clean up this mess."

After making an emergency bandage from a piece of paper towel tucked in the pocket of her shorts, she disappeared into the cottage, still talking about letting go of the grief. Although her expressions of concern disappeared with her, I knew the litany all too well. I had been hearing those same thoughts from my family for months, a cacophony of advice I had come to the Island to escape.

My husband often declared that Susan was the only person who could get away with telling me truths I would not accept from others. Our relationship has always been like that, saying what needs to be said, hardly ever taking the easy way out of a conversation. Susan is better at it than I am. But then she has had more experience.

When we met, over twenty years ago, she was recently divorced from a man who had been abusive and hateful. She and her nine-year old daughter had packed up what they could carry in her small VW and had driven from Oregon to Maine in four days to escape the ravages of a marriage that her family said should never have taken place. That perspective was of little help to her when she had arrived home, tired and frightened and needing their support instead of their condemnation and self-righteousness.

Ten years later she met the love of her life and they were married on Valentine's Day. This impulse seemed the one incongruous event in her story that up until then had been told with words of mistrust, sadness and anger. I have often thought since that perhaps that February afternoon was the one, truly happy moment of her life, a time when she threw all caution to the wind and shamelessly enjoyed the romance of the day.

Since our arrival at West Point, we have relaxed into the rhythm of the Island, settling into a routine of sorts that includes taking a chilled glass of wine out to the deck around eight-thirty to watch the sunsets. Each evening's solar display has been more spectacular than the last. The glorious panoramas of color have inspired wonderful conversations about creation and community and the connectedness of all beings.

Our theologies have developed from very different backgrounds, but our beliefs and conversations are framed by a common thought: that there is one God, or God-dess as Susan says, and that all of creation is holy. We both struggle with the patriarchal focus of the church, and yet we arrive at different points of view after hours and hours of discussion. Sustained by the bond of our special friendship, we encourage each other to a higher awareness of the potential of all relationships. This heightened awareness is often painful, however, as those we love do not understand the intensity of our thoughts or the intent of our actions.

While Susan lives most of her life in the full light of this intensity, I cannot. I am awed by her energy and tenacity to call those around her to acknowledge the ways in which humanity abuses itself and the rest of creation. She accomplishes this, not by berating others, but by pointing out where harmony exists. Her descriptive commentaries about the wildlife communities in the salt marsh located behind her home are insightful and thought provoking, especially when they are published in the same context as political editorials about domestic violence or any of a hundred other social conflicts. A month on the Island has provided her with a good deal of background material for her winter's work.

On our early morning walks along the beach, we have harvested enough sea glass to fill a one pound coffee can. Another holds small, oval-shaped red, white and black rocks worn smooth and polished by the tidal action of water and sand. The cool, flat stones remind me of the worry stones of the '60's.

Many of our afternoons have been spent visiting friends made on past visits. This Island community has deep roots. Because my grandmother was born here, Susan and I have been welcomed everywhere, as though we were members of each family. The graciousness and hospitality is of an era that has partially disappeared back home.

Last night Susan's husband called to say that her mother was ill and that she should come home.

Susan returned to the deck with a broom and dustpan. "I'm really concerned about leaving you alone, Annie. Are you sure you want to stay another month?" she asked, handing me an antiseptic swab and a band-aid from her shirt pocket. Quick and efficient as usual, she had thought of everything.

"Yes, I'm sure. I've come home, Susan," I said, forming the words slowly as I unwrapped the original makeshift bandage now stuck to the wound on my thumb. The bleeding had stopped. I looked at her with tears in my eyes and then looked back at the dark waters of Northumberland Straight. "I belong here, Susan. The Island is where I'll hear God's voice again, and then, maybe, find the peace of mind that has eluded me all these months."

When Susan finished sweeping up the broken glass, she sat down next to me. The warmth of her hand in mine was reassuring. We relaxed into the silence, listening for the faint and distant sounds usually muffled by the commotion of life. Susan smiled at the light-hearted twittering of thrushes that nest in the dunes. The mournful moan of a distant navigational buoy resonated deep within my soul. In the dim light of the passing day, we watched the waves slowly roll to shore, one by one, remembering…

We talked late into the night about whether or not I should stay alone, mostly to convince her, that after a month on the Island, the depression was under control. With her help over these last few weeks, I have put perspective back into my life. Now, in the days and weeks ahead, I look forward to rediscovering the passion that used to rise up suddenly, filling me with life and love and laughter.

"I'm sure everyone back home thinks I came up here just to escape, and in some way they're probably right. But I had to do it," I sighed. "Making this break with all the old routines and expectations of others is just what I needed to let up on myself."

Susan laughed and hugged me. "Annie, you are a master of understatement."

I laughed with her. She was right. For years I have been running from one crisis to another trying to help everyone else, trying to meet the expectations of family and friends as well as my own. Taking time for any self interests turned into guilt instead of renewal. No wonder I have been exhausted.

Susan set her alarm for seven, said good night and made herself comfortable on the old sofa in the living room. I stayed outside on the deck to enjoy the night sky for another hour. The Morris chair, tipped back to a reclining position, was the perfect place to stargaze. With no moon, no clouds and no city lights, the heavens here are black and deep. I counted five shooting stars, a satellite and a couple of planes before finally giving in to sleep. Waking a short time later, I quietly tiptoed across the living room to the bedroom. Sleeping under the star-filled canopy was tempting, but even the old, lumpy bed was more comfortable than that chair.

The next morning Susan was packed and ready to go when I awoke. She brought me a hot cup of coffee and a cinnamon bun dripping with butter. As she put the tray down on the bed she said, "You're on your own now, Annie. I'll call you when I get home and often after that. No lies, okay?'" She looked into my eyes for agreement, remembering the day she found me curled up in my bed at home. "Give me a hug and I'll get out of here." She hugged me, holding me for several minutes and then said, "I love you, sweetie. Take good care of yourself."

In an instant, she was gone. I heard the car start, back up, and bump down the path to the main road. Silence settled into the room. I was alone for the first time in twenty years.

Chapter 2

July – 1993

This is my first full day alone on this magnificent Island. God has created a wondrous gift…a glorious afternoon…bright sun, clear blue sky, temperature in the high 70's, and a gentle, warm breeze. The colors are brilliant, enhanced by the sun…the sea, a calm blueberry pool…the sand, a rich red-brown ribbon of color marking the transition point between the sea and the blue-green dune grass…the sky, a deep, powdery blue peppered with cotton-ball clouds. Further down the beach to the west, red-faced sandstone bluffs rise up from the ocean's edge like crumbling canyon walls that mimic the curves of the shoreline for miles. An emerald green tuft of grass runs along the top, interrupted here and there by a fence post. This must be the most beautiful place on earth.

My body and soul are overwhelmed with emotions. Grief. Relief. Anger. And yet I feel free! I miss him. I miss who he was and all that we had together. It has been nine months since he died…nine months of tears and regrets…depression and illness. But today, resting here in this heavenly spot, I feel alive! Free and alive!

♪♪♪

Listening to the soft sound of the waves lapping at the red sand beach below the deck, I relaxed into the bed-pillows, thanking God for my good friend who had insisted on this sabbatical of sorts from the familiarity of home. The coffee and cinnamon bun that Susan had left on the side of the bed were wonderfully delicious. As I ate, I browsed through the paper, and then curled up with my pillow, intending to sleep just a few more minutes. I awoke hours later, the sheets and pillow soaked with perspiration. The hot, summer sun had warmed the cottage to an uncomfortable temperature. After opening doors and windows to welcome the cooler ocean air, I hurriedly dressed and left the cottage, skipping down the back steps and over the boardwalk to the beach below. The mile-long walk to the Lighthouse and back would be an excellent first step toward renewal.

The journey to the Lighthouse produced a rare find of blue sea glass, but more than that, that first solitary walk along the water's edge began a devotional ritual. With each step I took away from the cottage, I gave to God all the cares of the previous night; and with each step back, I asked for fresh and fulfilling experiences that might heal my soul. Upon my return to the cottage, I relaxed into the welcoming softness of the cushions in the old Morris chair.

Located a mile north of the West Point Lighthouse and Cedar Dunes Provincial Park, the small cottage is nestled in a high dune overlooking the red sand beach. Over the years, wind and water have pushed the dune higher around the little building, leaving only the roof and the outer rail of the deck visible from the beach below.

Built over fifty years ago, the cottage has withstood the ravages of hurricanes, tidal surges and cruel winter winds. The original cedar shingles have weathered to a soft blue grey. This past spring, the owners freshened the white paint on the shutters and trim around the windows and doors. On the west side of the building, a broad deck reaches over the dune toward the water. From its outer rail, the beach is visible for miles in both directions. Since my trip to the Island last summer, a bright yellow, canvas canopy has been installed along the west wall. Stretched over an aluminum frame attached to the roof, the canvas provides shade from the hot afternoon sun, as well as a pleasant shelter from early morning rains.

Susan and I learned early on, however, that the canopy must be wound up before a bad storm. On one such occasion, we found ourselves laughing and screaming at the same time, when the cold rain poured down our backs as we hurriedly secured the new canvas. We spent the rest of the afternoon sipping hot coffee laced with kalua, while we listened to k.d.lang and played hearts.

The owners have recently added white plastic furniture with decorator pillows for those who wish to spend more time in the sun. The old Morris chair, a remnant from a distant time, doesn't belong outside, but it is far more comfortable with its soft, newly upholstered cushions than the hard plastic chairs. To make my ocean-side retreat complete, I have added a small pine table found in the corner of the bedroom. If we should have a bad storm, there will be a lot of bulky furniture to return to the safety of the cottage, but right now that risk is worth the effort.

This afternoon a group of six people approached from the direction of the Lighthouse, stopping at a natural break in the sand where the outgoing tide had created a cluster of small streambeds that drain the incoming waves back into the sea. The walkers chose that spot to sit and rest for a while before turning back. When they looked up and saw me on the deck, they waved and then responded to an invitation to join me.

Pausing on the boardwalk that runs along the side of the cottage, they clustered together like visiting carolers at Christmas, explaining that they were traveling with a bus tour from Massachusetts. I repeated my invitation and shared with them what I knew about the western end of the Island. The local folklore about ghost ships and our own Northumberland sea monster captivated them. I suggested that they visit the West Point Lighthouse Museum to talk with the curator. A climb to the top, although difficult and a bit intimidating, was worth the effort not only for the view, but also for more storyboards of shipwrecks and folklore.

"Why is the sand so red up here?" asked a woman wearing a white tennis visor and pink sunglasses.

"There are iron particles in the sand, that when oxidized, stain the sand this reddish color," I explained. "At least that's the scientific answer. The Micmac creation legend is a lot more interesting though."

After hearing the story about the Great Spirit forming the Island from a red piece of clay and Glooscap carrying it on his shoulders to the "laughing waters" of the Gulf of Saint Lawrence, they agreed that the Micmac legend was a great deal more entertaining. We had a pleasant visit laughing easily together and sharing stories about the Island and events from back home. When they left, they thanked me and told me that they were surprised by my hospitality. I explained that it was the "Island Way."

Alone again, I reclined the old chair, closed my eyes and released the stress of difficult memories, as I listened for the unmistakable sounds of life by the sea. Bits of conversation were blown my way on the wind: children squealing when the waves caught them and splashed over their knees; young lovers laughing as they chased one another, spinning themselves around, hugging and kissing in the bright sunshine; older lovers, wearing wide-brimmed straw hats, calling to one another as they stooped to pick up sea glass and an occasional shell. I loved sharing the wonder and excitement of the Island with them.

Chuckling, I thought about my heightened state of relaxation. My body had become so limp, I believed I might melt and seep through the cracks in the deck onto the cool sand below. I dozed off thinking how grateful I was for this time alone.

Voices from the beach woke me. I popped up like a rabbit from a hole. A young couple turned around abruptly when they saw me. Others waved and called out to me, "Hello! Nice day, eh?" In the distance, a lone walker slowly made her way along the beach to the braided ribbons of water flowing back into the sea. She walked through the little streambeds as though her thoughts were of another world. When she stopped and wrote a message in the sand with the driftwood stick she was carrying, I could not see the marks she made, but I imagined that she had written the name of someone she longed to see. She turned then toward the sea, raised her arms, still holding the stick, and yelled. The on-shore breeze captured her words, lifting them over the dune. "I miss you!"

My heart ached for her as she returned to the Lighthouse, her head down, the stick dragging along beside her leaving a line in the sand to mark where she had been.

Another walker approached from the northern side of the shore. Tall and lean, wearing a red windbreaker, he walked with a distinct limp. "Great day, isn't it?" he shouted to me.

"Yes!" I agreed, smiling and wishing I had my camera nearby to capture the surprise of the splash of red against the backdrop of the silvery blue water. He waved, continuing his solitary walk toward the Lighthouse. Perhaps he's another traveler from Massachusetts, I mused.

The wind picked up suddenly, so I moved inside. The cottage is very cozy with a large, comfortable front room that serves as both living room and dining area. A sliding glass door opens to the deck near the kitchen table and three cottage style windows, along the west wall behind the sofa, frame the magnificent overview.

There is an efficient kitchen area along the southwest wall with a small window over the sink that faces the Lighthouse. In the darkness of night, its beacon casts a distinctive arc of light across the water. The northwest wall has no windows, a concession to the harsh winds that blow from that direction. The back half of the cottage contains a large bedroom, a bath and a hallway that leads to the back door.

The furniture is old, but functional. The bed isn't very comfortable, but the sofa in the front room makes up for that. While Susan was here, we fought good-naturedly over who would sleep there, each devising a number of games from which the winner got the "sofa-prize." Now that she has left, I have it all to myself. A writing desk, a hutch filled with two sets of china, a portable television perched on a homemade shelf, a small woodstove, an overstuffed chair that matches the sofa and three end tables, each with a distinctive table lamp, complete the simple furnishings. On the walls and shelves is an assortment of souvenirs, golf paraphernalia, and photographs of the owners' family gatherings. Near the woodstove rests an old pair of wooden shoes from Holland. A croquet set is tucked in the corner by the front door, its colorful wooden mallets and balls scarred from years of wear and tear.

As I turned from watching a small brown bird repairing its nest in the dune, I noticed a pottery vase filled with pink and white wildflowers. A piece of blue notepaper peeked out from beneath it.

My Dear Annie, I have thoroughly enjoyed our month on the Island.
The peace that I found here with you will fuel my soul throughout
the coming winter. Stay well and be good to yourself.
I love you, dear friend. Susan

When the tears started, I couldn't stop them. The profound sadness born of grief poured out of my mouth and eyes, choking me at first, then draining me dry. I wept for my husband, myself, Susan, and for all those who had been abused by others who claimed to be human beings. Exhausted, I burrowed into the comfort of the sofa and slept.

The dreams were more peaceful than they had been for weeks. In them I found myself walking on the beach, wading through soothing, cool water that lapped at my feet, or sitting on the sand at night wrapped in the midnight sky. When I awoke, the morning sun was shining through the bedroom door, spilling its light across the living room floor.

I stretched and groaned when I stood up, laughing at the distressing sounds that bounced off the morning silence. At the kitchen sink, I splashed cold water on my face, poured myself a glass of orange juice and stepped out through the sliding glass door to the deck. The new day had brought with it the sounds of an early morning symphony. Like a great machine working somewhere over the tops of the waves, fishing boats from nearby harbors created a continuous drone that signaled another day's harvest from the sea. Birds of various sizes and colors chatted about the day's business. Five Canada geese flew overhead, one behind the other, honking as though they were talking about the weather and making their plans to leave for the south. A crow called out as it flew straight as an arrow over the deck. "I'm passing through. Get out of the way!" Seagulls screeched at one another over bits of food floating in the water.

The waves were much bigger this morning, their rhythm slow and easy. Funny, I thought, the things you notice when you purge your soul and allow your mind to rest.

After a breakfast of scrambled eggs and one of Susan's cinnamon buns, I dressed in shorts and a t-shirt and left the cottage by the back door. After taking a few steps, I heard a faint sound. Cocking my head sideways like a robin listening for worms, I heard it again. Someone was singing on the beach.

As I crested the top of the dune, I saw her. A young child about nine, wearing sky blue shorts and a white t-shirt with a rainbow across the back, sang and danced barefoot on the red sand like an Irish leprechaun. Her dark, auburn hair had been pulled back into two long pigtails that bounced as she bounced. Completely absorbed in her singing and dancing, she squealed with delight as she chased the waves and they chased her. I was mesmerized as I stared at a little girl who could have been me, pigtails and all.

When she saw me, she froze. I waved and smiled. She relaxed a little, lifting her hand, palm up in reply, but I could sense that she was frightened.

"Hi there, I'm Annie York," I called out gently. "I liked your song. Will you teach it to me?"

"Hi," she said shyly. "I didn't know anyone was watching me." She scuffed at the sand with her toes as though to rub out where she had been. "You probably think I'm silly."

"No, not at all. You looked like you were having a wonderful time. I'm sorry if I spoiled your fun." When she lifted her head, I noticed a dark spot under her left eye. "Are you staying in a cottage near here?" I asked, wondering where this delightful child belonged.

"We're camping at the park next to the Lighthouse. My folks know I'm walking on the beach. They don't mind." Her words hung in the breeze as she ran toward an incoming wave. She giggled as it splashed against the front of her legs, getting her t-shirt and her face wet.

Concerned that she had wandered so far away from her parents and the park where they were camping, I said, "I usually take a walk to the Lighthouse every day. Would you like to walk along with me?"

"I guess." She didn't sound sure about going with me, but when I turned away from her toward the Lighthouse, I was relieved to see that she had followed me. As we walked in silence for several minutes, I became aware of the surf once again, the rhythm of the waves, and the soothing feel of the water on my feet. The child returned to chasing the waves, giggling as she ran just ahead of the incoming flow, daring it to get her wet.

What an enchanting child, I thought, laughing with her. "How long have you been on the Island?" I asked, as she continued teasing the waves.

"We got here last night," she hollered, running ahead of me, "but it was too windy to set up the tent so we slept in the car." She returned to my side and stopped. "My Daddy is setting up the tent now, and I wanted to help, but he told me to go play, so I decided to walk on the beach." She spoke hurriedly, expressing her thoughts all at once and in hushed tones, as though each word was extremely confidential.

"What's your name?" I asked.

"Millie!" she said with great pride.

I laughed and said, "I'm glad to meet you, Millie."

"Me too," she shouted over her shoulder as she ran ahead of me, waving her arms like a bird. Soon she was swooping back, running around me, and asking, "Do you live here, Annie?"

"No, but I'm staying in that cottage back there where I first saw you."

"Oh," she said, stooping to pick up a piece of green sea glass. "I've found lots of this stuff on the beach," she said, pulling a handful from her pocket. "Where does it come from?" When she turned her face up to me with her question, I smiled at the serious expression on one so young. Her eyes squinting against the glare of the sun, her cheeks peppered with freckles and flushed from exertion, her mouth pouting with thought, she answered her own question. "Does this come from the ocean?"

"Yes, it does. Some of it is very old, washed up from a sunken ship. Feel it," I suggested, rubbing the smooth glass between my fingers. "The water and the sand polish the sharp edges, so by the time it washes to shore, it feels like this."

She chose a large amber piece from her collection and rubbed her fingers over it. "Suppose this one came from a sunken ship?" she asked, the excitement of new information raising the pitch of her voice.

"Could be," I replied, captivated by her curiosity.

"Are there lots of different colors?" she asked, racing up the beach to look for more bounty from the sea.

"Yes. Blue and red are very rare and very special."

"Wow, look at this one!" she exclaimed, picking up a large green piece. "It looks like jelly candy." She laughed, as she continued her treasure hunt, unaware that we were halfway back to the park.

The ocean spilled cool water over our feet from one side, and red sand dunes, spotted with patches of sea-green dune grass and an occasional dwarfed and misshapen evergreen, undulated at varying heights on the other. Behind us, great red bluffs towered at the water's edge, their lush green pastures on top a haven for grazing black and white dairy cows. Just ahead, an unusually high tide had formed a terrace of sand, a perfect vantage point to observe the sights and sounds of the shore.

"Want to sit down for a few minutes?" I asked, dropping to the sand.

"Okay," Millie said, sitting close to me as young children often do. She looked up at me with surprise when she realized just how close she was, and scooted away so our bodies were no longer touching.

Strange, I thought, this little girl is a complete stranger, and yet I sense an immediate bond with her. Maybe that's because she looks so much like me when I was that age, or maybe I sense something more. Whatever the reason, she's an intriguing child.

"Where do you live, Annie?" Millie asked, as she investigated a razor clamshell. She put it in her pocket, and then looked at me for my answer.

"I'm from Maine," I replied, scooping up a handful of cool sand, letting it filter through my fingers. "I'll be here for another few weeks. What about you?"

"We live in New York, and we're going to be here for a couple of weeks, too." Her words tumbled out of her mouth in a distinct and rapid-fire speech pattern I was beginning to enjoy. "Gosh, I hope the wind doesn't blow as hard as it did last night. Did you hear it?"

"I must have slept right through it. The wind blows a lot up here, though. I guess I've gotten used to it. Did it frighten you?"

"Sort of," she answered, looking up at me, "but Mommy hugged me tight in the back seat of the car."

I leaned back on my elbows, my face to the sun. "You've had quite an adventure, haven't you? Is this your first trip to the Island?"

"Yes, and I just loved the ferry ride from New Brunswick. Daddy let me run all over that boat," she exclaimed, jumping up and running circles around me to demonstrate her story. "Of course, I couldn't get lost," she giggled, "because...well, because I was on a boat." She laughed again and soon had me laughing with her.

We talked about her school and her friends. She told me she was hoping to get a puppy for Christmas, but that depended on how well she did in school and whether she kept her room clean.

"What kind of puppy do you want, Millie?" I asked, remembering the German shepherd I had as a child.

"I'd like one like my friend Trudy has. It's not very big and really cute. I don't know what you call it, but she got hers at the dog pound. Mommy said we could go there right after Thanksgiving to see what they've got. I hope Daddy can go with us." Her large, blue eyes glistened with tears of excitement as she shared the promise of her new puppy.

Thinking about the overcrowded animal shelter I had recently visited in Maine, I said, "There's going to be a special little dog just waiting for you Millie. I just know it. And that little dog will be so lucky when he goes home with you."

"Thanks, Annie. I can't wait." Unable to contain her excitement any longer, she ran toward the surf. "I better go back to the park before my Daddy gets mad at me for being gone so long." As she started to run toward the water, she turned back to see if I was coming along. The sun highlighted the red-gold strands of her hair. Freckles danced across her nose and spilled onto her cheeks. In that instant I thought, "God, why did you send this angel to me?"

As Millie and I approached the Lighthouse, her energy shifted. Her smile was gone and the bounce in her step was replaced with a slow-paced shuffle through the sand. I sensed she was thinking about something quite serious. "I'm glad to know you, Millie. Come by any time to visit or walk on the beach. And bring your Mom. I'd love to meet her," I added, watching her walk away.

"Thanks, Annie." She waved, turned and ran toward the park, the red ribbons on her pigtails flying in the breeze. I hoped I would see her again.

The gift shop at the Lighthouse was crowded with tourists, and the restaurant bustled with the noise of table conversations and food preparation. While I waited for a lobster roll to go, I wandered through the museum dedicated to the first lighthouse keepers. How different, I thought, to live in a place where each room was on a different floor. The main parlor, located on the first floor, was now the museum, and the bedrooms, located on each of three floors above, were now additional rooms at the inn. I paid for my sandwich and walked back to the cottage wondering if I would ever know the rest of Millie's story.

As I walked up the wooden boardwalk built over the dune to protect the grasses from being trampled, I thought again about that black mark under Millie's eye. Children often get hurt playing. Scraped knees and elbows are common sights, but that was definitely a black eye. I hoped the uneasy feeling growing in my stomach wasn't a sign that my intuition was working overtime. She was a dear little girl, full of life and joy.

Before I could dwell on such negative thoughts any longer, I heard the noisy cough and sputter of an old truck as it rumbled up the lane behind the cottage. Three teenaged boys wearing baseball caps sat shoulder to shoulder in the cramped front seat. They were looking for friends who had vacationed nearby the previous summer. I recognized one of them and waved. Steve Phillips asked if I knew where Megan Brown and her parents were renting this summer. I gave the boys the information they wanted and watched them drive away, their three heads bobbing in unison in the front seat of the old pickup truck as it bumped along the road.

Belonging is almost instant here. Island people are open, warm and very generous, welcoming visitors into their homes with gracious words and big smiles. Many of the Island families that my husband and I had met over the years came by to visit soon after Susan and I had arrived. Their love lifted my spirits more than anything or anyone else had since my husband's death, except, of course, for Susan. She, too, was overwhelmed, particularly the day Ernest came to see me. One of a few remaining members of a generation born in the early 1900's, he was blessed with amazing good health and a profound appreciation of his ancestral home at West Point.

He knocked hard on the back door, opened it, and called out to me. Before I could get back there to greet him, Ernest had stepped through the door, his right arm outstretched, a huge bouquet of fresh wildflowers clasped in his hand.

"Here you are, Annie, my girl, fresh from the fields!" And with that he scooped me up into a bear hug, tears spilling out of his big, blue eyes. "How are you, darlin'?" he asked, as he put me down and reached in his back pocket for a clean, white handkerchief.

"I'm okay, Ernest, especially now that I'm on the Island. And I'm so glad to see you," I said, standing on tiptoes to kiss his cheek. "These flowers are gorgeous." We walked arm and arm to the kitchen table where most of our visits took place.

"Ernest, I'd like you to meet my friend, Susan," I said, handing the flowers to her. "She's been my lifesaver these past months. I don't know what I would've done without her."

In a blur of motion, Earnest stood, grabbed Susan, and hugged her, lifting her off the floor. She laughed as he put her down, surprised at his strength and his spontaneity. As she looked into his face, she was stunned by the look of love she saw there.

"Susan, my girl, I want to thank you for taking such good care of Annie," he said, wiping his forehead with his handkerchief. "She means a lot to us up here. Especially to me. I look forward to her visits every summer, and to her letters all winter. Keeps me going, she does!" He looked over at me, his eyes still glistening from the emotion he had brought into the cottage with him.

"Ernest, you old devil," I said, laughing, "you certainly know how to turn a girl's head." I gave him another hug and a kiss on the cheek, and then we all sat down to talk about what had been happening on the Island since the past summer. In November, Ernest's older brother had been taken to a nursing home in O'Leary. After about a month, he had adjusted quite nicely, but Ernest missed him terribly.

"Does your daughter stay with you now?" I asked, sitting down across from him.

"Yes, she does some, Annie. But this past winter was terribly lonely when no one was around, especially after my brother left. Your letters were a Godsend. When you stopped writing there for a while, I got terribly worried, but then you sent word that you would be here in June. I knew then that the Island would help you." He patted my hand and leaned back in the chair.

"I have Susan to thank for that. She called the Crawford's and made all the arrangements to rent the cottage again this summer. As much as I love you, I don't think I would have had the courage to get myself up here without her."

Susan reached over and squeezed my hand. "You needed to be here, Annie, and now I know why."

"By the way, young man, where have you been?" I asked, laughing as Ernest's face reddened at my term of endearment.

"I've been away, off Island, for longer than I intended. Been going to graduations and weddings of some of my grandchildren and great-grandchildren. And, honestly Annie, I hope that's the last of it for a while. I don't like being off Island. This is where I belong, and you, too, Annie my girl." He put his big, calloused hand over mine.

Ernest's smile lit up the cottage. At 90 he still had the energy of most people thirty years younger. He and his wife, who had died about twenty-five years ago, had raised twelve children at West Point. Ernest had made his living from the sea, crewing on the original Blue Nose Schooner as a young man and then owning his own lobster boat later in life. The young men of the harbor respect him and look out for him when he visits with them at the end of a long day of fishing. Although they might be dead-tired, they take time to talk with him, telling their sea stories and listening to his.

That's the Island Way of Life…love of family and friends…genuine concern and respect for elders…and gracious hospitality for visitors. Ernest embodies that Island spirit. Perhaps that's why I love him so much.

Over tea and cookies, Ernest talked through the afternoon, telling Susan all the wonderful stories he had told me about his trips on the Blue Nose and his life as a lobsterman. We heard the amazing story of how he had rescued two men from a sinking boat and how he had rowed a small boat to safety in a terrible storm. Susan fell in love as well that afternoon.

"What a wonderful man!" she exclaimed after he had left.

"Yes, he is, Susan. I wish he were forty years younger, though. I would never leave this place again." I sighed, poured myself a glass of wine and went out on the deck to watch the sun go down.

Chapter 3

August – 1993

Just a few days have passed since Susan left the Island. She has called twice asking probing but concerned questions, assuring herself that I'm okay. I was relieved to hear that her mother had recovered from a painful gallbladder attack.

Susan is a true gift of God, for without her friendship I'm not sure where I would be today. Certainly not here in this peaceful place where the cares and concerns of home lie dormant so that I may rest. Everything is easier here, even sleep. The nightmares no longer haunt the early morning hours. Sleep has been peaceful and restful. And until last night, my dreams have been nondescript experiences of motion as though I were floating on warm currents of air or water.

But last night the motion was insistent, palpable and foreign. The fluttering inside my abdomen was disturbing at first, drawing me out of deep sleep to a semiconscious state. In that state of heightened awareness, yet still asleep, I felt a baby moving inside my body. I actually felt the baby's foot with my hand as it kicked against my stomach. As I continued to dream, I struggled to sit up, but the child inside didn't want me to move. I'm not sure how long all this activity continued, but eventually I was fully awake and soaked with my own perspiration.

Not having any children of my own is the biggest void in my life, Now, I've had this strange dream, and like a wondrous gift from God, I have actually felt a child's life inside my own. What an amazing sensation. For a few moments I was pregnant, carrying a child that was ready for birth. What a precious gift!.

Life! That's the gift. God is giving me life!

♪♪♪

The morning began with the wind blowing a shutter off the southwest side of the cottage. I heard the hinge rip away from the window frame, and when the shutter slammed back against the cottage, adrenalin shot through every nerve in my body leaving me weak and jittery. I was still trembling when I opened the sliding glass door to retrieve the furniture on the deck. The old chair was heavy and bulky as I moved it into the cottage, but the physical activity calmed my nerves.

Strange, but quite distinctive gurgling sounds from the kitchen signaled that the coffee maker had finished brewing its magic potion. As I poured my first cup, I recalled the dream from the night before and the wondrous sensation of that baby in my belly. Remembering the feeling of those little feet pushing to get out, I felt warmth from that tiny body and that made me laugh. To have a child manifested in this special way had been an answer to prayer. I rubbed my stomach and smiled. Perhaps that child *was* born in the night, and she is sitting right here at the table drinking coffee and eating the last of the cinnamon buns.

"Susan, how I wish you were here," I said out loud, as I raised the last bite of my cinnamon bun in a mock toast. "To life!"

The wind continued to blow, every now and then wafting up under the eaves and lifting the shingles on the roof. The steel grey sky was mirrored in the water of the Straight. Dark, smoky clouds sat on the horizon, heavy with the day's rain. What a contrast to my dream. No life in the sky. No one walking on the beach. I was very much alone, and yet I felt another presence.

As I stood up to put the dishes in the sink, I noticed the man with the limp walking toward the Lighthouse. He was dressed in jeans and the red windbreaker zipped up half way over a white sweater. He looked up toward the cottage and waved. I waved back. He jammed his hands into the pockets of his jeans and leaned into the wind. The red windbreaker billowed out on both sides like a parachute threatening to pull him all the way back to where he had started.

"Well now, there must be a cottage in those dunes up the beach. I wonder who he is? And I wonder why he's walking on the beach in weather like this?" I said out loud, as I rinsed out my coffee cup and placed it in the dish drainer to dry.

Thoughts of my husband tugged at my heart. The first time we met I knew that he was someone I would love forever. Reluctantly, each of us had gone to a summer dance with friends who happened to know each other. When we were introduced, he asked me to dance, pressing my body against his, never saying a word. The sweet smell of the man and the gentle rhythm of the waltz captivated my soul. A year later we were married.

Life was wonderful. Each of us had a career. Each of us loved what we were doing; he a design engineer for an aeronautics company, and I a sales manager for an electronics company. We worked long hours during the week and spent every weekend at our cottage retreat in Northeast Harbor.

We arrived late every Friday night, exhausted from the week's busyness and stress. Saturday mornings we enjoyed sailing, walking on a nearby beach, or visiting with friends. Later in the day, our family would arrive for a late afternoon barbecue.

Sunday mornings were reserved for our private, intimate moments. We slept in, read the Sunday paper in bed or out on the deck, drank lots of coffee and ate lots of doughnuts. Those were the best hours of our week. We savored each moment, sometimes making love among the comics and sports sections strewn over the bed. In the late afternoon, we would pack the car and drive back to our house in the city to start another week.

We pursued our dreams together for fifteen years. Our daily routines were busy, familiar, and successful. We were unaware of the subtle changes taking place in our lives from the stress of longer hours at work and less leisure time together. The changes in our relationship were subtle, too, as stress became the third partner in our marriage.

A year later my husband suffered his first heart attack. It was what the doctors call a warning. Both of us took a three-month leave of absence and went to the cottage at Northeast Harbor to sort things out.

Our Sunday mornings changed. We still slept in and read the Sunday paper, but coffee and doughnuts were taboo. The lovemaking changed as well and then stopped altogether.

We had been back to work for about a year, when I noticed that my husband was no longer enjoying his job. He was nervous and irritable. Our long conversations over supper had dried up to inane small talk. While life had changed dramatically for him, I was sailing along in the same old routine, driving myself and everyone who worked for me ten and twelve hours a day to get the work done. I was making good money, enjoying my job, and spending less and less time at home.

Two months later, he suffered his second heart attack. This time there was damage, leaving some paralysis in his right arm and right leg. After a prolonged period of physical therapy, he was able to walk with the help of a cane.

Life was never the same for us after that. My husband could not cope with the physical changes to his body. He grew more and more despondent as life passed him by, leaving him alone and bitter with his thoughts.

I talked with him, argued with him, sympathized with him, and cried with him. Nothing helped. If he couldn't be the man he used to be, he just wanted to die. None of this made any sense to me. Life was for living, even if life changed. But the depression had its claws into him and fought me hard for two years. Depression won, for two years later he suffered a massive heart attack that left him unconscious until he died.

We never had a chance to say good-bye. We never had a chance to tell each other how much we still loved each other. We just never had a chance.

So he died alone and bitter, and I carried the guilt of being alive and full of life despite my grief. I grieved over our lost years. I grieved over the loss of a man who had been so vital, so creative, and so tender. I grieved because I missed the intimacy of our lost relationship. When had we lost all that?

I couldn't identify the moment when we began to distant ourselves from one another. I wanted to blame the heart attacks, but understood that I, too, had some responsibility in it. I had been wrapped up in my career and had stopped listening. He had been wrapped up in his fears and in his fate as a tragic victim and had stopped talking. As he was drawn deeper and deeper into the depression, our last two years became a living hell. The seeds of my own depression had been deeply planted.

Friends and family noticed the changes but were too shocked or too upset to say anything to either of us. We were no longer invited to parties or gatherings and that hurt us both. Life had evolved into a dull routine, both of us getting through each day doing what was necessary and avoiding what each of us wanted to talk about most. We had loved each other deeply once and, ironically, it was that love that held us together. We just couldn't manifest it anymore in the ways that nurtured and cared for our souls. The emptiness became more than either of us could endure.

We made one last trip to the Island last year hoping to recapture some of the love and joy we had shared with each other and our friends. Because of his physical limitations, he could not walk on the beach and did not want to visit with anyone. Depression settled in even deeper, until I was forced to pack up our things and head for home. Our expectation of a summer-long experience of warmth and renewal evaporated with each mile that passed on that eternally long drive home.

Then life stopped one October morning and all of the pain, all of the fear, all of the risk of hurting each other didn't matter any more. We were both free.

Chapter 4

August – 1993

    The sweet, pure fragrance from the fields surrounds my deck like an invisible veil of fog. At this early hour, the heavy, rumbling sounds of boats and machinery are stilled. Even the sea is at rest. Songbirds wake, fluttering in the trees, offering their delightful melodies. This is, indeed, God's re-creation of the new day.

    Yesterday's howling winds are gone, sucked into a black hole somewhere, waiting for another day to stir up the anxieties generated from its energy. Are my feelings of grief like that, under control for now, yet ready to spring to life with the force of the wind?

    Just a few months ago, I was trapped in a prison of grief…unable to eat…unable to concentrate…unable to connect with anyone around me. Life was empty and lonely. I felt like such a fraud. I wore a mask that said, "Oh sure, I'm okay," when inside I was screaming, "Help me! Love me!" I couldn't find anyone to take away the pain. The overwhelming weight of it became so unbearable that I nearly died.

    So what has happened? I still need and desperately desire the intimacy of a loving relationship. But right now, right this minute, I'm not so consumed by it. I feel more peaceful and more hopeful than I have in years.

    But I'm scared…scared that all those feelings of panic will return, that I will not be able to recapture this feeling of peace and well-being when I return home…that the wondrous relief from the weight of the awful emptiness will suddenly evaporate.

    This morning the waves of anxiety are not as terrible. I can feel them coming, but they do not last as long. The world outside is bright and fresh and there is hope. That's enough for now.

♪♪♪

    She rapped lightly on the door. When there was no answer, she opened it and poked her head into the hall. "Hello, Annie. Are you there?"

I was struggling with the fourth corner of a fitted sheet when I heard Millie calling to me from the back door. "Come on in, Millie. I'm in the bedroom."

She peeked around the corner of the door, a broad, impish grin on her face, and held out a huge bouquet of yellow and white daisies. Standing in the shadow of the door, her hand extended the daisies into the ray of sunshine coming from the back window, as though God had put a spotlight on her gift.

"I was walking up the road early this morning," she said, swallowing her words as she tried to catch her breath, "when I saw a whole field of these flowers. I thought you might like some." Her cheeks were flushed with anxiety. She looked at everything around me, but not at me, as though she was unsure if she'd been bad or good.

"They're wonderful, Millie," I said, giving her a reassuring hug. "Let's see what we can find to put them in."

Millie followed me into the kitchen, watching as I rummaged through the cupboards looking for a suitable container for the flowers. After a good deal of banging and clanging of the pots and pans under the sink, I found the old aluminum coffee pot without any "innards" that had served as a vase a few weeks ago.

"This will do," I said. "We won't be using this for coffee, so we might as well recycle it as a vase. There," I exclaimed, placing the pot in the middle of the kitchen table, "that looks lovely. Tell me, Millie, what have you been doing for the past few days?" I asked, walking back into the bedroom to finish making the bed.

"Well," she paused, "we went over to the other side of the Island yesterday. There was a great place with a water slide and a miniature golf course. See, Mommy bought me this neat t-shirt." She pulled her shoulders back and pointed to the colorful flags sitting atop the park name printed on the front of her pink shirt. "We had a good time," she chattered on, "but by the time we got back the wind had blown our tent over. It took my Daddy a long time to fix it. Some of the other campers had problems too. Did you, Annie?" Millie said all this with the same force and speed of the wind the day before. By the time she finally stopped talking, her eyes were glistening with a hint of tears.

"One of the shutters blew off the cottage and flew over into the dune," I said more composed than I was when it happened. I motioned to her to help me put the light comforter on the bed. "I looked for it for almost an hour this morning before I found it. I'm going to try to hang it back on the window before I leave."

Millie wandered out of the bedroom toward the front door. As she walked away from me, I noticed an angry bruise on the inside of her left calf and another mark on the back of her right arm. That old homesick feeling punched me squarely in the stomach causing acidic bile to rise up in my throat. I could feel the heat in my face.

"Millie, did you have some sort of accident at the fun park yesterday?" I asked, as I stepped into the living room.

She was investigating the croquet set in the corner. She froze in place when she heard my question. My intuition told me that she wasn't going to talk about it, so I said, "I remember one time, when I was about your age, my father took me to the circus. There were some rides there, too, and I was determined to go on the bumper cars."

Millie rubbed the rough edge of one of the croquet mallets, her head down, listening to my story. "Well," I continued, as Millie slowly worked her way across the room to the sofa, "there were some rough kids in some of the other cars, and by the time we got through, I had black and blue marks all over me from getting bumped so many times. I've never been on bumper cars since then."

Millie sat on the edge of the sofa, looked up at me, tears pooling in the deep blue of her eyes, and then started to sob. I went to her immediately and sat down next to her, putting my arm around her. She hugged me and continued to cry, softly at first then open-mouthed, gulping sobs until she choked. I knew instinctively what had hurt her so badly, but I hoped I was terribly wrong.

"Millie, dear, who has hurt you so badly?" I asked softly.

"Oh, Annie, my Daddy hurt me," she said, trying to calm down, inhaling abruptly between words. "I don't, think he, means to do it, but he gets so mad!"

"I'm so sorry, Millie," were the only words I could think to say out loud. Curses and accusations were screaming inside my head at a man I had never met.

Calmer now, Millie continued to tell me what had happened when they returned from the amusement park. "When Daddy couldn't put the tent back together quick enough, he got mad and hit me with the tent pole." She started to cry again, swallowing and sniffling between words. "It hurt, so I cried, and that's when he grabbed my arm, and shook me, and shook me, until he scared me so much, I stopped making any noise."

I tightened my grip, holding her close to me, wanting to protect her from her own words. She told me her mother intervened, taking her to the bathhouse for a hot shower. When they returned, the tent was standing, the beds neatly arranged inside. Her father had left for a walk on the beach.

Millie and her mother slept huddled together that night. Unable to sleep, Millie left the tent at the first sign of dawn, not knowing where she was going, but knowing she didn't want to be there when her father woke.

"When I found those pretty flowers, I thought about how nice you were to me on the beach the other day, so I picked some for you. I hope you're not mad at me for coming here," she started crying again.

"Oh, no, Millie. I'm glad you did come here," I said, wondering what I was going to do now. "It's dangerous for you to be walking alone so early in the morning, though. I'm glad you thought about coming here where you're safe." As if to assure myself, I said it again. "You're safe here, Millie."

My God, this child *is* being abused, I thought, remembering the black eye from the other day. I held her in my arms, rubbing her back and rocking her as I hummed a favorite tune. Within minutes, I felt her body twitch as she relaxed and fell asleep, her head on my chest, her arm still wrapped around my waist. She was exhausted from the emotion and lack of sleep the night before. I held her until my own tears abated, then laid her back against the cushions and covered her with an afghan.

As she slept, I prayed and wondered what I could do to help her. Perhaps I should walk back to the park with her and meet her parents, I thought. And then what? Confront her father? Right! He'll tell me to go straight to the devil, and I'll never see her again. And what might he do to her? I could call the RCMP, but I'm not sure whether the local authorities here in Canada will want to become involved with an American family's problems. And even if they did, her father could lie and say that she really was hurt on the rides and just looking for attention.

I sat in a chair near the sofa forcing myself to calm down by knitting on the sweater I was making for one of my nieces, looking up every once in a while to see if Millie was awake. About a half hour passed and I was just wondering if I should wake her, thinking that her mother must be frantic with worry, when Millie suddenly popped up off the sofa like a jack-in-the-box. Her eyes darted around the room as she tried to get her bearings. "Gosh, I must have fallen asleep. How long have I been here?" Her face was flushed from tears and sleep, her hair matted to one side of her head.

"Not very long, about a half hour or so," I said, putting the half-finished sweater back in the basket as she stood and walked toward me.

"Thanks, Annie," she said leaning over my chair and kissing my cheek. "I'd better be getting back to the park before my Daddy gets mad again." As she spoke to me in the rapid-fire manner that I was getting used to, she backed away from me toward the door. She had it opened and her foot on the first step of the stairs before I had a chance to react. "Millie, wait a minute! I'd like to walk back to the park with you and meet your parents."

"Oh, no, Annie!" she cried, her whole body shaking with dread. "If my Daddy knew that I was here with you, he'd be awful angry."

"Why is that?" I asked cautiously.

"Because you would have seen my bruises, and he would know that you must have asked me about them." She had stepped back into the cottage, her arms outstretched, her hands emphasizing each word.

I felt the knot in the pit of my stomach tighten. Millie's answer was the answer of an experienced victim. She knew what made her father mad because she had been through this before.

"Okay then, I'll walk back with you just as far as the Lighthouse. But before we leave, I wish you would write down your home address and telephone number. That way, if your father decides to leave before I see you again, I can get in touch with you back home."

After she had carefully printed the information I had asked for, we left the cottage. She was quiet as we made our way across the beach to the Provincial Park. When we reached the Lighthouse I pulled her to me and hugged her. "Will you come back tomorrow, so I'll know you're okay?"

"Yes, I promise, Annie," she said, as she wrapped her arms around my waist. She looked up at me then and said, "Don't worry, Daddy is always nicer to me after." She stopped abruptly. "Well, he's just nicer." She buried her head against my body, her words of gratitude muffled in the folds of my shirt.

"You're welcome," I said putting my hands on her shoulders and gently pushing her away from me so I could look into her eyes. "Come back to the cottage any time you need to or want to, okay?"

She nodded, hugged me again and ran toward the park. I wasn't pleased with the outcome of the conversation, but I was afraid to push her too hard. If she came back tomorrow, we'd talk. If she came back……

Chapter 5

August – 1993

As promised, Millie came by the cottage yesterday morning to assure me that she was okay. She was excited because her mother had promised to take her to a matinee at the Confederation Theater in Charlottetown. The bruise on her arm was fading, but I couldn't see the one on her leg because she was wearing long pants. I walked most of the way back to the park with her, hugged her and let her go.

I am worried about her and haven't slept well for two days. Each time I doze off, I dream, and somewhere in the dreams Millie gets all mixed up with me. I woke up about an hour ago struggling with the blanket that had become twisted around my body and feeling cold from the sweat of anxiety and fear. The hot tea tastes good and has warmed me, but the uneasiness has settled in my stomach like a heavy stone.

Much like a boat on a stormy sea, the cottage sails the dunes, rocking back and forth to the rhythm of the blowing wind. The light from the reading lamp shines out through the window onto the sand, but only a few feet beyond is darkness. The incoming tide pounds ashore just below the deck.

If I can't sleep, I might as well write, and in the writing perhaps I will remember what it was like to be Millie's age, so full of life and yet so afraid and so ashamed.

For forty years I forgot. For forty years I truly believed that my childhood was happy. Even though my parents were divorced when I was six, even though we moved so many times, my memories are that life back then was okay. But it wasn't.

When I was six, my mother, brother, and I left my father and the little white house that had been our home. She was trembling when she hugged me out of bed before dawn. There was unmistakable panic in her voice when she whispered her love as she helped me get dressed. There were tears in her eyes, the right one blackened by his fist, and there was a scary black mark along her neck. Every part of our life changed that dread-filled morning, as we tiptoed across the second floor landing, afraid of waking the sleeping giant on the other side of the bedroom door.

Over the next few years, we moved from one apartment to another, each time getting farther away from my father. I loved him. I didn't understand why we didn't all live together any longer. I didn't understand that he had made those black marks on my mother's face and neck. I just didn't understand.

For seven years we moved nearly every year, changed schools too many times, and left friends behind. We were latchkey children, home alone after school until my mother got there from work. I was too young to be responsible for my younger brother during those long afternoon hours.

When I was an eight-year-old child walking home from school, some neighborhood boys put their hands up my dress, laughed, and tried to steal my innocence. They were rough and ugly boys. I ran home to our empty apartment, crying, wondering why those awful things were happening and why my father wasn't there to protect me.

Childhood was lost to me. My innocence was replaced by shame. I felt ugly and unwanted. Now as an adult, I look back at that little girl, and as I understand more of what was happening to her, I feel so much grief. She was neglected, abused, molested, given far too much responsibility for her age, and expected to do what she was told regardless of how hard it was. She trusted everybody around her but some did not respect her trust in them. I wonder if they ever thought about that?

All these dark memories hurt more than I have the capacity to endure. Only with the help of those who understand and my own self-determination have I been able to peel away the shame and see there a child of God who is a vital human being full of love. I pray to God that Millie does not have to suffer these things. Writing has helped, but my soul aches.

♪♪♪

The long, hot shower was soothing, relaxing the knots in every muscle of my body. As I opened the small bathroom window to let out the steam, I discovered that a cool wind was blowing out of the Northwest. "Tomorrow will be a good day to drive along the North shore," I thought aloud, remembering that a northwest wind loosens the Irish moss from the sea floor and pushes it on shore for harvest.

After cleaning up the kitchen and writing a quick note to Susan, I pulled on a warm sweatshirt and struck out for the Crawford place just down the road. While Susan was on the Island, we visited with Linda Crawford often, talking about gardens, and good books, and our sexual fantasies. We laughed a lot on those hot, sunny afternoons in the shade of her porch, sipping cool drinks and acting like teenagers, much to the disgust of her two teenage daughters. Linda has become a good friend over the past five summers.

Her family reunion has evolved into an annual event on this end of the Island. The Crawford's invite the locals and any vacationing neighbors, a custom that started five years ago when they first visited the Island. That year the family reunion had been small, with only 23 making the trip from Maine and a few other points in the U.S.A. But this year, Linda's list of relatives numbers nearly 60, and with the usual group of locals, there will be over 100 attending the dinner and the barn dance.

Linda, a tall, well-built woman, well kept and efficient, is very adept at planning an event such as this. At home in Ontario, she manages their 200 acre farm, mowing fields, mending fences, and tending flower gardens scattered around the house and throughout the sprawling yard. In the early spring she retreats to her sugar shack in the woods to boil maple sap into gallons of syrup for special breakfasts and family gifts. A sign on a nearby tree reads, "Linda-ville, Population - 1." The sign was a Christmas gift from her children.

During the winter months, Linda and her husband, Barry, cook breakfasts and lunches for passing snowmobilers who stop along the trail that passes over their farm. Because she has so much experience responding to the hungry winter travelers at home, the Island family reunion has become just one more event, perfectly planned and always successful. Each year Linda has a surprise or two to keep everyone interested and excited about gathering so far from home.

"Linda? Are you here somewhere?" I had entered the large farmhouse from the back porch. A squeaky screen door opened into a hallway that led to a roomy, country kitchen. The smell of bread baking in the oven of the converted old-fashioned wood range was instantly familiar. There were dozens of fresh doughnuts cooling on the counter and three blueberry pies waiting to be attacked by hungry monsters. "Have you been cooking since dawn?" I asked to an empty kitchen. "Linda, where are you?" I shouted.

"Down here!" I heard her voice coming from behind a door at the far end of the kitchen. As I opened it, she said, "Is that you, Annie?"

"Yes. What in the world are you doing down there?" I called from the top of the stairs.

"I'm looking through this old stuff for ideas for the barn dance. I was thinking of asking people to wear costumes, but I think it's too late to get the word out to everybody down in Maine. What do you think?" The turquoise kerchief tied around her head was covered with dust. Her husband's denim work-shirt with its sleeves rolled up, hung down to her knees. She looked like a little girl playing house.

"Well," I replied as I neared the bottom of the rickety cellar stairs, "you've got two weeks. What kind of costumes were you thinking about?"

"Western. I've got a terrific surprise for everyone this year. I thought we could dress in western clothes and dance to country music," she said, her voice muffled now as she disappeared behind a stack of boxes. Re-appearing on the other side, she bent over to investigate a tattered rug rolled up against the rock wall of the old foundation. "There's a great country-western band that plays over in Tyne Valley. They've already agreed to be here."

"Sounds wonderful and lots of fun," I said helping her roll out the rug to get a better look at it. "I've got a beautiful pair of cowboy boots and a great hat at home," I continued as we rolled the rug back into place. "I'm sure if I called Susan, she would get them over to one of your relatives who's coming up for the event. And I bet if you called a few relatives in Maine, they would pass the word."

"Thanks, Annie. That's all I needed…just a little encouragement." She continued to rummage around in a corner of the musty cellar. "Oh, Annie, look at this!" She had pulled a crackled piece of oilcloth away from a workbench, discovering a handsome saddle. "I wonder how long this has been down here?"

"Yes, and I wonder who used it. It's magnificent!" I said, caressing the worn leather.

The saddle was made from dark, heavy leather with bits of silver worked around the edges. The initials K.M. were burned into the leather under the saddle horn. On each side of the saddle there was an intricate design burned into the leather that included fishing boats, lobster traps and the West Point Lighthouse. The saddle was worn, but in relatively good shape. The two of us groaned as we struggled with the weight and awkwardness of it. By the time we had pushed and bumped it up over the stairs into the kitchen, we were laughing so hard we collapsed over it onto the floor.

Linda pulled a kitchen stool from under the counter so we could heave the saddle onto it. "This is going to be perfect!" Her face, streaked with dust, sparkled with joy.

I laughed at her spontaneous outburst. "Linda, what are you up to? And what is the terrific surprise?" I asked, still admiring the saddle and the craftsmanship of the designer. In the light of the open kitchen, the leather work was even more stunning.

"Have you seen a single man walking on the beach this last week? He usually wears a red windbreaker." Her eyes twinkled with mischief.

"Yes. He's waved to me a couple of times. Do you know him?" I asked, drinking down a glass of water to chase away the dust of the old basement.

"Yes! That man is Casey MacDonald!" Linda's voice trembled with excitement.

"Who is Casey MacDonald?" I asked, leaving my glass at the sink before sitting down at her large kitchen table. Like many Island homes, people gathered around the centerpiece of the spacious kitchen. A long bench on one side and four kitchen chairs on the other complemented Linda's large, oak table. She had placed a red and white square cloth in the center of it and topped that with a cobalt blue vase filled with yellow wildflowers. Better Homes and Gardens would be proud. "Should I know him from one of your reunions?"

"Heavens, Annie, don't you know Casey MacDonald, the American movie star?" To emphasize her point she passed one of her daughter's movie magazines to me. Casey MacDonald's picture was on the cover.

"Of course, everyone knows him," I said without thinking. And then, as what she had said registered, I sucked in my breath. "Are you serious, Linda? That man walking on the beach is this Casey MacDonald?" I exclaimed pointing to the picture.

"In the flesh! Last week he appeared at my back door looking for a telephone. I knew who he was the minute I opened the door," she said, removing the bandana on her head and stuffing it and the dusty shirt in a laundry bag. "I managed to talk with him as though he were my brother. I invited him in and gave him some lemonade and a bag of doughnuts to take with him, then left him alone in the kitchen while he made his phone calls. When I returned, he was gone, but he left me this note." She crossed the kitchen, the note in one hand and a glass of iced tea in the other. She handed the note to me as she placed the glass in front of me, then returned to the counter for a plate of molasses cookies.

Casey MacDonald had found one of her blank recipe cards and a pencil and carefully printed:

Mrs. Crawford, Many thanks for the bag of doughnuts and the use of your phone. If I can return the favor, please call on me.
Casey MacDonald

"Well, I bet old Casey doesn't know what he's in for now!" I laughed, my mouth full of molasses delight. "Is that why you want to have a western theme for your reunion this year?"

"You betcha, pardner!" Linda drawled, as she washed the cooking dishes that had yielded the delicious treats spread along the counter. "Mr. MacDonald is staying at the old MacDougall cottage. I thought I would walk over there and ask him to the party. Why don't you come with me?"

"Sounds like fun, but we've got to keep our cool. We can't be acting like a couple of teenagers all agog over a movie star for heaven's sakes," I said waving my hands in the air like a screaming fan at a Beatles' concert. "The man probably came here for privacy."

"Yes, I thought of that," she said, chuckling at my antics. "He may not want to come to the party if he's here for a rest." Linda rarely sat down with me when I visited in her kitchen, instead keeping busy with the culinary chores she loved. She had placed the doughnuts in a huge, glass container on the counter. The pies were stored in the small pantry just to the left of the cellar door. "He told me he was walking on the beach to strengthen the muscles in his legs. Did you notice that he was limping?"

"Yes, I did. Now that you mention it, I remember reading that he was thrown from a horse in his last picture. He was in the hospital a couple of weeks and there was some problem with the studio about finishing the picture. At least that's what the gossip magazines had to say."

"Let's take a walk and find out!" Linda said with great anticipation.

Each of us looked in the mirror and then laughed. "Who are we kidding?" we said in unison, nudging each other out through the door. Still laughing, we shared some of our more embarrassing moments as we crossed the clover field.

The MacDougall cottage had been built in the 1930's a good distance from the water. But, over the years, storm surges and high tides had pushed the sand back and up forming a high dune that crowded both sides of the cottage so that its occupants no longer had much of a view to either side. Someone had recently painted the weathered clapboards white and put green shutters on all the windows. A small shed, similarly cradled by sand, sat just to the right of the cottage. Several gnarled, black spruce trees lined one side of the dirt driveway. A path found its way through the dune grass and led us to the back stairs. The inside door was open. As we looked through the weatherworn screen door, we could see into the front of the cottage and out through the windows to the porch. No one was there.

"Hello-oo." Linda's voice was carried over the dune by the wind. "Hmmmm. I guess he must be walking on the beach," she said with a hint of disappointment. "Let's go look."

As we scrambled down the stairs and around to the side, we were both startled when the door to the shed opened and Casey stuck his head out to see who was there. "Oh, hi, Mrs. Crawford. I'm busy working on a two-seater bicycle. There's not much room, but come on in!" he said, disappearing behind the door.

The small shed was dark and musty, the only light filtering through a small window in the back and a bare light bulb hanging on an orange cord hooked over a rusty nail. Aluminum framed lawn chairs with frayed seats hung on one wall, a stack of firewood filled the far, left hand corner, and jars of nails, nuts and bolts and other hardware filled two shelves haphazardly attached to another wall. A green, metal toolbox lay opened next to the two-wheeled curiosity in the center of the shed.

"I found this bicycle hanging from the rafters and decided it was a good challenge for me. Got it pretty nearly ready to go." His smile was handsome and his blue eyes snapped with the electricity of a child finding the best gift ever under the Christmas tree.

"You'll have to find someone to ride that thing with you, Mr. MacDonald, and show you around the Island," Linda offered.

"Exactly!" he said, laughing. "How about you, Mrs. Crawford?" He looked up at her as he kneeled beside the front wheel. "Dare to risk a ride with an old cowpoke?"

"No way! No offense intended, but I have never really cared for bicycles." Linda noticed Casey looking in my direction. "Oh, my goodness, where are my manners? Mr. MacDonald this is my friend Annie York. She's staying in that cottage in the dunes just down the beach."

"Hi, Annie, glad to meet you." He stood and reached out a big hand to shake mine. "Are you the person I've been seeing on the deck early in the morning?"

"One and the same," I said, feeling the warmth of his hand radiate up my arm and into my neck. He noticed that I was blushing and broke the awkward silence by looking over at Linda. "So, Mrs. Crawford, what's up?"

"Well, Mr. MacDonald..." she hesitated.

He rummaged through the toolbox looking for a smaller wrench. "Please, call me Casey," he said, finding the wrench and trying it on a nut under the front seat.

"Casey." She said his name as though for the first time. Talking to him seemed very easy, but there was that edge around the conversation, for he was, after all, a pretty famous guy. I had not seen Linda flustered before, but I could tell that she was having trouble coming up with the words to invite him to the barn dance.

"Casey, you probably came to the Island to get some rest and relax and get away from the stress of being recognized," she said, the words tumbling out of her mouth like dozens of tiny marbles. "And so if you want to say no to my request, please feel free to do so."

"Whoa, girl. I've already heard about your barn dance...that you invite your neighbors to join you and your family. To tell you the truth, I was beginning to feel left out. I hope that's what you came here to ask me." His gracious reply surprised me.

"Yes, it is." Linda was visibly relieved. "The dance is a week from Saturday, and I would like you to be the guest of honor. You see, every year I plan some sort of surprise. Everyone expects it. And to tell *you* the truth, I was beginning to think that this would be the year when I'd have to give up on that idea. And then you came to the door to use the telephone." Linda moved slightly out of the shadows into the light of the doorway. The color in her cheeks had deepened to a deep rose by the surprise and excitement of the moment.

"I would be happy to come to your barn dance, but I wish you wouldn't make a fuss. I am here trying to relax and get away from all the nonsense of publicity." He paused a minute while he tightened a nut under the rear seat of the bicycle. Then he looked up at Linda and said, "Here's an idea. If you need some sort of surprise, set up a square dance, and I'll call it for you. I had to do that in one of my movies last year and it was great fun."

"That's wonderful!" Linda was thrilled. "I'm going to ask people to wear western clothing to give us a sense of a real, country hoe-down!"

"Great. I've got some stuff with me that should work out just fine. What time does this shindig begin?" he asked, smiling.

"The festivities start at two in the afternoon. We usually have a softball game to get things started, then the cookout at six and the barn dance after that. Come over whenever you want"

"Thanks, Linda. I'll be looking forward to it." He wiped his hands on a rag and pushed the door open for us. "And, Annie, will you be there, too?" he asked, turning to me.

"Yes," was the only word that would form in my mind.

"Good." He smiled and continued to look at me as he spoke. "Linda, I'll see you before your dance, so if there's anything I can bring, don't hesitate to ask. Okay?"

Linda and I backed out of the shed and managed to wait until we were at the end of the driveway before grabbing each other like two schoolgirls who had just been asked to the Saturday night dance by the most popular boy in the school. Without saying a word, we rushed back to Linda's kitchen, nearly tripped each other trying to get through the door, and collapsed at the kitchen table.

"Wow, is he gorgeous or what?" I was still shaking from the intensity of the meeting. "No matter what, Linda, no matter how much of an adult I think I am, I just don't meet major movie stars every day. My heavens, that was Casey MacDonald!"

"Careful, girl, you're drooling!" Linda was having fun and so was I, laughing and truly enjoying life for the first time in a longer while than I wanted to remember. The traumas of the last few years and the memories from the night before had been forgotten for an afternoon while two grown women acted silly and actually had some fun doing it. It felt good.

After we came back down to earth, Linda and I talked through the afternoon about the upcoming family reunion, planning every detail. She fed me egg-salad sandwiches made with her homemade bread. The hastily created egg-salad was warm and the fresh bread burst with the flavors of wheat and yeast. Her blueberry pie was lightly flavored with cinnamon, a secret that both our grandmothers had passed along to us. She sent me home with a dozen fresh doughnuts and two more pieces of the pie, saying, "You never know, Annie, you just might have company!"

As I walked back to the cottage, I thought about why I hadn't told Linda about Millie. What a different focus our afternoon would have taken. Linda was excited by and involved with her plans for the reunion. How could I spoil that? But, I argued with myself, she would be the first person to throw all that aside to help a child. What could she do? What can anyone do?

By the time I walked through the back door, I had imagined the worst for Millie and was feeling selfish and helpless. Trembling, I looked for a clue that Millie might have been there in my absence, but there was none. In an effort to calm my nerves, I decided to walk on the beach to stretch now aching muscles and breathe in some clean air.

As I walked toward the Lighthouse, I hoped to see Millie any moment running toward me, pigtails flying behind her. But she wasn't on the beach. When I finally arrived at the Lighthouse, I decided to walk over to the park to investigate. Their tent was still set up in their campsite, but their car was gone. "Good," I thought, "they're just away for the day."

The wind had picked up again and the western sky boiled with charcoal clouds. Hoping the weather pattern would change soon, I hurried back to the cottage and fastened the shutters over the windows to protect them from any flying debris. Thinking that the power might go off, I filled a couple of buckets with water and set out the candles and matches.

Soon the wind was blowing a gale, threatening to rip the shingles off the roof. In staggered intervals, great gusts of wind and red beach sand slammed the northwest wall. A heavy downpour slashed at the front wall of the cottage, turning the sliding glass door opaque. A small stream of water seeped under the front door finding its way down through the cracks in the wooden floor to the storage space below.

Just as I burrowed into the protection of the wonderful, old sofa, the lights went out. Well, I had expected that. Like Noah and his family drifting at sea in the ark, my little ship in the dunes was all closed in, riding the crest of the waves, holding back the torment of the storm. The fire spit and crackled in the woodstove as the wet piece of wood I had placed on top of a pile of kindling finally fell into the flames.

I lay there wrapped in a blue and white quilt I've carried with me through life. It was made and given to me by my grandmother when I was in high school. With my eyes closed, I took a deep breath, smelling the sweet essence of mint and ginger in the small pieces of fabric that recorded the memories of my family.

The wind howled unmercifully throughout the night. The sand and the rain pelted against the clapboards with every gust. In the early hours of the morning, the wind lifted something heavy and threw it against the northwest wall of the cottage. The thud lifted me off the sofa putting me on my feet before I was fully awake. I stood there for a moment shaking uncontrollably, then fell back onto the sofa, wide-eyed and fully alert, terrified. The soft texture of the quilt caressed my cheek as I wrapped myself in it once again and snuggled down into the sofa and the pillows in an act of self-protection. I slept. I was five years old again.

♪♪♪

The truck was spinning in the sand, riding around and around in a great circle. I could hear her screaming, pleading with him to stop…to let her in. I could hear my brother crying and my father laughing. The laugh wasn't a happy laugh, but a spiteful, hateful laugh as he floored the accelerator again and again, spinning the wheels of the truck in the sand.

Now she was on the running board, looking in the window, fear in her eyes as she looked at each one of us. "Stop," she screamed. "Please, stop!"

I started to cry. "Daddy, Daddy, what are you doing? Let Mommy get in!" I grabbed his arm and pulled hard. He turned to look at me, letting the truck slow down. It was then he stopped the truck. My mother jumped in, and we went home.

♪♪♪

The early morning was chilly. The howling wind had not let up. I wanted to burrow further into the sofa, under the cushions where the warmth of my body had been stored throughout the night. I lay there for an hour hoping the storm would pass, but it didn't.

I added a few sticks of cedar and a couple of dry logs to the woodstove and tiptoed across the wet floor to make a cup of hot tea on the gas burner. Returning to the sanctuary of the sofa, I quickly wrapped up in the wonderful old quilt. The hot tea and a couple of Linda's doughnuts warmed my soul. I tried to read, but the cottage was too dark because of the closed shutters. The sweet aroma of the burning cedar relaxed me and, again, I slept.

♪♪♪

"Go to bed, Annie," my father said in a soft, soothing voice. I was sitting on my mother's lap, her arm was around me and her hand was on my leg. As my father talked, her grip got firmer. "Annie, it's late and you should go to bed."

"No, Daddy, I'm scared! I want to stay with you and Mommy." My mother was trembling as I buried my face in the softness of her sweater.

I learned much later that I saved my mother's life that night. I was my father's pride and joy, the love of his life. Because I was frightened, he calmed down. He had been in a rage, a rage that usually led to terrible, brutal beatings. But that night he picked me up from my mother's lap and read to me until we both fell asleep over the book. My mother left us in the big chair in the corner of the living room and went to bed in peace.

♪♪♪

The dreams continued. I drifted in and out of consciousness, chasing and being chased by the demons and monsters of the past. A loud knocking on the door broke the hold of unconsciousness.

"Annie! Annie! Are you in there?" The voice sounded like it was coming up through a pipe. I was tangled up in the quilt and still numb from sleep, but I recognized Millie's voice.

"Just a minute, Millie. I'll be right there," I mumbled as my arms and legs moved in slow motion.

"Annie!" She couldn't hear me above the noise of the wind and the banging of the shutters. My arms and legs felt like lead, but I finally extricated myself from the quilt and ran to the door. She was gone.

The wind blew the door out of my hand, and it slammed back against the wall. I hurried back through the cottage and out onto the deck to look down the beach, but I couldn't see very far through the heavy rain. Grabbing my jacket, I flew out the back door and ran down the beach toward the park, but Millie was nowhere to be seen, so I returned to the cottage trembling from the cold rain and the anxiety for a lost child.

The small woodstove was my only source of heat. Another dry log added to the bed of coals from last night's fire caught quickly. The warmth from the fire, dry clothes and another cup of hot tea chased away the bone-chilling cold, but I couldn't get Millie out of my mind. Had I imagined her knocking at the door? I didn't think so. I drank more of the hot tea and then rummaged through a back closet for the old yellow slicker that hung there. It wasn't very glamorous, but it would keep me dry. I struck out for Linda's, regretting that I hadn't shared Millie's story yesterday when I had the chance. Now there wasn't time to explain anything, except to tell her that I was looking for a terrified nine-year old girl and wondering all the while if I was losing my mind. Was I still dreaming or was this real?

Linda hadn't seen Millie. The heavy heat from the wood stove warmed her kitchen. The smell of cinnamon and nutmeg was inviting, but I was convinced that Millie was in trouble.

"Annie, I don't think you should go back out in this storm by yourself. I wish Barry was here to go with you." She handed me a towel to dry my face.

"Linda, I know that kid is out there somewhere and needs some help. Look, I'll go over to the MacDougall Cottage and see if she's there. If she isn't, I'll come right back. Okay?" I handed her the damp towel.

"Okay, but for crying out loud, be careful." She hugged me and stood back from the door.

When I stepped out onto the porch, a gust of wind blew me back against the door. Pulling the strings of my hood tightly under my chin so only my eyes were exposed to the rain, I leaned into the wind and made my way toward the dunes. I was fifteen minutes traveling the distance it took Linda and me five minutes to travel the other day.

Casey opened the door immediately. "Hi, Casey, do you remember me?" I shouted, releasing the ties on the hood of the slicker so he could see my face.

"Sure. Annie, isn't it? What are you doing out in miserable weather like this? Come in, come in," he said as he held the screen door open for me.

I stepped past him into the warmth of the cottage. "Have you seen a little girl about nine? She has dark auburn hair done up in long pigtails."

He scowled. "No. My God, is she lost in this storm?"

"Yes, I think she is." Small puddles were forming around my feet.

"Is she your daughter?" he asked, closing the door. A strong gust of wind shook the cottage, and we both jumped.

"No. No. It's a long story, really," I stuttered, staring through his front windows at a small, tattered flag waving franticly in the wind. In that moment, my entire attention was focused on the wild motion of that flag, blown about by the strong winds. Was Millie out there in that madness?

"Annie?" Casey's light touch on my arm broke the momentary spell. "Why do you think the little girl is out in this storm?" The six-foot-four man stood before me in his stocking feet, dressed in tattered jeans and a soft cotton shirt hanging loose over a white t-shirt. His sandy brown hair was mussed suggesting I had interrupted a nap.

"She came to my cottage about a half hour ago," I said, pushing the hood further back from my face. "I was sleeping like the dead when she knocked, and by the time I got to the door, she had gone. At first, I thought I had dreamed it, but the more I thought about it, I realized that she had actually been there." While I talked, Casey reached in a closet for his jacket. "I looked for her on the beach, and walked back toward the park where she and her family are staying, but I never saw her. The only other direction she might have gone is this way."

"Hmmm." I could see by the frown on his face that Casey was concerned. I remembered reading that he had two children of his own, one about the same age as Millie. "Maybe she found shelter in that old shed. Let's take a look." He led the way out the door and down the steps. When we stepped into the opening between the cottage and the shed, the wind blew me against him. He reached out instinctively, grabbed my arm, and held the shed door open so I could look inside. The beam of light from my flashlight caught a flash of bright yellow in the far corner. "Millie!" I cried.

"Oh, Annie," she screamed as she ran to me and hugged me around the waist. She was trembling and soaking wet. "Annie, I was so scared. When you didn't come to the door, this was the only place I could find to get out of the storm. I didn't know where I was!"

"You're okay now, Millie," Casey said, picking her up. "Let's go inside and get you dried off." Millie wrapped her arms around his neck as he ducked through the small opening and sprinted through the rain to the back stairs of the cottage. She was giggling when he put her down on the top step, opened the door for her, and with a sweep of his arm said, "After you, my lady."

"Millie, I'm Casey MacDonald. Glad to meet you," he laughed as the three of us stomped through the entryway into his small kitchen.

Millie looked up at him, smiled and said, "Hi, Casey MacDonald."

"I think there's some hot chocolate around here somewhere. Why don't I brew up a few cups, and you two can go in here to dry off," he said as he led us into a back bedroom where he found a couple of big, terrycloth bath towels that smelled like vanilla ice cream. When he stepped out into the kitchen, Millie hugged me, put her cold, wet face against mine and whispered, "Thanks, Annie, for finding me. I was so scared."

"I know, honey. I was scared, too." I held her for a few minutes, giving thanks to God that she was safe.

The slicker had kept me relatively dry, but Millie's sweatshirt was soaked. We both laughed as I tried to pull it, heavy with water and inside out, over her head. Like a wet bathing suit, it just wouldn't budge. Millie's muffled giggles made me laugh, too. Finally, she put her arms straight up and one last pull revealed a red face covered with dancing freckles.

"There," I said throwing the heavy, wet mass on the floor. Millie quickly removed her t-shirt and shorts and I wrapped her up in one of the terry-cloth bath sheets. Her bruises from the other day were healing nicely, but I noticed a fresh one at the base of her spine. As I dried her back she winced, and then she hugged me and held on. We didn't need to say anything. She knew I had seen the bruise.

"Millie, how did you happen to be out in this terrible storm?" I asked, taking her wet clothes into the adjacent bathroom to wring them out in the tub.

"Oh, Annie, when the storm got bad last night we got in the car to keep dry." She followed me into the bathroom and watched as I hung her clothes over the shower bar to dry. Shivering, she held the bath towel closed in front of her with both hands. "When Mommy and I woke up, Daddy started to scream at us. That's how he sounds just before he starts to hit me. So I told him I had to go to the bathroom. The little building where the bathrooms are is right beside our campsite, so they let me go alone." She looked up and was surprised to find me staring at her, my arms locked in place over my head, the wet t-shirt suspended in air. "Annie," she said, "are you okay?"

Shocked by her story, I cleared my throat and finished draping her clothes over the bar. "You were very courageous to walk on the beach in that storm, Millie," I said, my voice under control, "but that was very dangerous, too."

"I know, Annie, but as soon as I got out of our car I was too scared to get back in. When I couldn't find you at your cottage, I thought I was going back to the park. But I got all confused and then I found that shed." She shivered again and pulled the towel tighter.

"Well, thank God you're all right," I said, hugging her and rubbing her back to warm her body. We fashioned the big towel much like a Roman toga, wrapped a smaller towel over her shoulders, and went back to the kitchen where we found Casey stirring a pot of hot chocolate.

The MacDougall cottage was somewhat smaller than mine, its open front room cramped by the addition of a breakfast bar separating the kitchen from the living area. A door in the center of the front wall opened to a small deck beyond. Red and white café curtains, tied back at the sides, framed the two windows on either side of the door. A matching valance hung over the six-pane window in the door. A small red and white enamel table with its two matching chairs was tucked under the kitchen windows. The living room, sparsely furnished with two pieces of wooden-framed furniture, narrowed at the far end to accommodate a corner bookshelf laden down with books, candles, shells, and small pieces of driftwood. Sea glass spilled out of a hand made berry basket sitting on top of an old trunk.

"Mmmmm, that smells good, Casey," I said, refocusing my attention back to the kitchen and helping Millie onto one of the stools tucked under the lip of the breakfast bar.

Casey poured three cups of hot chocolate then leaned on the counter. "Are you warm enough, Millie?"

"Yes, thanks," she said, as she sipped the steaming liquid. "Mmmm, this is good."

"That's my secret recipe, Millie. My kids love it." Casey looked at me over her head and silently mimed, "What now?"

Before I could say anything, Millie asked, "Are you the Casey MacDonald who is in all those westerns?" She was relaxed now, holding the mug of hot chocolate, and chewing on one of Linda's doughnuts.

"That's me!" Casey said, pouring a little more hot chocolate into Millie's cup.

While Millie concentrated on dunking her doughnut into the steaming brown liquid and eating the mushy end before it fell off, Casey and I walked to the back door. "Casey, this is putting you in an awkward position, but do you mind if I leave Millie here while I go back to Linda's to call the park? I think hearing from me would be less of a shock for her parents, than wondering what on earth she's doing here with you. Don't you?"

"You're probably right, Annie," Casey whispered, "but let's make sure Millie is comfortable with your idea."

In her innocence, Millie was thrilled to spend time with Casey who promised to tell her stories about the moviemaking business. As I approached the back door, I could hear him whooping and hollering as he pretended to be a cowboy, riding a broom around the kitchen. She was squealing with delight at his antics. I hurried back to Linda's home to tell her I had found Millie and to call the park to tell her parents. Linda couldn't believe it.

"You mean she was hiding in Casey's shed?" she asked, hugging me through the door.

"Yes. She got turned around on the beach, and that was the first place she found to get in out of the rain. You know, he's quite a guy."

Linda smiled knowingly. "Yes, he is, but watch out girl. He's also dangerous!"

"Right. Like he's going to be interested in me." I shook the water out of the slicker and hung it on a peg in the entryway, then hurried to the phone. The park ranger assured me that she would immediately inform the Carters of Millie's whereabouts. Linda was waiting at the door with a plastic bag filled with homemade goodies.

"I left your number at the park," I said, pulling on the cold slicker, "in case Millie's parents get antsy and want to talk to her. If they call back, send one of the kids over. Otherwise, we'll wait out the storm for a few hours while her clothes dry out. Then we'll take her back over there."

"If she were my kid, I'd be over there right now," Linda exclaimed.

"I know, but perhaps it's better this way for now," I said, as I hugged her and pulled my hood back over my head.

"What do you mean, Annie?" she asked, her frustration turning to concern.

"I'm worried about her, Linda. I promise to come back and tell you all about it, but right now I've got to get back to Millie. I've left that little girl alone with a total stranger. She assured me she'd be okay for a few minutes, and I'm sure she is, but I don't want to be away any longer than necessary." I hugged her again, took the bag of food she had prepared for us, and left her standing in her kitchen, a deep frown obscuring the plain beauty of her face.

Breathless from my struggle to cross the field against the wind, I stumbled through the back door of Casey's cottage. As I kicked off my sneakers and hung my wet slicker on a peg in the hall, I could hear them laughing easily together.

"Annie," Millie said turning on the stool to face me, "Casey was just telling me some secrets about making his last western. And he told me that we could come visit on his next movie. He's making it near Lake Ontario. That's only a few hours from our house!" Her cheeks were streaked with rosy excitement.

"Really? That's great," I sighed with relief, giving her a hug. "Look what I brought back with me. Linda is so thoughtful. She sent these peanut butter and jelly sandwiches and these chocolate chip cookies just for you, Millie."

The three of us sat at the small kitchen table eating Linda's sandwiches and cookies and drinking more hot chocolate. Casey had many more stories to tell us about the movie business. For a few hours, Millie forgot the reason she came to be with two strangers in the first place. Casey's silly facial expressions, strange voices, and funny stories made her laugh. Best of all, Casey made her feel good about herself. I was impressed with her questions and her interest in the minute details she longed to understand. As I watched them together, I marveled at the ease with which they interacted; and chuckled to myself, thinking that there hadn't been any need to hurry back or to leave poor Linda standing alone in her kitchen imagining the worst possible scenario.

"Sounds like the storm has let up, Millie," Casey said, as he picked up the sandwich wrappings and put them in the paper bag. "Your clothes are probably dry by now. Why don't you get dressed, and I'll take you and Annie back to the park."

I could see the look of horror on Millie's face. Casey noticed it too, but didn't react. Instead, he said, "If your sweatshirt is still wet, put on that flannel shirt hanging on the hook behind the door."

When Millie and I were in the bedroom, I suggested that it might be a good idea to have Casey take us back to the park. "Your father will see that you're okay," I said slowly, "and maybe Casey's presence will help. What do you think?"

"I don't know, Annie," she whimpered. "I'm scared to go back there." She sat on the edge of the bed, shivering, as I helped her get dressed. Casey's flannel shirt with the sleeves rolled up fit her like a coat.

"I know, honey. I wish you could stay here a little longer, but I'm sure your mother must be worried sick about you." As I said this, I wondered why her mother had not come banging on Casey's door looking for her daughter. Perhaps this was her way of protecting Millie until her husband calmed down. In any event, the entire situation was more than I could understand.

The three of us bundled into Casey's Jeep and bumped down the old dirt driveway to the main road. The fury of the storm had passed, but the damage from it was visible at every turn. A large spruce tree had been turned up by its roots, taking half the pavement with it. Another tree lay over the corner of a house, exposing the contents like the backside of a dollhouse. The owners were competing with the wind to tie down a big, blue tarp that had covered their boat the previous day.

When we arrived at the park, Millie showed us where their campsite was located. As we pulled in beside the car, her mother jumped out and ran toward her shouting, "Millie. Millie. I was so worried about you. Why did you disappear like that, honey?" Millie ran to her and buried herself in her mother's arms.

The door on the other side of the car opened and her father's head appeared over the roof of the vehicle. He walked slowly around the back of the car to meet us. Millie's father was not a handsome man. His long, black hair was combed straight back and gathered in a ponytail at the base of his neck. There were dark circles beneath small, dark brown eyes and an ugly, red scar that ran from beneath his right ear along the edge of his chin.

He introduced himself, thrusting a big, calloused hand toward Casey. "Bob Carter," he said, straightening his tall frame.

"Casey MacDonald, and this is Annie York." Casey's voice was deep and somber. He was beginning to understand the situation.

"Thanks for helping my kid. I can't imagine what got into her." He shuffled his feet as though he wanted to say something more, but didn't.

"No harm done, Mr. Carter," Casey said. "We've had a lot of fun this afternoon. Your daughter is a beautiful child."

"Mr. Carter, I'm glad to meet you," I said, stepping toward him, my hand outstretched to shake his. "I met Millie on the beach a few days ago, so I guess that's why she felt she could come to my cottage for help. Evidently she got turned around on the beach in the storm." My breath caught in my throat when he took my hand, but I decided to take a chance right then and kept talking, hoping I didn't sound like I was making it up as I went, because I was. "Mr. Carter, I'm up here doing some writing and I need help with my research. If you folks are going to be here for another week or so, do you suppose Millie could come by each morning and work with me?"

"Well, I don't know. What would she be doing?" By now, he had his hands shoved into his jeans pockets, his shoulders hunched up as though someone was about to hit him. I calmed down.

"I'm writing about the plants and grasses on this part of the Island," I said convincing myself, "so I need to collect specimens. Millie has a natural curiosity, and I think she would be a great help to me. We would walk the beach and record various plants in the dunes. We would also take some short trips to gather plants from some of the surrounding fields and woods. I'll pay her, of course."

"Millie, does that sound like something you'd like to do?" her mother asked, kneeling beside her to talk with her.

"Oh, yes, Mommy, could I?" Millie hugged her around the neck and whispered something in her ear.

Millie's mother looked at Mr. Carter for the answer. Neither Millie nor I believed he would say yes, but he surprised us both.

"I don't see the harm in it," he shrugged.

"Oh, Daddy, thank you." Millie ran to him and hugged him. He patted her head with his big hand. His reaction to her was stiff, as though the tenderness was foreign to him. Millie's mother looked on as astonished as I was, tears in her eyes.

"Wonderful," I said. "Millie, why don't you come over in the morning when you get up? The earlier the better. Okay?"

"Okay, Annie. I'll see you then." She continued to stand by her father, her arm around his waist.

"Yes, well thanks again for helping her," Mr. Carter said. And with that they disappeared into the car. Millie waved to me through the back window.

As Casey and I drove back to my cottage, he said, "Seems like there's more to that little girl's story than meets the eye."

"You're right, Casey. Would you like to come in for a cup of coffee, and I'll tell you as much as I know about it?"

"Sure." He turned off the ignition and threw the keys into the center console.

While I made the coffee, Casey wandered around in the small cottage, looking at the photographs, picking an odd-shaped rock off the mantel at the far side of the room, turning it over in his hands before gently putting it back. When I poured out two cups of coffee and placed them on the kitchen table, he quickly walked back across the room to hold the chair as I sat down. We talked about Millie at first. I told him what I knew about her and my concerns for her. He was upset when I described the bruises, and like me, wanted to do something about it immediately. But as we weighed all the possible alternatives, we discovered that there was little we could do except be there for her and keep an eye on her as much as possible.

"At least her father is going to let her come to the cottage every morning. Perhaps that will help keep her out of harm's way for a few hours a day," I said hoping my initial lie had not been apparent to him.

Casey's eyebrows knit together as he looked at me over a suspended coffee cup. "Is that what you do for work, Annie?"

"No. I just made up that story. Well, not really made up," I blushed. "I've been thinking about cataloging the plants that grow along the shore for a couple of years now. I don't know what made me say it out loud, except I just wanted to do something to help Millie. So the story I told her father wasn't entirely untrue."

Casey chuckled. "I thought you must be a famous botanist or something."

We laughed easily together, talking through two pots of coffee. Late afternoon passed unnoticed into early evening. Just outside the cottage the rain stopped, the sun filtered through a veil of clouds resting along the horizon, and the seagulls pursued their evening ritual. Just inside the cottage two people from vastly different lives found common ground around their concern for a nine-year-old child. Conversation about careers and hometowns and family grew out of that common bond.

Since neither of us had eaten any real food that day, except Linda's sandwiches, I rummaged through the refrigerator and managed to find enough eggs, mushrooms and cheese to make an omelet. I had a piece of ham left over from yesterday's dinner and some boiled potatoes that turned into some pretty good home fries. I laughed to myself as I served up Linda's two pieces of blueberry pie.

"Man, this is like being out on the set when we film a western. Mighty good eatin', Ma'am," Casey drawled and laughed.

"Thanks. It was nothing, Cowboy." I smiled, remembering Casey and Millie deep in conversation, he with a dish towel wrapped around his throat like a western bandana, she with a towel toga, her pigtails dripping little spots of water on the floor behind her.

"Annie, what are you doing here by yourself?" he asked, eating the last bite of blueberry pie.

I had been waiting for that question. Telling him my story would make me much too vulnerable to him, and I wasn't sure I wanted to expose all those feelings. So I just said, "Oh, I come here every year for a vacation. I love this place, and Linda and her family have become close friends. We keep in touch over the winter. I wouldn't miss one of her reunions. You know that's going to be a good time this year," I said, changing the subject.

"Yeah, it sounds like fun. I just hope she doesn't make too much over me. You know the limelight can get pretty hard to take. That's why I'm up here." Casey stood up and stretched by putting his fists in the small of his back and leaning backward. As he did so, he looked up at the clock over the sink. "Wow, I've been here longer than I thought, Annie. You probably have things to do."

"Nothing very pressing. I'm on vacation, remember?" I hesitated a moment, began to speak, then thought better of it.

"What?" Casey asked, a smile causing a dimple to form in his right cheek. His sandy hair, combed to one side, hung loose over his forehead.

Talking over my shoulder as I walked toward the sofa, I said, "It's none of my business, really, but I wondered about that limp. Didn't I read somewhere that you got hurt filming a movie out west?"

Casey settled himself in the upholstered chair that faced the sofa and the windows behind it that framed the view of the water. "On our last shoot, I was knocked off my horse during a cattle stampede. A couple of the cattle ran over me and did some damage to my leg. Tore this quadriceps muscle up quite badly." He reached down and rubbed his leg just above his knee. "We were able to finish the movie after some fast editing to write in the accident, but I was dog-tired. My production company wanted me to fly to South America to start another movie right away, but I wasn't in any shape to do it. There were a few legal hassles about it, but when you're a star you can get away with a lot."

"So is that why you came up here, to get away and rest that leg?" I asked, leaning back into the sofa as I relaxed.

"That and I needed some time away from family, too. My wife and I haven't been getting along this past year," he said leaning forward, his elbows on his knees. "God, Annie, you make it too easy for me to talk about some pretty personal stuff. Maybe this is more than you really want to know."

"Nonsense," I said, waving my hand, sounding braver than I felt. "Perhaps talking about it will help."

"It's difficult for her and the kids because I'm away so much, and the tabloids are always making something out of nothing. During this last negotiation of the South American deal, things got pretty tense, and we said some things that will be hard to take back. So I decided that I needed some breathing room. A friend of mine had heard about this place. In fact, I think he's related to Linda in some way." He relaxed and leaned back in the chair. "I called and was able to rent the cottage for a month. It's just what I needed to put a little perspective back into my life."

"Perspective. Interesting word. When you've got it, or think you have, all the baggage that you're carrying seems to fall away like some wonderful miracle, doesn't it?"

"Sometimes. But in my case, I'm afraid perspective has only managed to help me see my problems in a clearer light. It's tough, Annie, to keep so much inside all the time. My kids are everything to me, and I think I've been denying the truth so that I don't hurt them. But in the process, I guess I've hurt them anyway. Sometimes you just can't win, and all the perspective in the world doesn't help at all." As he talked, Casey maintained eye contact. "What kind of problems wait for you back in Maine, Annie?"

"Oh, just the ordinary life sort of things. You big movie stars wouldn't appreciate any of it." I laughed as a blush started to make its way up from my neck to my cheeks.

This was the second time Casey had encouraged me to open up and failing, decided to change the subject. I breathed a sigh of relief as he shared some fascinating stories about the film business. He was wonderful, answering all my silly questions about whether or not he did his own stunts and what some of the other stars were like. Suddenly he noticed the color in the evening sky.

"My God, Annie, isn't that beautiful?" he said, looking over my head at the colorful scene framed by the windows.

Turning, I gasped in appreciation at the beauty before us. "Let's go out on the deck to get a better look."

The storm had passed leaving behind a comforting silence. The sun had dropped like an egg into the ribbon of violet sky that sat along the horizon, a perfect backdrop for the azure blue water. We stood on the deck with our hands on the rail, both looking out at the sunset, our arms just brushing against one another. The gesture wasn't much, but he leaned against me for a second. His face never changed. He kept staring straight ahead, then turned to me and said, "It's been a day, hasn't it Annie? I better get back."

I walked with him through the cottage and out the back door to his Jeep. "Thanks, Casey, for your help with Millie. I think meeting you was a big treat for her."

"Well, meeting you has been a big treat for me. I'll see you, Annie."

"I hope so, Casey."

He started the truck, smiled and was gone. "Yes, Casey, it has been a day all right," I whispered into the cool night air.

I went back to the deck and watched the color of the sky continue to change along the horizon. The red sand beach was deserted. A golden cast from the setting sun magnified the driftwood and seaweed strewn about from the storm. Then the bright orange ball of fire disappeared into the water.

"Tomorrow morning I'll comb the beach for unusual pieces of driftwood and more sea glass for my collection," I thought out loud. "Millie should be here, too. We'll have a good time investigating the gifts from the sea. And the mossers will be up on the North Shore. If Casey has never seen them harvest sea moss, I think he might be quite fascinated by it.

"Now would you listen to me, talking like that man is going to be that sociable. I've got to forget Casey MacDonald! Besides," I laughed, "if he heard me talking out loud like this, he would be certain that I'd lost my mind." I waved at an older couple walking on the beach, then settled into the old Morris chair and watched the dusk turn into night.

Part Two

Letting Go

Chapter 6

August – 1993

The air is fresh and clear as though the storm has sucked all the impurities away with it. The sunrise brought with it a cloudless blue sky and a gentle breeze from the south.... air that is warmer than it has been in several days.

I am always amazed at how different life can be from one day to the next...how unexpected events and people we've never met before can change the course of our life's journey. But then, perhaps, that was the course designed for us all along, and the change is really in our understanding of where our particular path leads.

But be careful what you wish for, the old saying goes. Each morning, as I've walked on the beach, I have asked God to fill my life with fresh and fulfilling experiences. Both Millie and Casey have become unexpected co-travelers on my summer journey to wholeness. Each one of us is terribly wounded, dealing with a crisis. Perhaps each one of us has something that the others need. Has God led us to this beautiful place to help one another, or was our meeting just coincidence? And if we are to help one another, what can we do, here in a foreign country, to help that precious child without jeopardizing her welfare? Report him or keep silent? Or is there another solution?

We are an either/or society. Things are good or bad, dark or light, right or wrong. The answer to a hard problem is either this or that. Our society doesn't push us hard enough to think beyond the possibility of two answers or two options...when, in reality, we might find there a myriad of solutions.

I remember seeing a greeting card in a little shop in a coastal village that read... "Beyond the field of right, and the field of wrong, there's another field." Inside the card it read..."I'll meet you there." I've never forgotten that card because it taught me that there is always another way to look at things. Sometimes that other way is hard to find, and sometimes we never do find it; but nevertheless, the other way exists somewhere in the universe. And with that thought, there is hope.

♪♪♪

I looked down the beach toward the park expecting to see Millie running toward the cottage, but she was not there. I wondered what was keeping her.

While I waited, I decided to check the shutters for any damage caused by the storm. I discovered that the hinges had been stressed by the wind so that some of the screws had pulled loose. Not wanting to experience another bump in the night, I removed the weather-beaten boards and secured them under the cottage. As I gave the cumbersome objects a final shove, I noticed a piece of dark wood sticking out of the sand next to the deck. Most of it was buried in the dune. Now curious, I got down on my knees and scooped the sand away with my hands, unearthing a board about two feet long and a foot wide. I gasped when I discovered "The Lady Ann" printed in faded black letters on the grey-blue board.

"It's the name of a boat," I exclaimed. "This must be what hit the side of the cottage the other night." I touched the name painted on the piece of wood and smiled. Of all the namesakes to discover in the sand next to this particular cottage, how strange that it was this one. A good sign, I thought.

My eye caught a movement on the beach, so I looked over the dune expecting to see Millie but the figure turned out to be a big, black lab, nose down, chasing the scent of some imagined prey. The lab's owners were further back, trying to catch up, calling the lab's name in vain. They looked up and waved. I put my hand over my head in a feeble attempt at civility. Where on earth was Millie?

I waited another hour, but she never came. The walk to the park seemed to take forever. My legs trembled from the forced march across the beach. My heart raced from worry and my lungs burned from the exertion. When I got to their campsite, my heart stopped. There was nothing there. No tent. No treasures from the beach on the picnic table. No wet towels hanging over the fence. They were gone.

I rushed to the ranger's hut to inquire about them. "Good morning," I said gasping for breath. "Can you tell me if the Carters have left the Island?"

A pleasant looking young woman looked up from a small desk. "The Carters? Oh yes, they packed up everything this morning and went over to Cavendish for a few days. I think they got tired of sleeping in their car," she chuckled. "But I'm sure they're coming back. Let me check." She rummaged through some papers on her desk until she found a small notebook marked 'Reservations.' "Yes, here it is. They made reservations for that same campsite for Tuesday night."

"Thanks," I said, as I waved good-bye to her. I was relieved that they were planning to return, but there was an uneasy feeling in the pit of my stomach. Fearing the worst, I hoped I was wrong. The request to have Millie help me had seemed like a good idea at the time, but asking Mr. Carter on the same afternoon that we brought her back from her great escape was probably a big mistake. I hoped that Millie wasn't paying for that mistake.

I was shaking. The old anxiety was trying to get its claws into me again. Instead of walking back to the cottage where I would be alone to anguish over brutality too horrible to imagine, I turned toward the harbor thinking that I would inquire about a boat named the 'Lady Ann.' Perhaps that would help keep my mind occupied until I could calm down. To my surprise, I found Ernest talking with some tourists about the lobster season. After they left, I sat down next to him and asked about the missing boat.

"No. No boat in this area with that name," he said, smiling his greeting at me. "Could have been in the sea for a long time, you know, Annie." Ernest was sitting on a couple of lobster traps whittling a dolphin out of a piece of driftwood. His blue eyes sparkled with the youthful gleam of a nineteen-year old. White tufts of hair stuck out on both sides of the old cap that covered his balding head. Like most men, Ernest looked so much younger with his cap on.

Because he had been a fisherman for fifty years, he liked to walk down to the harbor to sit on a stack of discarded lobster traps and wait for the boats to come in with their catch. He is a kind and generous man, still interested in the younger men who have their own boats, still knitting heads for the traps. The heads are the nets that fit down inside the traps to hold the bait and trap the lobsters. Ernest has developed a special contraption to make them, expertly weaving the green nylon cord. He demonstrated his handicraft for me a few summers ago. You just roll the contraption in under your kitchen chair, tie the cord to a ring fastened on a post out in front of you, put your feet on a piece of wood that protrudes out from each side of the post, then pull tightly on the cord so you can knit the head…much like doing macramé.

"What's wrong with you, girl? Are you having a bad time of it up here all alone now that your friend has gone back?" Ernest was such a dear man. He could always tell when I was upset about something.

"I'll admit I was lonely at first, but the Island has worked its magic." I paused, not sure how to continue. "But I met a little girl from the park the other day and I think her father is hurting her. She was supposed to come over to the cottage this morning to help me with a project, but she didn't show up. I went looking for her and found out that they've gone over to Cavendish for a few days."

"Bad business it is." Ernest's blue eyes darkened as he talked.

We both looked up as a boat navigated through the opening at the far end of the wharf. The harbor is a self-contained area with its wharf built up like a great breakwater. The wharf was designed in the shape of a huge square with an open water area in the middle so the boats can maneuver to unload and moor for the night. There is a paved area on two sides of the square, so the trucks are able to drive up to the boats when they are tied off to the wooden pilings that line the water side of the wharf. The opening to the sea is not direct, but doglegs to the left around the outer protective side of the square. The boats make their way out easily, but coming back in, especially when there are high rolling waves, is a bit tricky. The captain has to guide the boat straight in and then make a ninety-degree left turn into the protected harbor. My heart has been in my throat many times as I've watched them maneuver through a pounding surf.

The boat was slowing, making its way to the side of the docking area. It was the "Andrea Lea," Ernest's son's boat. Lindy waved when he saw me. I stood and waved back at him and yelled, "Hello!" Then I turned to Ernest who was putting his whittling knife and the little dolphin into a small canvas bag.

"Now don't go worrying about that little girl, Annie," he said, as he pulled the drawstring tight on the bag. "There's nothing you can do for her if she isn't even here. Do you think she'll be back?"

"Yes," I said, as I brushed a piece of wood shaving off his shirt. "I hope so, anyway. The park ranger said they have reservations for Tuesday night."

"Good. They've probably gone to the other side of the Island looking for better weather. If there was any problem, he wouldn't bring her back here." He stood up to greet his son.

"Oh, by the way, have you heard whether or not they're harvesting Irish moss yet after the big storm?" I asked when he bent over to give me a hug.

"Yes. They're harvesting up at North Cape. Quite a sight it is! You going up for a look?"

"I'd like to. There's a fellow visiting over at the MacDougall Cottage who might like to see that, too." The smile I tried to hide gave me away.

Ernest looked at me over the top of his glasses, a twinkle in his eye, and a smile making up around the corners of his mouth. "A fellow?"

"Yup. There's a movie star from the United States staying over at the MacDougall Cottage." Ernest's eyebrows shot in the air. "I met him with Linda the first of the week," I continued. "Nice guy! Thought I would ask him if he's ever seen them harvesting Irish moss. If not, maybe he would like to ride down there." I was trying to act nonchalant about it all, but Ernest could see right through me.

"Now this sounds as good as one of my fishing stories, Annie. A movie star you say? Who?" Ernest was chuckling.

"His name is Casey MacDonald. He's been in some westerns, mostly. Linda invited him to the reunion, and as far as I know he's going." I linked my arm in Ernest's and walked with him toward the Andrea Lea. She was moored at the innermost end of the harbor so that the crane stationed there could lift the heavy-laden lobster crates to the scales.

"MacDonald, you say. Wonder if he's related?" Then Ernest laughed that wonderful belly laugh that started at his toes and worked up through his body until he was shaking all over. I laughed with him.

"He's certainly not as good looking as you are, Ernest, but maybe he is related." We laughed even harder as Ernest gave me a big hug. I kissed him on the cheek and headed back to the cottage. When I looked back, he waved. I returned the wave and wished again that Ernest were about forty years younger. Now there's passion for you! There's the ability to touch another's soul. I had felt it the first time I met him.

The couple with the black lab approached me on the beach. They had finally managed to get their pet under control. With his tongue hanging out of his mouth dripping saliva, he was walking obediently beside them as they returned to the park. We nodded our hellos as we passed one another. Funny, I thought, some people are so shy, and others will stop and talk for hours as though they've known you forever.

When I got back to the cottage there was a note tucked into the handle on the back door.

Annie, Stopped by to ask you to go for a ride with me on the two-seater.
If you get back before noon, come on over.   Casey

I looked at my watch. It was 11:30. I hurried inside, changed my shirt for something a little more attractive, combed my hair and put on a little makeup...but not too much. By the time I reached Casey's cottage, a small clock inside was chiming the noon hour.

"Hi, Annie. I was giving up hope that I'd see you this morning. Thought you might have gone away with Millie." He opened the screen door and beckoned to me to come in. He was dressed in jeans and a light blue shirt the same color as his eyes. I could feel the warmth of a blush rising up my neck.

"I was expecting her," I said, as I followed him into the cottage, "but when she didn't show up, I walked over to the park to find out what might have happened to her. They've gone over to Cavendish for a couple of days."

"Oh, oh." Casey's sweeping motion of his hand suggested that I sit down on the sofa. "I hope her father wasn't mad because she disappeared like that. Could you find out if they're coming back?"

"Yes. The ranger told me they'd be back Tuesday night. I hope they stick to their plans." I relaxed into the sofa and realized that this was the first time I had sat down since I panicked and raced down the beach to look for Millie. As my nerves loosened against the soft cushions, I felt like a Raggedy Ann Doll.

"I hope so, too," he said, returning from the refrigerator with two soft drinks. "I'd like to see Millie again. Grape or orange?" he asked, a bottle in each hand.

"Orange, thanks." The cool soda was instantly refreshing. "Gosh, I wish there was something I could do for her!" I exclaimed.

"You already have, Annie. It was obvious the other day that you've earned her trust in a very short period of time. You've accepted her just the way she is. For abused kids who carry the shame of their abuse, that's a big deal." Casey sat in the chair facing the sofa, leaned back and crossed one leg over the knee of the other, much more relaxed in his own space.

"You talk as though you know something about that," I said, as the fizz of the soda went up my nose and made me sneeze.

"I do," he said, handing me a tissue. "But let's not spend time imagining the worst. We've just got to believe that Millie's okay; otherwise we'll drive ourselves crazy." He changed the subject before I could reply. "What do you say? Let's give that old two-seater a try." He sat forward in the chair eager for my reply.

"I would love to, but I was talking to a friend down at the harbor, and he told me that they're harvesting Irish moss at North Cape. It's a kind of seaweed that comes ashore after a strong northwest wind," I explained. "But North Cape's really too far to ride on a bike. Want to take the Jeep and go up to see how they do it? It's quite a fascinating process."

"How far is it?" he asked, sounding somewhat disappointed.

Too late, I realized that Casey was excited over his handyman project and might not have wanted to ride all the way to North Cape to see a primitive harvesting procedure that, for some strange reason, fascinated me. "It's about thirty miles or more. Too far for the first trip on the bike, don't you think? But that's okay, we could ride up there another day," I added quickly.

"Nonsense. Let's see what's in the refrigerator and pack a quick lunch. There must be some place at North Cape where we can stop to eat it." He popped out of the chair, extended a hand to me to pull me up off the sofa, and said, "North Cape it is. The two-seater can wait for another day."

We raided his refrigerator managing to find some cold cuts, cheese, lettuce and tomatoes. Using some of Linda's homemade bread, we made a couple of Dagwood sandwiches. In addition to the remaining chocolate chip cookies, a couple of apples and two bottles of water, we threw in some paper towels and closed the lid on the small cooler.

Casey grabbed an old quilt he had found in the bedroom closet and tossed it into the back seat of the Jeep with the cooler. He opened the door for me, then ran around the front and folded his tall frame into the driver's seat. Smiling, he said, "Okay, Annie, lead the way!"

I laughed at his boyish enthusiasm for the anticipated adventure and thought that this simple type of activity must be very foreign to a man who just a few weeks ago was stressed by family and work related problems. "We'll just follow this road up along the coast," I said, pointing to the map. "It's really a pretty drive, and there is a nice spot up there where we can stop to have lunch."

As we drove along the shore road, I told him about Ernest MacDonald and the others I had met at West Point in the five years I had been coming to the Island. Most of the people around West Point were fishermen or farmers. They were all people that he would meet at Linda's barn dance.

"I would love to make a movie up here sometime. This is such beautiful country. Just look at that scenery." Casey slowed the Jeep and pulled over to the side of the road. He was enchanted with the red bluffs, the acres of golden barley and the white and pink blossoms on the sea of green potato plants. The farmers had planted every inch of field, running their crops right to the edge of the red sand bluffs.

"Wait until you see how they collect the Irish moss. I think that's one of the most interesting harvesting processes on the Island." I absent-mindedly put my hand on his arm as I talked, then quickly pulled it away. My husband and I had spent many hours riding around the Island, exclaiming about its beauty, me sitting next to him, my hand on his leg, as we bounced over dirt roads and talked about retirement.

Casey sensed my withdrawal. "You okay, Annie?"

"Yes, thanks. Just remembering." We drove the rest of the way in silence.

North Cape holds many surprises as you drive into the large parking area. The longest natural rock reef in North America runs out into the water at the tip of the Cape. At low tide you can walk out there a country mile it seems to see the "meeting of the waters" as the Gulf of St. Lawrence and the Northumberland Strait tides converge. Eight gigantic windmills stand like sentinels in what is Atlantic Canada's first wind farm. A large building houses a wonderful restaurant that overlooks the reef, an interpretive center where you can learn about shipwrecks and ghosts, and a gift shop that sells local crafters' wares. There's a lighthouse that warns ships of the two-mile long reef and an excellent coastal nature trail.

Casey was surprised to see so much activity. "This is an amazing spot, Annie. I had no idea this was here, or I would have been up here sooner."

"Let's go look for the mossers. They're usually right over there after a big storm," I said, pointing toward the other side of the parking area. We were standing on the northern most point of the Island. A red sandstone bluff pushed up by strong winds obscured a roadway that led down to the beach. Looking over the top of the bluff, Casey was surprised by the activity below. Two large, Belgian work horses, ridden by young men in their twenties, splashed in the rolling surf.

"Those horses are beautiful, Annie." As we stood on the bluff watching the teamwork of the men and the horses, Casey put his arm around my waist. The young men wearing rubber waders were astride their horses and working parallel to the shore in water up to the horse's belly. A scoop or rake, attached to the horse's harness by two long poles, much like those on a rickshaw, was dragged along behind the horse. As the horse waded through the surf, the scoop gathered up the moss that had been loosened from the sea floor and washed inland by the storm. The horse pulled the scoop ashore, where a man waiting on the beach tipped it up to empty it. Then, using a large pitchfork, he tossed the moss into the back of a pickup truck.

"Looks like an ancient harvesting process, doesn't it? The whole family gets involved. They take that moss that's in the back of the truck to their homes and spread it out all over their front lawn, driveway or anywhere else where it can dry. Then it goes to the plant."

"What do they do with it?" Casey asked, still mesmerized by the horses.

We started to walk back to the Jeep. "Irish moss is a source of carrageenan, a powdery substance that's used in puddings, toothpaste and even beer as a thickener or stabilizer. It might not look like it, but this is quite a cash crop for this Island. They harvest a lot more of it by boat. On our way back to West Point, we'll have to stop at the Seaweed Pie Café and get a piece of their famous pie."

"Seaweed pie? You've got to be kidding!" Casey's expression reminded me of a gnome and made me laugh.

"The pie looks and tastes a lot better than it sounds, Casey. In actuality, it's just a vanilla pudding pie. They use the carrageenan to thicken the pudding. I think the folks who run the café get a kick out of seeing people's faces when they read seaweed pie on their menu. They used to put green food coloring in it," I laughed, "but I think too many people really did think they were eating seaweed. I suspect they sell a lot more of it now."

"Speaking of menus, let's eat. Aren't you hungry?" We retrieved the cooler and the old quilt from the back of the Jeep, and found a perfect spot near the top of another bluff that looked back down the west coast. Casey spread the quilt over the tall grass that was peppered with timothy and wild mustard, before dropping to his hands and knees to pat it down. The sun was warm and bright in a cloudless, blue-white sky. Mercifully, there was a pleasant breeze that kept the mosquitoes away.

We ate our Dagwoods and watched the boats running along the coast. Casey pointed out two playful seals fishing for their lunch, then lay back on the quilt, putting his hands under his head and shutting his eyes. "Annie, it just doesn't get much better than this, does it? I haven't been this relaxed in years. Thanks."

I sat next to him, looking out at the water, my arms hugging my legs, my chin resting on my knees. "I know. That's why I come to the Island, especially this year."

"You never did tell me why you're up here by yourself. Care to talk about it now?" he asked, squinting at me as he kept his hands behind his head. "I'm a good listener, Annie."

I talked to him for over an hour telling him nearly everything about the last few years of my life. He was a good listener, responding with a nod or a touch to let me know he had heard everything I had said. He was like Ernest, right there with me, connected.

"Life is difficult as they say. But Casey, I wasn't prepared for all this. I have so much inside me that I want to share with someone. Someone who loves life as much as I do. Someone with the same passionate feeling for the sea and the stars and little kids. There's so much energy inside me that there are days I can barely stay contained. Does that make sense to you?" I rested on my side, leaning on my elbow, my hand holding my head.

"Yes, it does. Living with someone who has given up on life can't be easy. Now that it's over, and you've had time to grieve and to think, your love for life has picked up where it was arrested. These last few years must have been just awful for you." Casey turned toward me, mirroring my body position.

"They were, Casey. There were so many choices to make, and it seemed that no matter what I did, the choice I made was wrong."

"I'm sorry, Annie. Life stinks sometimes. But not today! Today is perfect!" He stood up, reached down for my hands and pulled me to my feet. We were standing close together like two people who are about to dance. "You're choice was right today, Beautiful," he said, starting to put his arms around me. But just as quickly he turned and bent over to pick up the quilt. "Come on, Annie, we better pick this stuff up and head back to West Point."

He took my hand and we slowly walked back to the Jeep. When we got in, he touched my cheek, then placed his hand on the back of my head and gently pulled me to him. His kiss was soft and warm. He leaned back, then looked into my eyes and pulled me to him again, this time taking me in his arms, holding me tenderly while rubbing my back. My head fit perfectly under his chin; my mouth pressed against the indentation in his neck where his collarbones meet. I kissed him there. He was warm and smelled of aftershave. He kissed me on the top of my head before pushing me away just as gently.

Casey coughed and cleared his throat. "Let's head back, Annie."

We drove toward West Point without talking. The afternoon air was warm and as soon as I put my head back against the seat, I fell asleep. When Casey turned the Jeep into the drive that led to my cottage, he touched my arm and woke me. "Annie, we're back."

"Oh, Casey, I'm sorry. I haven't been very good company." I was embarrassed.

"Nonsense. You looked like an angel. So peaceful. Thanks for a beautiful day."

As I closed the door, I looked through the open window and said, "I really enjoyed the afternoon, Casey." He smiled, put the transmission in reverse, turned the Jeep around and was gone without a word.

Chapter 7

August – 1993

Intimacy is a wonderful word that conjures up memories of romantic moments lying in bed with my husband, feeling as though we were fused together. He would lie next to me with one leg over mine, put his head on my chest and hug me like a child. I would caress his head and talk softly to him until he fell asleep. Those were marvelous, intimate moments that I will cherish forever. I did not feel vulnerable then, but those were the few times he would be that vulnerable with me. I loved him so much.

Now vulnerability scares the devil out of me. Vulnerability is a state of pure abandon. To be truly vulnerable to another person is to give them access to your life…to hand them your heart with the trust of a five-year-old. I did that once. I'm not ready to do that again.

But vulnerability is only one side of the coin. The other side is protection. For me that protection became work. Work hard. Work long hours. Force the feelings down until they are mired in the muck of denial. And then, there were no feelings at all. Protection. No life. No love.

And so, it would seem, that both sides of the coin may lead to a terribly wounded soul. Another interesting thought. Odd that I'm thinking such negative thoughts, when I feel so much alive.

No, not odd, I guess. I've met a man who is full of passion. Red warning lights are going off everywhere. I'm just working through the trauma of the last two years. I've just begun to feel alive and free again, to dare to feel the passion again. How can I risk this?

Passion is the fuel of life. Passion is the music that takes you soaring through magnificent white clouds on a summer day. Passion is lying on the beach at night willing yourself up into the stars to play with Orion and drink from the Big Dipper. Passion is feeling the pain of the universe and crying until you hurt. Passion is loving someone throughout eternity: backward where you meet as children and forward where your ancient selves no longer anguish over the frailties of humanness. Passion is life! To truly live is to have passion for something outside yourself. In those truly passionate moments of my life, I have felt energized, free and limitless.

But does every day have to be a choice? Perhaps. This feels like a major crossroads. Back where I have just traveled are the ravages of a relationship that died right before my eyes. Ahead lies the promise of new life, but I am not sure I'm willing to take that risk.

♪♪♪

When Casey's Jeep turned the corner at the end of the driveway, I went into the cottage, crossed through the living room and back out again onto the front deck. I sat there until the sun set, its rays spreading a bronze-rose glow across the horizon and up into a jet stream that streaked across a clear sky. The night was warm from a balmy southern wind. I sat there until after dark watching the sky, taking in the breathtaking spectacle of the clear night and the millions of stars. I could see into deep space. There were so many stars that I imagined that it was snowing in the heavens. I fell asleep in the old Morris chair and awoke with a start.

I wasn't sure what it was that woke me. The balmy breeze had turned cool so I gave up the old chair on the deck for the warm, comfortable sofa in the cottage. With my grandmother's quilt pulled up around my chin, I fell asleep within minutes. My dreams were jumbled and disconnected images of my first year of marriage: the fishing trips, our first vacation to Hawaii, and the times at our camp in the northern woods of Maine. When I woke, I felt drained and emotionally exhausted. My neck and shoulders ached, and so did my heart. The loneliness and sadness triggered by the dreams sat on my chest like a boat anchor. The old feelings of depression were pinning me to that sofa, holding me there, squeezing the life out of me.

It was then I began to cry, softly at first, and then great, racking sobs. Wailing, really, eventually burying my head in the pillow and screaming out my anguish. I fought the depression in the only way I knew how at that moment, by releasing the terrible hurt that lived so deep inside my soul. And by releasing it, I had to acknowledge it. As I stared at the naked truth of the hurt, I cried harder until I was choking and gasping for air.

I thought about my father and how much I loved him. Then I thought about my mother and all the terrible things that he did to her. How had she dealt with that hurt and fear herself? I loved her with all my soul and couldn't believe that my father truly understood how devastating his actions were, to her especially, and to my brother and me. But then, how can anyone rationalize abusive behavior like that? How does a child reconcile her total trust in her father with the monster he was when he was drunk? As I continued to think about my parents and wonder how that sort of thing comes about, I had, of course, gone into my head. And as I went into my head, I calmed down.

Groaning, I threw back the quilt and sat up. I was still wearing the same clothes I had worn the day before. As my head cleared, I thought about yesterday's adventure with a movie star.

Casey MacDonald. How on earth could it happen that he and I had crossed paths now when I'm so vulnerable to his touch and to his kindness? His kiss was warm and wonderful. The sheer tenderness of it filled me with feelings I hadn't experienced for years. His lips felt good on mine. His hands carefully held me to him as though he knew how fragile the moment truly was for me.

"Well," I thought out loud, "he's been there before. I can't get carried away with one kiss." But our afternoon was more than one kiss. He was kind and seemed truly interested and concerned about me. "Right," the little voice in my head warned. "Be careful!"

The morning was already warm. The long, hot shower soothed away the aches of the night, and the soft, citrus fragrance of my shampoo made me hungry. Piling note cards, pen, stamps, and a novel that would have to be started again on a breakfast tray with coffee and a couple of Linda's doughnuts, I carefully maneuvered through the sliding glass door onto the deck. Newsy messages to my nieces and a few friends were easy to compose, but I decided to wait a few days before writing to Susan. No matter what I said, she would be able to tell that the demons had surfaced again. I wanted to try to handle them on my own for now.

Later in the day I walked across the field to Linda's farmhouse, stopping every now and then to pick wildflowers. I needed to put some perspective on my afternoon with Casey, and Linda was just the person to help me do that.

My rapping at her back door went unheard. One of the children was screaming at another about using something that wasn't his. Children must be the same in every time and place, I thought. My brother and I used to sound like that years ago. "Helloo-oo," I called, opening the screen door and leaning into the entryway so I could see into the kitchen.

Linda was sitting at their large kitchen table drinking iced tea and browsing through a gardening magazine. "Hi, Annie. Welcome to chaos and confusion." She turned and yelled back into the house. "Settle down up there, Kevin, and leave Rebecca alone. Why don't you and Brian come down and make some popcorn. You can watch that new video your Dad picked up last night." She turned her attention back to me and said, "Barry rented one of Casey's old movies last night when he returned from Charlottetown. Thought we might get a kick out of it."

Linda was beautiful in her own way. When she smiled, she glowed. Her eyes were a deep, rich brown with flecks of butterscotch in them, and she still had the remnants of childhood freckles across the bridge of her nose. Her light brown hair was streaked with grey, but the way it was changing color was beautiful and natural, the grey growing in as blonde highlights. She kept her thick mop of hair short and styled. No muss. No fuss. Efficient, just like everything else in her life.

When she saw the bouquet of flowers, she pointed to the pantry. "You'll find something in there, Annie, to put those in."

The pantry held wondrous treasures of another time: old cookie and tea tins, Fiesta ware dishes with their splash of color, several pickling crocks, cast iron fry pans, and dozens of antique kitchen utensils hanging on a pegboard at one end of the counter. High on the innermost shelf, I found a large, garnet red vase. "How's this?" I asked, holding up the vase with both hands.

"Thanks, Annie. The flowers are beautiful. Let's put them right here." She moved the sugar bowl from the middle of the table to the far end next to the salt and pepper shakers.

As I made myself comfortable on the long bench that rests along one side of the table, I asked, "By the way, where's Amy?" Rebecca and Amy were sixteen-year old twins, one an introvert, the other an extrovert. Rebecca was tall, blond and very serious. Amy was shorter with chestnut brown hair and full of the devil. They both excelled in school. Rebecca was the president of her class and one of the best on the debating team. Amy was a star outfielder on the girls' softball team and a whiz with computers. As usual, Rebecca was in her room reading and putting up with the antics of her younger brother.

"Where else?" Linda closed the magazine and pushed it aside. "She's over at the Brown's with the rest of the teenagers on this part of the Island. I wish Rebecca would join them and live a little. She spends too much of her time up in that room."

"The Brown's must have a houseful. Steve Phillips was driving in every road from his house to the Harbor looking for Megan's cottage the other day."

"Is that right?" Linda laughed. "Well, I really appreciate Doug and Monica's support of those kids. They have a good time over there and stay out of trouble. By the way, speaking of trouble, what happened the other day with Millie? And what did you mean that it was better that her parents weren't there to get her?" Linda had placed her arms on the table using them for support as she leaned toward me.

"I hardly know how to tell you this, Linda, because I know it's going to upset you." I put my hands on hers as a gesture of concern. "Millie's father has been hitting her."

"What?" Linda gasped. She leaned back quickly, her hands held out in front of her, palms open, as though to defend herself against the words.

"The first day I met her, she had a black eye," I continued, consciously keeping my voice as calm as possible. "I wondered about it, but chalked it up to little girls easily getting hurt playing. Then she came by the cottage the next day with terrible bruises. Her father got angry when we had that storm the other night and their tent blew down. When Millie tried to help him put it back up again, he got mad," I paused.

"And?" Linda said, her voice deep now, like the soft growl of a female dog protecting her litter.

"He hit her with one of the tent poles." I looked down into my lap, ashamed in some perverse way at knowing such horrible details.

"Annie, she can't stay with a man like that!" Linda's eyes were wild with fear. She stood up, quickly walking around the table to sit on the bench beside me, her back leaning against the table.

"I know, but what can we do?" I asked, turning to face her. "If we report him to the authorities, they'll probably just warn him and let him go. He'll take Millie and her mother home, and we'll never see her again. God only knows what he would do to her then." I took a breath.

"When Casey and I took her back to the park, I asked Mr. Carter if Millie could come over to the cottage each morning to help me do some research on collecting and cataloging plants and grasses."

"Oh, what a good idea, Annie!" Her facial expression changed instantly, the deep lines along her forehead disappearing as she smiled.

"I thought it was. But when Millie didn't show up yesterday morning, I went looking for her. They've gone." Linda started to speak, but I interrupted her. "Wait. I asked the park ranger if they were coming back, and she said they had reservations for Tuesday night. My God, Linda, I hope they do come back." I was trembling. When I looked at her there were tears in her eyes. We sat on that bench in silence for several minutes, Linda holding my hand, staring out the window.

"How can anyone do that to a child?" she whispered, as though afraid to hear her own words.

"I don't know. Millie's such a dear little girl, so full of love and life. Casey was wonderful with her. He told her all about movie making and shared some inside information. She loved it!"

"He's charming. You have to give him that. Still, I wonder what we could do to help Millie when she gets back?" Linda crossed her kitchen to get a phone book. "I'll call the local RCMP Officer and ask him what can be done to help her."

I heard the concern in her voice as she talked to the RCMP Officer, but the frown on her face suggested bad news. There was really nothing anyone could do since they were U.S. citizens. Trying to prove the man was hurting Millie would be almost impossible as he could say she fell down or bumped into something. Because they couldn't detain him without proof or witnesses, he could pack up his family and go home. Up until this point, no one else had seen his actions. I remembered that the park ranger said they were a "nice little family."

"Well, that's that I guess." I was disappointed and angry. "When they come back, Linda, I'm going to see to it that Millie comes over to the cottage every day. The more she's out of his sight, the better. There's more than one way to fight that man," I said sounding braver than I felt.

We didn't speak for several minutes, each of us thinking about Millie and how frustrated we felt about the situation. There didn't seem to be any real solutions that would actually help her. I just didn't know enough about her background or the full extent of the abuse. To get involved here in a foreign country might mean putting Millie in more danger. To not get involved seemed immoral.

Linda broke the silence. "So, Annie, what did you do all day yesterday?" Completely unaware that she had left the table, I was surprised to hear her voice coming from the other end of the kitchen "I walked over to your cottage, but you weren't there," she explained as she placed a glass of iced tea in front of me and returned to the other side of the table.

"When I finished talking with the park ranger, I knew I didn't want to walk back to the cottage. I was afraid that being alone all afternoon would resurrect too many old memories." We both jumped when an ice cube cracked in my glass as though to emphasize the point.

"The next best thing was to walk over to the Harbor and talk with some of the folks who show up there when the boats are coming back. Ernest was there, sitting on a pile of old lobster crates, whittling a dolphin out of a small piece of driftwood." Remembering that picture of Ernest made me smile. When I looked up at Linda, she was smiling as well. She loved Ernest as much as I did.

"He told me that they were harvesting Irish moss up at North Cape, so I thought I would invite Casey for a ride along the western shore to check out the mossers. But when I got back to the cottage, Casey had tucked a note in the door asking me to go for a ride with him on that two-seater bicycle."

"Good heavens," Linda cried, "you two didn't pedal that thing all the way to North Cape!"

"No," I laughed. "We packed a picnic lunch and drove up there in his Jeep."

When our eyes connected, I could see a brief flicker of concern. "A picnic lunch?" she said slowly. "Did you have a good time?" She was still looking at me, searching for some hint of what the day might have been like for me. Linda, one of my best friends, was very much aware of the roller coaster ride I had taken over the last year.

"Yes, we did," I paused. "He kissed me," I said into the void of silence, then smiled, and let out a long sigh. "What am I doing, Linda? The man's married. Besides that, he's a movie star for crying out loud. What does he want with me?"

Linda just looked at me, saying nothing.

"Hello?" I said to her, knocking on the table.

"I don't know what to say, Annie. Casey is a great guy, but you do realize that he'll be leaving in a couple of weeks and chances are you'll never see him again?"

"Tell me about it. I thought about that all night. Passion and peace. You know passion is a wonderful thing. It's life giving. I've been through a living hell over the last couple of years, Linda, dying by inches, but I feel more alive today than I have in a very long time. And it's really not just because I spent time with him. Maybe this is just what I need to understand that a relationship, whatever it is, is still possible for me."

I didn't say anything about the wave of depression that had engulfed me earlier that morning. Perhaps it was because she knew all about the awful months at home after my husband died, or perhaps it was because I just didn't want to give the depression any life at all by talking about it. Furthermore, I had overcome the awful feelings on my own for the first time and was still feeling quite vulnerable.

"I'm not fooling myself," I added quickly. "When he leaves here, he'll forget all about me."

"That's what I'm worried about," Linda whispered.

"What do you mean?"

"I don't think he will forget you, Annie. You're a kind and caring person. Special. You're the type of woman who gets into a man's blood and drives him crazy, especially if he can't have you." Linda's face was flushed with worry.

"Linda! Don't be silly!" I cried, surprised by her words.

"I'm not being silly. I'm telling the truth. You have a way with people, Annie. You talk with them, not to them. You make people feel special. And people who are in crisis, or who are lonely, feel your tenderness and care for them. You've been a wonderful friend to me. And Susan has told me on many occasions how much she loves you. Honey, you're special! If that part of you connects with Casey, he's going to be in trouble. Mark my words! I doubt if he runs into many people like you in his business." She sipped her tea, leaned back against the chair, and relaxed into the conversation.

"I appreciate what you are saying, Linda. Really, I do. But I'm no more special than you are." I was beginning to feel ridiculous.

"Yes, you are, Annie. I don't take time with people like you do. Look at Ernest for example. That man loves you! You go down there and talk with him, not just to be kind or social, but because you like him and are genuinely interested in what he's doing. All men love that! Heck, everyone loves that."

"Well, I am genuinely interested in what he's doing. He's a terrific person and...interesting!" The hard bench seat was feeling very uncomfortable all of a sudden.

"Right. I know that, too, but I don't go down there and listen to him tell me the same stories every summer. I don't go down there and get involved with knitting heads or making fudge with him. But you do. You do that with everyone. My kids think you're great for the same reason. You talk with them and help them to understand that they're valuable people, because you give them all of yourself, Annie." She stressed these last few words with a tap on the table. "That's what you do. You give them all of yourself, and that's what scares me."

"Why?" I asked, but I knew the answer.

"Honey, you gave your husband all of yourself and it almost killed you. This time you've got to go in with your eyes wide open. You won't be able to change who you are, and I wouldn't want you to, but you've got to take a good hard look at what you're doing and set aside some energy and strength for the time when Casey leaves for home. Can you do that?"

"I don't know. Anyway, we're talking as though Casey and I were having a hot and heavy relationship. All he did was kiss me!"

"What about the rest of the trip?" Linda asked as she crossed the kitchen to the refrigerator to get a large pitcher of iced tea. She refilled her glass, poured another for me, then cut two pieces of fresh blueberry pie and brought them to the table.

"We went up to North Cape to watch them harvesting Irish moss. He was particularly fascinated with the way the horses work in the surf. We must have stood there for over an hour. Then we spread an old quilt out in that grassy area on the west side of the Cape and had a picnic. There was a warm breeze blowing the fragrance of wildflowers across the field and the boats were droning up and down the coast. The whole experience was," I paused searching for the right word. "Healing. The whole experience was healing, Linda," I repeated, looking into her eyes for understanding. She nodded the way my mother used to when I would bring stories of teenage catastrophes home from school.

I moved on the bench, now straddling it. As I turned toward the window, I noticed the family dog, Barnie, chasing a rabbit around the corner of the barn. When I turned back to talk with Linda, she was holding her fork in mid-air, as though frozen in time waiting for me to speak again. Breaking the spell, I continued, "Casey asked about my life back in Maine. I guess I was relaxed enough to tell him how things have been for the last few years."

"How do you feel about that?" she mumbled, eating the last bite of pie.

"To tell the truth, I feel a little vulnerable, Dr. Crawford," I laughed.

She wiped a spot of blueberry juice from her chin with a corner of her apron. "I'm sorry, Annie, but I'm worried."

"I know, and I appreciate your concern. Really I do. Casey is a good listener, just like you and Barry. He told me a little about his own childhood. Not an easy one I gather. I think that's why he identifies with what Millie is going through. Anyway, when we got back in the Jeep, he leaned over and kissed me. Then he leaned back, and I thought he was going to say something and start the car, but he didn't. He put his arms around me and pulled me to him and hugged me. It felt good, Linda." I sighed and shoveled a fork full of pie into my mouth.

"Of course it did," she agreed. "No one has done that for you in a very long time. That's what scares me. Annie, I want you to be happy. I just hope that both of you can let go of it when he leaves. Your lives are worlds apart. And there's the fact that he's married. I know that he and his wife are separated right now, but honey, that's not divorced! You just don't need any more emotional trauma in your life. Please, just take it easy and think about what you're doing every step of the way."

Linda stared at me, tears in her eyes. I was listening to her but thinking about Casey, too.

"Why is it that I feel like I'm talking to the wall?" Linda shouted. Then in a calmer and softer voice she said, "I'm sorry, Annie. That's how I get when I'm worried about the girls."

"It's okay, really, and you're not talking to the wall. I hear you, and I love you for your concern," I said and smiled at her. "Honestly, this scares me, too, but I may have the chance to experience something rare and wonderful. I would love to just get to know him. He's really a great guy."

"Uh, huh." Linda sounded unconvinced.

"I know better than you do that happiness doesn't last forever. I also know that the happy times in my life are wonderful memories that often help me through the bad days. Not taking a risk because of fear is paralyzing, numbing. I've been doing that for years, and I'm tired of it."

"We've been taught well, haven't we? Relationships are supposed to last forever. Passion is dangerous, not for the *genteel*." She laughed, making a quote sign with her forefingers and thumbs.

"You're right, though," I said, draining my glass of iced tea. "We've been taught to expect certain things for ourselves. Find a Prince Charming, get married, and live happily ever after. Like every guy out there *is* a Prince Charming and you only have to find yours. Ha! Life just doesn't work that way. Expectations like that will let you down every time."

Linda picked up the dishes and carried them to the sink. "Expectations can set us up for terrible disappointment, especially if we close our minds to any other possibilities. More often than not, what we thought would happen doesn't, and then, sometimes, by God's grace, what does happen is something you never dreamed was possible." She rinsed the dishes, then bent over as she opened the dishwasher and placed them in the bottom tray.

"Remember when Barry had that skiing accident and we thought we would lose the business because he couldn't work for over a month? He had no idea that Jim, his most experienced cabinet worker, had a degree in business management. Back then Barry didn't ask a lot of questions about a person's background, he just evaluated them by their woodworking skills. Anyway, Jim stepped in for that month and did a wonderful job. Now he splits his time between managing and woodworking. That's why Barry can spend more time up here with us each summer."

We talked through a good part of the afternoon, exchanging philosophies about life. "Thinking out loud" is what we called it, often working through some tough problems doing it. Susan and I have done the same thing. I felt blessed to have such a good friend so near on the Island. She pushed me hard to think about and weigh the consequences for both Casey and myself.

"There may not be any consequences to weigh, Linda. He's probably kissed a hundred women like that. It really was an in the moment thing. Besides, I actually fell asleep on the way back from North Cape. You know how easily I can do that when I'm riding in a car. I was terribly embarrassed. When he dropped me off at the cottage, he left without saying a word."

The brief silence that hung in the room was broken when Kevin blew into the kitchen, sliding across the floor in his stocking feet.

"Hey, Annie, do you want to see this movie? Casey MacDonald's in it!" His hands were in the air as though he were calling a touchdown.

"Sure, Kevin. Why don't you and Brian make some popcorn and then we can all sit down to watch. What's the name of it, and what's it about?"

He handed me the video so I could read the outer jacket. The movie had been made in the eighties. Casey wasn't the star but one of four space jockeys seeking some sort of adventure. Since his change of status as a leading actor, his movie studio had re-released some of his older movies with his picture prominently placed on the front for marketing purposes.

"This just might be fun, Linda. Casey wasn't a major star when he made this one," I laughed, as we followed one another into the large family room that overlooked the beach. The room was furnished with two over-sized sofas, several over-stuffed chairs and two bright yellow wicker rockers. Linda had covered the rockers' cushions with blue and white pinstriped cotton. The television and VCR sat prominently in the middle of a floor to ceiling shelving unit attached to one wall. Games, books, pictures, as well as an assortment of treasures found on the beach were haphazardly stuffed into every available space on the shelves. The sea of collectibles and souvenirs reminded me of a picture in one of my nephew's I Spy books. A large basket holding light blue yarn and a half-finished afghan sat next to one of the big chairs. Barry's sports magazines spilled out of a magazine rack next to another.

I curled up in one of the rockers and waited for Kevin and Brian to serve the popcorn and cold drinks. They were best friends and good kids. Brian had arrived the day before to stay with them until Linda and her family returned to Ottawa. He was the reason that Barry had been in Charlottetown. With the reunion just over a week away, Barry would be driving to Charlottetown often to pick up friends and family arriving at the airport there.

Kevin was big for his age. Only twelve, he was taller than his mother, and all arms and legs. Brian, on the other hand, would have to wait a few more years to reach his full height. He weighed in on the heavy side. They were quite a pair, both terribly self-conscious about their abnormal size in comparison to most boys their age. They were both scholastic achievers as well, another fact that put them at odds with the majority of students in the their sixth-grade class.

"Okay, Annie, start the movie!" Kevin plopped himself down beside the rocker and passed a big bowl of popcorn my way. When I pushed the play button on the VCR remote, the video whirred into motion.

We had to wait twenty minutes before we spotted Casey. He was floating outside a spaceship, a backpack with rockets propelling him through space to the far end of the ship to make a repair. Kevin and Brian loved it.

My reaction to seeing him on the screen surprised me. My heart pounded so hard that I looked around to see if anyone else could hear it. The heat rose in my neck and cheeks, but no one noticed that either as they were all glued to the screen to see what Casey would do next. Just as I was thinking that it was a good thing that Casey wasn't there to witness my adolescent reaction to a movie star I had just met, he walked into the room.

"Oh, no! I can't believe you folks spent good money to rent *that* movie!" he laughed.

I jumped at the sound of his voice and spilled the popcorn all over Kevin and myself.

"Yikes, Annie, when I said pass the popcorn, I didn't mean the whole bowl," Kevin laughed, as he began to eat the popcorn resting in the folds of his shirt.

"Oh, Kevin, I'm sorry." I was laughing, too, while crawling around on the floor trying to help scoop up the wayward kernels. The movie was lost in all the chaos much to the frustration of the two boys.

"Casey, what can we do for you? Do you need to use the phone again?" Linda was directing Casey's attention away from me as I continued to pick up pieces of popcorn that had managed to scatter in every direction.

"Uh, no, Linda, I was looking for Annie. I thought she might be over here." Casey looked back in my direction just as I stood up. Linda's eyebrows were nearly brushing the ceiling as she looked at me.

"Looks like I had better go home and clean up," I said, still wiping butter off my shorts and legs. With that I gave her a hug and walked out through the kitchen as Casey followed.

"Mind if I walk over with you?" Casey asked.

"No. Not at all," I said, pushing the screen door open.

Casey walked behind me as I followed the narrow path Linda had mowed across the field. When we neared the cottage, he said, "You know, Annie, I did enjoy our trip to North Cape yesterday. I'm afraid I was kind of rude when I dropped you off."

"You weren't rude at all, Casey. I guessed you probably thought I was a ditz, falling asleep like that," I laughed. We reached the back stairs and went in. I poured Casey a glass of iced tea and motioned to him to sit on the sofa while I went into the bedroom to clean up. Casey raised his voice so I could hear him.

"Annie, how long are you going to be on the Island?" I could hear the tinkle of the ice cubes as he tipped the glass to drink from it.

"A few more weeks. I have this place rented until the end of the month."

"Then what will you do?" His voice had lowered, and I didn't quite hear what he said.

I poked my head out of the bedroom and said, "What?"

"Then what will you do," he asked again.

"I'm not sure. Go home and find another job, I guess," I said sitting down next to him.

"I see." He frowned, started to say something, but stopped. He took a drink of the tea instead. Then he said, "Want to go somewhere tonight for supper? I understand that there's a restaurant over at the Lighthouse. Would you like to try it with me?"

"I would love to, Casey."

He stood up to leave. "Good. I'll be back around seven-thirty to pick you up."

"Uh, we had better call them, Casey," I said looking up at him. "People up here eat earlier than you folks in the city. They may not be serving that late."

I found the telephone number for the restaurant so that Casey could call them to make the reservations. He discovered that they were open until eight, so made the reservations for seven o'clock. He told me he would be back around six-thirty, kissed me on the cheek and left. I followed him to the door and watched him walk away. He waved after the door had shut and called over his shoulder, "See you at six!"

I laughed. This was going to be fun.

Chapter 8

August – 1993

The air is clear this afternoon. The mainland across the Straight looks as though it has been pushed closer to the Island. There's a lone walker at the far end of the beach, dressed in white, wearing a red cap. Tractors are moving on the road between farms, transporting huge, angular pieces of equipment for tomorrow's chores. These are days that memories are made of...days to cherish into my old age.

My little cottage-boat continues to sail the dunes high atop the world. Here we ride through storms and calm seas together. I wish I could sail her home for the winter. She's been a sanctuary for me...sacred space, where I have rested and known the healing presence of God. Perhaps I'll hear today whether or not the owners have accepted my purchase offer. Their decision to sell this particular summer is a gift from God.

The 'Lady Ann' nameplate, nailed over the door, causes me to smile at the coincidence. I wonder where her namesake lies...washed up on some distant shore, at the bottom of the sea, or high and dry in a drydock somewhere being lavished with TLC? I imagine that in her heyday, she sailed proudly on the open sea, sails unfurled and full of wind, white water splashing over her bow. Such contrasting images. Such a wonderful metaphor for life itself.

How do we ever know what others face? We see our next-door neighbor, the mail carrier, even movie stars, all smiling, confident, acting as though nothing in the world bothers them. But behind everyone's eyes there seems to be suffering of one sort or another. Everyone has it. Is suffering a universal language? Perhaps if we all talked to one another remembering the depths of our own suffering, love and compassion might finally overcome violence and cruelty. If there has to be a reason for pain and suffering, maybe this is it. But, understanding pain and suffering, in the same context as thinking about and worshipping a loving God, is very difficult.

Because Casey and I share similar heartaches of child abuse, last night we were able to touch each other in those ugly places hidden deep within our souls. Our stories are different, but the residual trauma is the same. The stark reality of Millie's experiences has triggered dark memories that have remained dormant for too many years. We have made an unusual connection…one that can never be broken…one that has existed forever…back to the beginning where the pain began and, now, forward through eternity where there is no pain, only joy. If I never see him again, I will know he's connected to me…and I to him.

♪♪♪

Casey knocked on the back door at six. "Annie!" he shouted through the screen.

"Come on in," I called to him from the bedroom. I was still fussing with my hair. The dusty rose dress, the only concession to civility in my summer wardrobe, complemented my complexion. A soft, butter-cream sweater completed my ensemble.

"Wow! You look beautiful," he said, as he handed me a single red rose nestled in baby's breath and polka dot tissue paper. "Thought you might like this." Casey looked like he had just stepped out of the pages of <u>The Great Gatsby</u>. He had draped a light yellow sweater over a crisp, white dress shirt, the arms of the pullover tied loosely across his chest. His blue eyes snapped with the electricity of the moment.

My heart skipped a beat as I accepted the delightful surprise. My husband had often given me a single rose for no reason at all. The words of appreciation caught in my throat. "The rose is beautiful, Casey. Thanks." Our eyes met and locked. In that instant I fell into a deep well, floating down until his arms reached out and caught me. He held me to him and kissed me gently on the top of my head. He smelled wonderful. How I wanted to tell him how good it felt to be held again and thought about in such a caring way. Instead, I mumbled something about finding a vase for the rose so it wouldn't wilt.

We decided to walk along the beach to the Lighthouse rather than driving over in the Jeep. I took off my sandals to walk near the water's edge. The damp sand cooled my feet, keeping me anchored to the ground. A deep blue sky with its fluffy white clouds hanging over the western horizon, promised a spectacular sunset.

Somewhere along the way, Casey took my hand. Our conversation focused on our concern for Millie and our hope that she and her family would return to their campsite. We agreed that each of us had fallen in love with her at first sight and that she was the embodiment of our lost innocence.

The Lighthouse and Provincial Park came into view as we rounded that part of the beach that juts out into the water. The impressive black and white structure with its strobe light warning ships of shallow water nearby stands guard on a great sand point surrounded on both sides by dunes that are covered with fragile, sea green dune grass. As we neared the boardwalk that crosses the dune, Casey stopped and put his arms around me pulling me close to him. He didn't say a word, but I could hear his soft breathing as his mouth brushed against my ear. Then he gently pushed me away, holding me at arm's length, and said, "Annie, let's make this a special evening."

"It already is, Casey," I whispered.

The hostess at the restaurant was nervous, obviously recognizing Casey as 'that famous American actor.' A few patrons, who also recognized him, approached our table to ask for his autograph. He stood to greet them, shook hands, signed napkins and the back of credit card receipts, and agreed with them that the Island was the perfect spot for a get-away vacation. When the last admirer waved good-bye, Casey sat down.

"I'm sorry, Annie, but I guess that's part of my job." He leaned back in his chair, shook out the folded napkin, and placed it in his lap. "I was hoping that tonight I could get away with eating in a public place without all the attention."

"I certainly don't mind if you don't. Anyway, those people were courteous at least, and seemed to sense that you wanted some privacy. I doubt if anyone else will be coming in this late. Let's order. I'm starved!"

Casey ordered a bottle of white wine. He poured each of us a glass, lifted his, clinked it against mine, and said, "To you, Beautiful. My life will never be the same." In that moment, his blue eyes conveyed happiness and sadness all at once. As the two feelings washed over me, I heard Linda's words of caution.

"What's the specialty of the house, Annie?" Casey's question quickly brought me back to the present.

"Lobster stew. Do you like it?"

"Yes, I love it. We made a movie in Camden a few years ago. I had my first lobster there. Bake-stuffed, I think."

I laughed. "Casey, that's a waste of a good lobster. The only true way to eat lobster is hot, right out of the shell, with plenty of real butter for dipping, but I'll vote for lobster stew as well, especially here." My mouth watered at the thought of the distinctive aroma and taste of the seafood delicacy.

"I've an idea, Annie. Let's go over to the harbor tomorrow and see if we can buy some lobsters right off the boat. Want to give it a try and show an old cowboy how to eat it that way?"

"I'd love it. I'll introduce you to Ernest. He'll be pleased that you came by to meet him."

Our house salads were served first, with fresh, hot, butterfly yeast rolls, an Island staple. When the bowl of lobster stew was placed in front of Casey, he whistled in surprise. Chunks of lobster meat rose up out of the steaming, hot milk. The red essence, sautéed from the lobster meat, blossomed across the surface of the hot liquid. Casey carefully tasted the stew, put his spoon down, patted his mouth with his napkin and said, "You're right, Annie. This is delicious."

Our conversation turned to one-syllable words and nods of agreement as we devoured the tasty stew. Casey straightened in his chair, threw his napkin on the table, grabbed his stomach and said, "Wow. What a meal."

I laughed at his smile of satisfaction and swallowed the last tidbit of lobster from my bowl. "I'm glad you liked it, Casey."

"Want dessert, Annie?"

"No thanks. I'm full, too. Let's take a walk on the beach and let some of this food digest."

"Good idea." Casey jumped up to hold my chair as I stood, brushing a crumb from the front of my dress. He paid the waitress, gave her a big tip, and autographed the order slip. As we walked across the restaurant to leave, I heard her gasp as she realized her good fortune. She hurried toward us, calling softly to get our attention. She blushed as she thanked Casey for the tip and the autograph. He leaned down and kissed her on the cheek, a gesture that deepened the redness already spread across her freckled cheeks and down into the neck of her uniform.

The night air was warm and pleasant, but I was glad I had my sweater. We walked over the dune on the special wooden walkway. The sun was setting, creating a magnificent orange-red glow that wrapped nearly all the way around us. The sea was calm, reflecting the solar display. The tide was low. There was peace everywhere.

Casey took my hand. As we slowly walked along the beach on the southwest side of the point, we could see the lights at the harbor. A few boats had been late getting in with their catch of the day. The drone of the crane's engine was almost musical in its rhythm as it lifted crates of lobsters out of the boats onto the wharf. The glow of the lights around the harbor shot up into the clear night sky, a beacon to any passing planes.

We stopped then to listen to the sounds of the evening. A campfire glowed in the distance at one of the campsites in the park. The campers' song and the distinctive smell of wood smoke drifted on the cool night air. The surf lapped softly against the sand, almost a whisper in the darkness that unfolded before us.

"Let's sit here and enjoy the moment. What do you say, Annie?" Casey asked as he offered his hand to help me sit down on a large, dry log that had washed ashore long ago. As we relaxed in the atmosphere of the night, our conversation led to stories about our lives and then to the anguish of our childhood. Talking with one another was strangely comfortable.

Casey recounted his early years. His father had abandoned them when he was four. His mother's boyfriends beat him and tormented him until he learned to hide under his bed until they left in the early morning hours of dawn. When he told me about the beatings, my heart pounded in my ears. He didn't have to describe the details. I understood.

When he was twelve, an uncle adopted him and did the best he could for him. He took him to his hunting lodge every weekend, where he taught him how to hunt and fish. The change of scenery was just what Casey needed, but the exposure to his uncle's friends was difficult. They were all alcoholics. Casey put many of them to bed when he was only thirteen, trying to reconcile their friendly behavior when they were sober with their crudeness when they were drunk.

At seventeen, he left his uncle's home, hitchhiking across the country to California. He was discovered three years later working as an extra on a multi-million dollar action film.

He had put his arm around me as he talked. My head rested in that special place under his chin. "Life has been less than boring since then, Annie. I've been lucky. My films get better and make more money every year. I love what I do."

"A lot of us love what you do, Casey." As I spoke to him, he took my face in one hand and bent forward to kiss me. Just as before, his kiss was warm and tender. My arms went around him as I responded with far more emotion than I intended.

As he stood up, he brought me up with him. With both arms around me he said, "Annie, you're special. I hope you know that."

"No one has told me that for a very long time."

"Shame on whoever it is that holds your heart." His grip tightened.

"Is this real, Casey?" I asked trembling.

"I don't know. What I do know is that from the first moment I met you I knew I wanted to get to know you. Now, here we are, on the threshold of something that could be wonderful for both of us."

"Or devastating," I said without thinking.

"Sit down, Annie, please," he said, his voice deepening. "You're right. If we do become good friends, as I believe we were meant to do, the consequences could be devastating for both of us. For both of us, Annie," he said accentuating each word. "But taking a chance would be awfully good."

I sat down on the log and waited for him to join me before I responded to him. The intimacy of the moment was gone. He reached for my hand, focused his eyes on mine, and waited. I took a deep breath and said, "I'm not ready, Casey. Not tonight. Can you accept that?"

"Of course I can. I'm not that guy you see on the movie screen, Annie. I hope you know that by now. I'm just a guy from a small town who made it big." Visibly agitated, he stood up again and looked down at me. "I'm not a movie star, Annie; I'm a human being. I care about you, more than makes sense right now."

"I care about you as well, Casey. But you have to understand that from my point of view you are a bit intimidating."

"Intimidating?" He bent his head back as he laughed. "Oh, Annie, you've got to let go of whatever fantasies or notions you've had about movie stars." He continued to laugh.

"No laughing," I said, embarrassed.

"I can't help it. You're too precious," he said, still chuckling as he took my hand. He pulled me up again and held me, whispering, "Annie York, I'm glad I met you." The silence of the night embraced us as we held each other. "Let's head back," he said abruptly.

We walked barefoot on the hard-packed sand, the waves tickling our feet. The moon was full and big, rising high over the water, casting a thin ribbon of light that extended across the Straight from PEI to the New Brunswick shore. The bright cast of the moon dimmed the brilliance of the stars. As we neared the cottage, we stopped to take in the breathtaking scene.

He held me to him and talked over my shoulder toward the water. "Annie, something special is happening between us. I felt it the other day at North Cape and, frankly, it scared me. That's why I left you so abruptly when we returned to your cottage." He paused and pulled away so he could look into my eyes. "You've helped me unearth memories that have been hidden and dormant for years. I haven't shared any of these thoughts or feelings with another living soul. I don't know if it's the Island, or where we are in our lives at this moment in time, or any of another dozen reasons, but I do know that when I'm with you, I feel a sense of well-being that I've never experienced before. I don't expect you to understand it, because God knows I don't understand it myself."

When he finished speaking, he hugged me gently waiting for my response. I put my arms around him and laid my head against his chest. His heartbeat was strangely comforting as my mind raced to comprehend the impact of his words.

"Casey," I said pulling away from him, "let's go slow and see where this takes us. Give me some time to get used to you as 'just that small town guy.' Okay? We've still got a couple more weeks on the Island to get to know each other. If this is right, we'll find our way. If you want to, that is."

"Of course I want to, Annie." He put his arm around my waist and walked with me back to my cottage. "It's late. Go in and get a good night's sleep."

He started to walk away, then walked back to me, took my hands in his and said, "Don't forget, we've got a date tomorrow for a lobster feed. Might be fun to learn how to eat them right out of the shell."

"I didn't forget!" I threw my arms around his neck and hugged him.

He kissed me passionately, held me for several minutes, then let me go and walked away. As I approached the steps to the cottage and reached for the handle on the screen door, I heard the Jeep start up, then its tires crunching in the dirt along the drive. I didn't look back. I didn't dare look back.

Chapter 9

August – 1993

The water is still…flat calm…eerily motionless. The usual wave action is absent as though I were sitting beside a huge, freshwater lake. The blue vastness of sea before me appears to be swelling, rising, as though to throw a tidal wave over me.

The sun is warm this morning, nurturing my soul. As it rises higher in the sky behind the cottage, the warmth of it soothes my back and neck, releasing some of the tension there. The air, soft on my face, carries the pungent smell of the red earth. There are few sounds, as though the whole world is holding its breath…waiting.

Waiting for what?

Answers?

Yes, answers, for there are so many questions. Am I crazy? Can I believe that a man like Casey could care for me? Or is this just a momentary fling for him… nothing more than a brief encounter to satisfy his needs? And if it turns out that that is the case, what will I do then? And if it turns out otherwise, what will I do then?

What was it that Linda and I were talking about the other day? Expectations? Seems a fine line between risk and hope. Isn't this a situation where I just shouldn't have any expectations? Right now is all I have. Right now, sitting here in this wonderful old chair in the midst of God's marvelous creation. This is good, right now.

Expectations will run me all around morality and integrity…brush up against loss and shame and worry…take me down the road of fantasy and unrealistic hope.

Last evening was a dream, a wonderful dream. My world has been so barren this last year. Casey's touch was magic, transforming the dry crust of grief into warm energy….energy that continues to fuel my soul this morning.

But no matter what happens, I will not let anyone or anything drape any more shame over me. I have had enough of that for a lifetime. I need to know that giving myself to a relationship is a good act. I can be responsible for myself…and I was. Whatever today brings is what it brings.

Now, all I have to do is listen to myself and believe it.

Right.

♪♪♪

I put the journal on the table, laid back in the old Morris chair and closed my eyes. The warmth of the sun, the soft texture of the cushions, and the memory of last night's ribbon of moonlight conspired to lift me and my chair off the deck. We floated across the golden path on the sea, gently bobbing and rocking under a blanket of stars. Casey's voice called to me, soothing at first, then urgent and high-pitched. As my state of consciousness changed, I realized that Millie was calling to me from below.

"Annie! Annie!" When I sat up to look over the porch rail, I saw Millie running across the boardwalk calling and waving to me.

"Millie! I'm so glad to see you!" I responded, but before I could maneuver out of the chair, she came in through the back door and exploded out through the screen door onto the deck.

"Oh, Annie, I've missed you so much!" She hugged me and cried. "I wasn't sure Daddy would bring us back here even though he said he would. He was so mad that day you and Casey saved me in that awful storm."

I gently pushed her back and looked at her. A faint green bruise was evident under one eye and she favored her right arm as though it hurt. "Are you okay, Millie? Has your father hurt you again?"

She looked away at the water. Then she sat down beside me in the chair. She tucked her left arm under me and laid her head on my shoulder. We sat there for several minutes, silent, understanding everything. I prayed to God for guidance and strength to help her. Just then Casey came through the door, a red, plastic bucket in one hand.

"Millie!" He put his arms out and she ran to him, hugging him around the waist. He looked at me over her head and frowned as he, too, noticed the bruise under her eye.

"So, Millie, did you have fun over in Cavendish?" Casey asked clearing his throat.

"It was okay. My arm has been hurting a lot so I couldn't go on any of the rides." She backed away from Casey, holding her right arm with her left hand.

"Oh? What's the matter with it?" he asked, as he looked at her arm.

"Oh…I…uh. It's better now. See?" She raised her arm, but I could see the pain in her eyes as she struggled to raise it over her head.

"Millie, have you been to a doctor?" I put my arm around her as she sat down next to me again.

"No. Mom says it will be okay. It doesn't hurt all the time." She looked up at me and smiled. The freckles dancing across her nose melted my heart.

"Really, Annie. I'm okay," she added, trying to assure me that her arm didn't hurt.

The rage was building inside my chest. I needed every ounce of strength I possessed not to storm over to the park and have a long talk with Millie's parents, but I was looking at the results of our last attempt to help her.

"Annie, I came over to see if you still wanted to go to the harbor for lobsters," Casey said, holding up the bucket.

"I was counting on it," I said, delighted that he had remembered.

"What do you say, Millie, want to go with us?" Casey asked, looking at me for agreement. I nodded.

"Sure! I told Mom I was going for a walk on the beach. She won't miss me for a couple of hours." Millie was animated now, the pain in her arm forgotten.

"I need to change my clothes," I said, as I jumped out of the chair. "You guys stay out here and talk for a minute. I'll hurry!" When I turned to close the screen door, Casey had straddled one of the white plastic chairs. He was leaning on it, tipping it forward toward Millie who had made herself comfortable in the Morris chair. Just as I entered the bedroom, I heard him ask again about her arm.

"Mommy gave me some Tylenol just before I came over here, and my arm feels a lot better now." When she saw the frown on his face, she said, "Really. It does." She leaned back in the chair and crossed her legs.

"I'm glad, honey," he said, accepting her denial of any pain. "But nevertheless, you don't deserve to be hurt like that."

"Daddy always says it's my fault, Casey. I must be an awful person, or else why would he hurt me so bad?" Millie whined, wiping the tears from her cheek on the corner of her t-shirt.

"Millie, honey, you're very special." Casey's voice was comforting and gentle. "I think you're very pretty and very smart. I have a little girl just about your age. You would like her, and I know she would like you."

"Then why does my Daddy hit me so much?" she cried.

"I don't know, honey, but I do know it's not your fault." He reached for Millie's hands, and as he did so, she jumped into his arms.

I quickly changed my clothes, then tiptoed across the living room and stood just inside the screen door for a few more minutes while they talked. Millie cried and hugged Casey, trusting him completely. In that instant, I knew that I could trust him as well. He held her and whispered words to her that I could not hear. My heart was full, and yet, it was breaking. I wiped the tears from my eyes and spoke to them as I stepped through the door onto the deck. "Okay, you guys, let's go!"

When we arrived at the harbor, we found Ernest talking with two other retired fishermen. The three of them were sitting in lawn chairs on an open deck that faces the wharf, each of them dressed identically in dark work pants, a plaid, short-sleeved, cotton shirt, and a cap. "Ernest!" I called to him over the noise of boat motors and machinery.

His blue eyes twinkled as they always do. He looked at me, and then at Casey, then back at me and winked. "So, Annie, my girl, is this the famous Casey MacDonald?"

"Yes. Casey, I'd like you to meet Ernest MacDonald." As I continued my introductions, Casey shook Ernest's big, calloused hand, and then extended the same greeting to his two friends. "You two fellows are probably members of the same family, Ernest. And this is Millie Carter," I said, putting my arm around her shoulder and pulling her close to me. "She and her family are staying over at the park."

When Ernest leaned down to shake her outstretched hand, he looked at me over her head. I knew that he had seen the spot under her eye and remembered our conversation about her. "Millie," he said with a catch in his throat, "I've got something here in my lunch pail that I save for special folks like you."

He reached into an old-fashioned black lunch pail and pulled out a piece of homemade fudge. Ernest's fudge was famous around the harbor. He wrapped pieces of it in waxed paper and brought it to the fishermen in the early morning before they left for their long day at sea. I was so pleased, that in this gesture of friendship, he was affirming Millie just as Casey had done at the cottage. "I made it myself, Millie!" Ernest grinned as he handed the sweet confection to her.

"Thanks, Mr. MacDonald." She unwrapped the fudge and took a big bite. "Mmmm, that's good. Peanut butter! My favorite!" The faint pink of a blush had spread across her face in reaction to the surprise of the peanut buttery taste.

"Millie, my girl, you can call me Ernest. I'm glad you like my fudge." Ernest closed his lunch pail, and leaned back in the chair. "Why don't you and Annie come over some day soon and help me whip up another batch." While Millie and I talked with him to set a date for our cooking lesson, Casey walked around the harbor wharf investigating the boats and the off-loading of the lobsters. I had pointed out the person to talk to about getting some lobsters for our lunch. He had reached that spot and was negotiating a good trade. I turned my attention back to Millie who was being entertained by three charming elders each telling their version of an amusing fishing story. Ernest was laughing so hard that he started to cough. When I looked again toward the lobster shack, I saw Casey sauntering along the wharf toward us, carrying the red pail made heavy with wriggling crustaceans. He was whistling.

"Wow, Casey, you sure bought a lot of lobsters." Millie's big, blue eyes were wide with excitement.

"Yup, I sure did. Let's go back to your cottage, Annie, and cook these devils. I'm hungry! Ernest, it was a pleasure meeting you." Casey reached toward Ernest and shook his hand, and then turned to the other two and did the same. "Perhaps we can talk more another time." As he spoke, Casey looked at Millie hoping that Ernest would understand that we wanted to get her back to the cottage. When I looked back, the three men raised their hands in unison and waved. I smiled and tried to imagine what they might have looked like as little boys.

Unaware of our concern, Millie followed us to the Jeep and happily watched over the bucket of lobsters, fascinated by their movement. Even out of water lobsters are fighters, their claws moving constantly as they try to find their way back to the sea. Pretending that he was afraid the lobsters would escape and attack him in the front seat, Casey hooted and hollered all the way back to the cottage. Millie was laughing so hard that when I opened her door, I found her lying across the back seat holding her stomach. I managed to pull the bucket of lobsters out of the Jeep onto the ground where Casey picked it up with both hands holding it out in front of him at arms length as he ran up the back steps and into the cottage.

I asked Millie to look in the cupboard for a large pot. "Is this one big enough?" she asked struggling with a big, black kettle.

"It sure is." The pot banged against the side of the sink as I slid it under the faucet to draw some water, then carefully lifted it out and put it on the stove to boil. While I rummaged in the refrigerator for fresh butter, I asked Millie to look for a cookbook in the pile of books strewn about on the shelves next to the desk.

Millie had relaxed since she arrived. She was having fun learning about lobsters and how to cook them. I didn't want to spoil her mood, but I was concerned about her arm and about her being away from her family for so long. "Millie, are you sure that it's okay for you to be here? I don't want you to get into trouble."

"Yes. Daddy went fishing today, and he won't be back until late this afternoon." She was down on her hands and knees at the side of the desk looking through the books on the bottom shelf. "Mommy knows where I am. She doesn't mind."

"Is your mother at the park by herself?" I said, looking for the source of the thumping and bumping coming from just below the window.

"Yes. She likes to spend time by herself. She says it helps her." She sat back on the floor, an opened cookbook in her lap.

Casey returned to the kitchen with a small wooden crate he had found under the cottage. He helped Millie step onto it so she could reach the lobster pot without getting burned. The water had started to boil, so I showed her how to take the lobsters out of the bucket without getting pinched. She squealed as she placed them carefully, one by one, into the boiling water. Between Millie's squeals and Casey's shouts of "Bonzai" each time she dropped one of the wriggling creatures into the pot, we were weak from laughter.

"There," I hiccuped, placing a lid on the steaming pot, "all we have to do now is wait."

"Millie, let's go out on the deck and see what we can do about setting the table." Casey had gathered everything he thought we might need in a large basket and was heading for the screen door. Millie followed him. The picnic table, new to the deck this summer, was the perfect spot for our elegant feast.

I found my camera and took candid pictures of the two of them working together. When they noticed me, they mugged for the camera with Casey leaning over Millie, both making faces at me. I took several pictures of them: one frowning the other smiling mimicking drama masks; Millie holding her fingers behind Casey's head in the sign of a V, an impish grin on her face, a grimace on his; and the last of Millie hugging Casey around the neck, their heads together. Both smiles were glorious.

As I went back into the cottage to check the status of the lobster pot, I heard Millie call, "Annie, come back so I can take a picture of you and Casey." When I stepped out onto the deck, Millie was pointing the camera at Casey as he leaned against the railing. She was having fun pretending she was the director of a film and Casey was its star.

"Now, why don't both of you lean against the railing?" she said, remaining in character. "Casey, put your arm around Annie." Casey acted as though he had never met me, putting his arm around me like a young schoolboy who didn't like girls. Millie was getting a kick out of it. "Oh Casey, for heaven's sake, get closer to Annie!" she giggled.

"How's this?" he asked as he pulled me closer to him in a bear hug.

"That's great!" She snapped the picture. "Now wait just a minute. I want to take another one." She bent over the camera to advance the film. Casey continued to hold me in a bear hug as he looked down into my face. I heard the camera click, but my total being was drawn into his blue eyes. I wanted to disappear into them forever. I heard him suck in his breath as I felt his hardness against my stomach, and I started to laugh.

"This is quite a predicament, don't you think?" he said chuckling, still holding me against him.

"Uh, huh. We could ask her to take another picture."

"Good idea." Casey looked over at Millie who was fumbling with the camera. "Millie, why don't you take one more?"

"Okay, Casey. Smile!" She lifted the camera to her face, squinted her right eye and looked through the viewfinder with her left. We both looked at Millie and laughed. She disappeared through the door when I asked her to check on the lobsters.

"You're driving me crazy, Annie. You know that don't you?" Casey walked away from me and sat down in the bulky chair.

"Well, Cowboy, the feeling is mutual, but we've got to cool it until we take her back to the park. I don't want to do anything that would make her self-conscious. She's dealing with too much already." I turned the plastic chair around and sat down facing him.

"I know. She talked with me about some of it before we went over to the harbor. There's got to be something we can do to help her, Annie. We just can't stand by and watch as her father hurts her like that." He sat forward in the old chair, his elbows on his knees, his arms extended, palms up. As he looked up at me, he frowned, and then turned to look through the door at Millie. She was standing on the stool carefully lifting the cover off the steaming pot.

"If we were home, we could report him," I whispered, looking in at her as well. "Although I'm not sure how much good that would do either. I wonder if there's some way we could talk to her mother. She's the one who has the power to do something about it. If she doesn't, she's just as guilty as he is. I wonder if he's beating her, too?"

"What a mess. I just don't understand how anyone can beat a child, and I really don't understand how a father could do that to his daughter. I know how much that kind of physical abuse hurts. She's got to be one tough kid." Casey's frustration was evident as he nervously tapped his fingers on his knee.

"She is a tough kid, Casey," I said, putting my hand over his tapping fingers, "but I'm worried about her arm. She's still in pain from that injury. Maybe we should take her back to the park after lunch and persuade her mother to go to the hospital with us to have it x-rayed."

"We can try, Annie. Don't be surprised, though, if Millie balks at that idea. She's scared to death of her father." He blew out his breath as though he had been punched and leaned back in the chair.

"I know. Think of what he's doing to her, not only the physical abuse, but the emotional trauma as well." My frustration had raised the level of my voice. I looked into the cottage once again, making sure that Millie wasn't listening to our conversation. Thankfully, she had her nose in the cookbook, her finger running along the words as she read the directions. "She actually thinks she deserves those beatings," I continued, lowering my voice to a whisper. "If she doesn't get some help now, I know only too well what that will do to her as she grows up. God, I wish there was something I could do."

Casey put his hand on my knee. "Annie, you are doing something. She adores you, and best of all, she trusts you."

"Let's give her a great afternoon, Casey," I said, grabbing his hands and pulling us both to our feet. "Then, let's see if we can persuade her and her mother to go to the hospital. If nothing else, we can get the injury recorded, whatever good that might do."

When we opened the screen door, Millie looked up, her blue eyes glistening with excitement. "This says we should cook the lobsters about eighteen minutes after the water boils the second time. I watched the clock and it's been eighteen minutes, so the lobsters should be done. What do you think, Annie?"

"Good! Let's take a look," Casey said, rubbing his hands together in anticipation. As he lifted the lid off the pot, the steam carried the pungent smell throughout the cottage. "The lobsters are bright red," he said, sounding surprised.

"Then they're ready," Millie and I shouted in unison.

Casey dumped them into the sink, put two for each of us on tin pie plates and carried them to the picnic table on the deck.

Casey and Millie were novices at eating boiled lobster. The shells were very hard, making their initiation that much more difficult. When I showed Millie how to break the shell on the claw, the juice squirted across the table and hit Casey in the chest. He pretended he had been shot and keeled over onto the bench. Millie giggled, then hiccupped, which made all of us laugh. Lobster juice and butter ran down our arms as we sucked the sweet meat out of the shells. When I opened the tail and extracted the green tamale paste, both Casey and Millie leaned back instinctively. Each of them tried a tiny taste of it, coughed and sputtered, and agreed that it was gross. By the time we had finished eating, we were covered with reminders of our meal and exhausted from laughing at each other.

"There now, Casey, doesn't that beat bake-stuffed? It's lots more fun to eat that way when the lobster isn't all covered up with stuffing."

"You're absolutely right, Annie. I've never tasted anything any better! And I've never gotten so messed up eating a meal!" Casey chuckled as he wiped the butter and lobster juice from his arms and face. "I'm going to run over to the cottage to wash up and put on a clean shirt. I'll be right back." He reached over the table and wiped butter off the tip of Millie's nose. "See you in a minute, Gorgeous."

After Casey left, Millie and I cleared the table, put all the dishes to soak, then went into the bathroom to clean up. "How's your arm, honey?" I asked, as I helped her put on the new t-shirt I had found for her in an O'Leary store.

"It hurts, Annie. I didn't want to say anything because we were having such a good time, but it really aches." She leaned against me and started to cry.

With my hand on her back, I gently nudged her toward the bed. We both sat down. "Millie, dear, I think we should drive over to the hospital to have your arm x-rayed. What do you think?"

"Could my Mommy go with us?" she asked looking up at me, tears spilling out of her blue eyes.

"Yes. When Casey gets back, we'll pick her up at the your campsite, then go right to the hospital. Okay?"

"I guess. I just hope Daddy doesn't get mad." She cradled her wounded arm with the other.

I heard Casey thump up the back steps. "Hey you guys, where are you?" he called from the living room.

"We're in here!" I shouted.

"Is it safe for a man to come back here?" he asked, poking his head around the door. As soon as he saw Millie's tear-stained face, his expression darkened. "What's up?"

"Millie's arm hurts badly. She's agreed to go to the hospital to have it checked out." Still holding her with one arm, I looked up at him for agreement. "Let's pick up her mother and take them to the hospital in Summerside."

"Millie, honey, are you okay with this?" He had knelt down in front of her, his hands on either side of her on the bed.

"Yes, Casey. My arm really hurts." She began to cry again.

"Let's go," he said suddenly, picking her up, being careful not to pin her arm against him. He carried her out to my car and put her in the front seat with him. When I hopped in back, Casey put the car into gear and drove slowly over the bumps in the driveway. At the end of the drive, we turned toward the park. Casey glanced at me in the rear view mirror, his face flushed with anger.

When we arrived at the campsite, I prayed that Millie's father had not returned. Much to my relief, his car wasn't there. Thanking God as I ran to their tent, I found her mother resting on the sleeping bags. She jumped up when she saw me and said, "Is anything wrong with Millie?"

"Funny you should ask," I said, regretting my reply as soon as the words were out of my mouth. "I'm sorry, Mrs. Carter, but Millie's arm is really bothering her. We think she should go to the hospital for an x-ray. Will you go with us?" While I had no right to make this decision for her, I didn't want to get into a long discussion with her about what was good for Millie.

"Yes, of course. She hurt her arm on one of those rides over in Cavendish the other day. Where is the hospital?" she asked, grabbing her purse.

"In Summerside, about an hour from here," I said over my shoulder as I walked back to the car.

"I better leave a note for my husband, just in case he gets back before we do." She nervously fumbled through her canvas bag for a piece of paper and a pen, wrote a short note and left it under a coffee mug on the picnic table.

When I opened the back door for Mrs. Carter, I heard Casey talking with Millie about a movie he had made in Wyoming, telling her all about the buffalo and the horses and the Indians. He was trying to get her mind off her pain.

"Hi, Mommy," she said as Mrs. Carter and I climbed in the back seat. "Is it okay if we go to the hospital?"

"Of course it is, Millie. Why didn't you tell me this morning that your arm hurt that badly?" She leaned over the front seat and kissed the top of Millie's head.

Millie didn't answer her. The ride to the hospital was quiet. We found the Emergency entrance, parked the car and went inside.

The attending nurse asked Mrs. Carter a few questions as she guided Millie into a wheelchair. She carefully examined Millie's arm, then didn't waste any time getting her to x-ray. Her mother went with an administrator to fill out forms. She returned to the waiting area a short time later, looking worried and tired. Her eyes were rimmed with red, and her hands shook as she folded the forms and put them in her pocket. Just as I was about to ask someone about Millie's progress, we heard Millie's voice. She was talking with the nurse who was pushing the wheelchair down the corridor. There was a bright, hot-pink cast on her arm.

"Oh, God!" her mother cried.

A doctor walked behind them. Dr. Green introduced himself and explained to us that Millie's arm had hairline fractures in two places. He wanted to know how it happened.

"Millie was thrown around on a ride over in Cavendish. She must have done it then," her mother explained.

Casey and I looked at each other and then at Millie. She was staring at me, her eyes wide with fear. I told her with a shake of my head that I wouldn't dispute her mother's statement, but I was furious. Much to my relief, the doctor did not accept the explanation. "Her injuries are not really consistent with that kind of activity, Mrs. Carter. Will you come with me a minute? I would like to talk with you in my office."

Casey and I sat down in two of the bright orange chairs that lined the wall of the waiting area. Millie's wheelchair faced us. "What do you think he's saying to her, Annie?" The fear expressed on her face was palpable.

Holding the arms of her chair, I leaned toward her and whispered. "Honey, I suspect that the doctor noticed the bruise under your eye. He's probably asking your mother some questions about how all this happened."

Millie started to cry. "Oh, Annie, my Daddy's going to be so mad."

Casey kissed the top of her head. "Let's wait and see what the doctor has to say, okay?"

The wait was long and silent. When Dr. Green and Millie's mother finally returned, she asked, "Annie, could Millie stay with you tonight?" Her words were spoken quickly, as though she was out of breath. "The doctor wants her to get a good night's sleep, and he's afraid that sleeping in the tent might be too hard on her. He's given me a prescription for her."

"Of course," I responded, totally surprised.

Mrs. Carter never said another word. Casey talked with the doctor a moment before joining us in the car. We stopped at the drug store in O'Leary to fill the prescription, took Mrs. Carter back to the campground and dropped her off at the gate. She assured us that she would be okay, kissed Millie, then closed the car door and walked away. I tried to feel sorry for her. At least in this instance, she was protecting her daughter.

Casey and I tucked Millie into my bed and sat with her until she fell asleep. We tiptoed out of the bedroom, leaving the door open just a crack, so we could hear her if she woke.

"She's such an angel. What an awful life she's had," I said, pulling one of the chairs away from the kitchen table. As I sat down, I looked up at Casey. "What do you suppose the doctor said to Mrs. Carter? I was shocked when she asked if Millie could stay here."

"I talked with him briefly before we left the hospital." Casey sat down next to me and lowered his voice. "I think he scared her. I'm sure he had a pretty good idea about those fractures, but what can he do? It's her word against his, even if he does report it." He put his arm across the back of my chair and leaned closer to me. "They're American citizens," he continued. "I wonder what the laws are up here for doctors who see cases of child abuse in families from other countries? He may have told Millie's mother that he was going to file a report. I have no idea. All I know is that I'm grateful that she asked you to bring Millie here."

"You know the doctor may have insisted on something like that," I said, our heads close together so we could talk without disturbing Millie. "This whole ordeal is triggering all sorts of horrible memories for me, though. What about you?" I reached for Casey's hand.

"Yes, the memories are there, Annie. Let's be thankful that we've got each other tonight, and we've got Millie here with us. We're all safe." He stood, leaned down to kiss me, then tiptoed across the floor to check on Millie. She was sleeping soundly.

We made lobster salad sandwiches and carried them out to the deck, staying there until well after dark. We talked about our lives back in the United States and the responsibilities we had waiting for us there. Casey had the movie to make in Ontario in a couple of months, but there was a great deal of pre-production work to be done in California. I had to resign from my job, sell a big house and basically start over.

"Life seems unfair at times, doesn't it?" Casey said, looking at the moon rising in the east.

"Downright unfair, Casey, especially for that little girl in there." A cool breeze brought the smell of the ocean over the railing. I shivered, crossing my arms in front of me, hugging myself. "Let's go in, Casey. I'm cold all of a sudden."

Casey wrapped his arms around me and rubbed my back to warm me. "Annie, would you mind terribly if I stayed here tonight?" he whispered in my ear. "It just seems important that the three of us stay together."

"I was hoping you would stay, Casey, but we're going to have to sleep on the couch."

"Sounds good to me." He gently pushed me away from him, kissed my cheek, then opened the door for me.

I quietly rummaged in my bedroom closet for another pillow, checked to be sure Millie was warm enough, then leaned down and kissed her. She was sleeping peacefully. The medication was doing its work well. Casey and I made ourselves comfortable on the old couch. Because it was so old, it was big and roomy enough for two. "This feels so good, Casey," I said, snuggling close to him.

"Yes, it does," he whispered, kissing my forehead. "I'm totally beat both physically and emotionally. You, too?"

"Mmm, hum," I responded, already comfortable in his arms. He pulled my grandmother's quilt up over us, kissed me again, and relaxed into the cushions.

I awoke around four o'clock and tiptoed across the room to check on Millie. She was sleeping soundly. I decided to lie down next to her so that I would be with her when she woke. Just as the sun peeked through the back window, she woke me. "Annie," she said as she patted my arm. "Annie, wake up."

I awoke with a start, not fully aware of where I was.

"Annie," Millie whispered. "I need to get up."

"Oh, good morning," I said, turning toward her. "How do you feel?"

"My arm feels awful heavy, but it doesn't ache like it did yesterday. I need to get up, Annie, and go to the bathroom." She had tossed the covers back and was trying to sit up. I hurried around the bed, and put my hand under her back to help her. She giggled as I tried to maneuver the sling over her head. Once she was comfortable in the bathroom, I hurried into the living room to wake Casey. only to find him at the kitchen sink making coffee.

"Mmmm, that smells good, Cowboy," I said, as I put my arms around his waist and leaned into his chest.

He wrapped one arm around me, kissed the top of my head and asked, "How's she doing this morning?" With his free hand he poured two mugs of coffee and passed one to me.

"Okay, so far," I said, breathing in the distinctive aroma of the morning brew. "Thanks, this is perfect," I said, taking a sip. I kissed his cheek, then walked back to the bedroom to check on Millie. She was sitting on the side of the bed waiting for me. The color of the cast seemed magnified somehow, like in those black and white television ads where one object is highlighted in color. A shot of adrenalin pulsed through me at the sight of it. Trembling, I sat down beside her. "How did you sleep, honey?"

"Great. It felt good to be inside a house. Thanks, Annie." She looked up at me and started to cry.

I put the coffee mug on the nightstand as I reached to comfort her. "What's wrong dear?" I whispered.

"I hope my Mommy is okay," she sobbed into my sweater. "I know my Daddy must have been awful mad."

I put my hand under her chin and lifted her face toward mine. "Millie," I said gently, "listen to me. I think the doctor at the hospital told your mother that he knew how your arm had been hurt. And I think he told her to talk to your father last night without you there. I suspect that your father is going to be okay about this while you're still on the Island. I just hope he doesn't pack up everything today and go home."

"Sometimes Mommy can talk to him and things are better for a little while," she agreed. She looked up at me, freckles dancing in the blush of emotion, blue eyes glistening with tears.

"I hope so, honey. Come on, let's get cleaned up. Casey's cooking us a great breakfast."

We both brushed our teeth, and then I brushed her hair and pulled it back into two ponytails. "There, that's the best I can do. My grandfather used to braid my hair, but I never did get the knack of it."

"Well, there's the two best-looking women in the world," Casey exclaimed as we walked into the living room. "How do you feel this morning, Millie?" he asked getting down on one knee to hug her.

"Okay," she whimpered.

"Just okay? Well, I'll have to whip up some of my famous eggs a la Casey for you so you can be terrific! How's that?" he asked, tickling her gently as he stood up.

He made her laugh, and he made me laugh. We sat at the picnic table on the deck enjoying our breakfast. The warm, morning air greeted us with the distinct smells and sounds of the beach. Much to Millie's delight, Casey described the plot of the new movie to be filmed near Lake Ontario. He was going to play a camp counselor in a family comedy about a troubled child sent to summer camp for discipline. The script called for lots of mishaps and misadventures that promised to be fun. When we finished our meal, he found a marker in the desk and autographed her cast with a flourishing signature under a heart and the words, "I love you, Millie." She squealed with delight and hugged him. "Thanks, Casey." Her words disappeared into his shirt.

"Oh, look, Annie," Millie said, pointing toward the ocean. "Isn't that a seal?" Casey and I looked over her head at the black object that had appeared in the water. Soon there were three of them cavorting in the waves.

The morning passed quickly, the trauma of the day before forgotten for a few brief moments. Hating to break the mood, I reminded Millie that her mother was going to pick her up before lunch. Before Casey left for his own cottage to change his clothes, he gave Millie a big, bear hug and told her that she could always count on him. He kissed me quickly and was gone.

Millie's mother arrived about a half hour later. She told me that her husband was angry at first when he found out that Millie was staying with me, but he calmed down when she told him that Millie's arm was fractured in two places.

"Are you staying for a few more days?" I asked, dreading her answer. I was relieved when she said, "Yes, we're on vacation until next week. He's agreed that we can stay here as we planned. And he's agreed that he'll leave her alone. That doctor was pretty clear about that. I don't know if he could do anything, but he threatened to and that seems to be making an impression on my husband." Mrs. Carter looked more rested than on any other occasion I had seen her. With her long, auburn hair tied back away from her face, she was an older picture of her daughter, freckles, blue eyes and smile.

"I hope so," I said, registering the amazing transformation. "Listen, if Millie needs to sleep here again, please bring her back. I love having her."

"We'll see. I don't know how to thank you for all you've done for her. Not too many people would get involved with a situation like this." She extended her hand to Millie in a gesture that suggested they should leave.

"Millie is a very special child, Mrs. Carter," I said, following them to the back door. "Casey and I both know the terrible consequences of child abuse. You need to know that both of us plan to keep in touch with her when we get back to the States."

She heard what I was implying. She turned to face me. "I understand, Annie. I've been urging my husband to get help for over a year now. Maybe this incident will do it."

"He's got to do something, and so do you before it's too late." The screen door slapped against the frame. We both jumped and looked out at Millie. She was walking toward the car, but I was sure she had heard every word we said. Mrs. Carter thanked me again and left.

My heart ached for Millie. My heart ached for any child who suffered from the abuse of adults. I felt heavy and tired. As I sat down on the couch, I cried, and then I prayed.

Casey returned dressed in tan khakis and a light blue, short-sleeved dress shirt. He told me that he had a message from California that he needed to go to Charlottetown to sign some legal papers.

"I'm sorry, Annie, but this South America mess just doesn't want to go away. How about coming along with me for the ride?"

"I would love it. Just give me a few minutes to get ready," I said, hurrying to the bedroom to find something clean and suitable for a trip to the city.

As we rode to Charlottetown, the largest city on the Island, I pointed out various landmarks and historic sites. The spectacular scenery across the interior of the Island rolled out ahead of us. Large tracts of land, fenced on either side by lush fir trees, were planted with golden barley or filled with clover. Horses and cows grazed in the warmth of the sun.

Once we arrived in the city, we drove up and down one-way streets looking for the lawyer's office. Casey completed his business quickly, then we walked for miles on the boardwalk at Victoria park, investigated a few gift shops, and browsed through a small art gallery. After a lovely supper at a local restaurant located along the city's waterfront, we started back to West Point.

"I would have loved to have gone to the Confederation Theater to see a play, Annie, but we've already had a long day, and we've still got a two-hour drive ahead of us before we get back to the cottage. Do you mind?" he asked, as he opened the car door.

"Not at all. I'm grateful that we could spend the day together. And honestly, I'm ready to head back as well. This whole terrible ordeal with Mille has been exhausting."

We talked about Millie and her parents as we drove west. There didn't seem to be any easy solutions. When we arrived at the cottage around nine, most of the color in the western sky was gone, leaving only a faint ribbon of light along the horizon.

Casey poured two glasses of wine and joined me on the deck. The warm and pleasant evening air brought with it the sounds of a bonfire party on the beach.

"They seem to be having a good time down there, Annie," Casey said as he passed a glass of wine to me and clinked my glass. "Here's to you, Beautiful."

We settled into our chairs listening to the sounds of the night. When Casey moved to stand up, I said, "Casey, will you stay with me again tonight and hold me? I'm so distressed over what has happened to Millie that I just don't want to be alone."

"I know, Annie. I was thinking the same thing. Come on. Let's turn in."

While I changed into summer pajamas, Casey stripped down to his boxer shorts. As we lay down on the old sofa, he wrapped his arms around me, whispered that he loved me, and pulled the quilt over us. When I heard him snoring softly, I relaxed and slept.

Chapter 10

August – 1993

I have taken refuge here on the deck to welcome a new day...to record both the wonderful...and the unspeakable...events of the last day.

It's very early. The dark of night is giving way to dawn as the sky brightens in the southeast, waking the songbirds and gulls. A thin layer of fog stretches between the Island and the distant shore, a fragile connection that will soon be broken by the warmth of the sun. Later this morning, the nearby farmers will be mowing hay on the honey-gold terrace of land that rolls out for miles between the coastal road and the red cliffs. The distant moan of an ocean buoy sounds its mournful warning. I feel that sound deep within my soul, as I think about Millie and her parents.

Children are precious, a true blessing from God. To hurt a child in any way is a dreadful act that diminishes everyone. Children are fragile human beings who, when abused, grow up to be fragile adults. There is nothing so wondrous as a child who feels secure and loved. And there is nothing so tragic as a child who does not believe in herself, because the ones who were supposed to love her, hurt her instead.

I did not sleep well last night, and when I did, I dreamed of hands reaching out of the depths of the sofa to grab and pull at me. Casey tried to comfort me, but the nightmares continued. In them Millie was running on the beach, crying, her arms dangling at her sides like those of a marionette. I ran after her, calling to her. When I put my hand on her shoulder to stop her, she turned around to face me. Her face was my face, swollen and red, one eye blackened by a blow from a fist, the other eye missing, leaving a gaping dark hole. It must have been then that I screamed. Casey gently woke me and held me, whispering words of love until the tears and the trembling abated. Calm once more, I slept until the harsh cries of the crows that nest in the huge pines nearby woke me. I slipped off the sofa, careful not to disturb the man who had been so tender and gentle throughout the night. As I bent down to kiss his cheek, I heard him snoring softly.

Breaking its bond with the horizon, the sun has risen and brought with it the promised warmth and light of day to my outdoor sanctuary. The new day has begun, chasing away the shadows of the night. I can hear the mowers in the distant fields now and can see the dairy cows grazing in the clover field to the northwest. A screen door slapped shut somewhere nearby and a car passed by the cottage as an Islander headed for work.

The Island is awake, its energy apparent in the sounds of morning. There's energy in me as well, nervous energy of panic and anxiety, born of nightmares and memories of a time when I was Millie's age. Feelings of homesickness have settled in the pit of my stomach.

I have learned so many other times to acknowledge the heavy sensation of dread, to give in to the need to cry, and to purge the sorrow buried so deep within. Denial kept the childhood demons of shame and ugliness at bay for forty years, until one day, a child younger than Millie, opened the wounds. She was the two-year-old child of a divorced friend, sent to her father on weekends, returning traumatized and silent. I helped by testifying for her mother in court, hoping she would gain full custody. And while we were successful, the terrible ordeal dredged up the emotions of my childhood.

For months, I thought I was losing my mind. I cried constantly. The dread and fear in my gut didn't make any sense, until I finally sought help. As it turned out, I was a forty-year old adult reliving my six-year-old feelings of abandonment and fear. Now those memories and feelings have been triggered once more, but this time I recognize them. Nevertheless, the enormous sense of grief is overwhelming.

♪♪♪

I set the journal aside, pulled my sweater around me for warmth and comfort, and let the tears flow. Thoughts of my own childhood experiences fused with the images of a child who looked so much like me. Not a coincidence, I thought. God brought us together for a reason.

I jumped when the screen door behind me slid open and Casey stepped onto the deck with two mugs of hot coffee. My morning muse was lost in the good cheer of his voice. "Good morning, Beautiful," he said, breathing deeply. "Looks like another grand day." As he turned toward me, I quickly brushed the tears away from my face with the sleeve of the sweater. He placed the mugs on the table and bent over the side of the chair to kiss me. "How long have you been out here, Annie?" he whispered, sliding his arms behind my back.

"A couple of hours," I mumbled into his shoulder. The warmth of his body and the tenderness of his kiss was a balm for my soul. I clung to him until the awkwardness of his position forced him to let go.

"Want to talk about it?" he asked, sitting in the chair next to mine.

"I've been remembering what it's like to be Millie's age and think that you're ugly and that no one loves you," I sniffed, reaching for a tissue. "Why do people do that to children? What's wrong with them?" I asked, blowing my nose. "Can't they see what they're doing?"

Casey shook his head. "I don't know. The whole thing stinks, but you've got to get a grip, honey. This thing is going to eat you up if you let it."

I took a deep breath and sighed. "I know. I'm so grateful you were here with me last night. Those dreams were just awful."

"I'm glad I was here, too," he said, looking at me over the rim of the mug as he sipped the coffee. "I can't imagine handling something like that alone." He inhaled sharply, then asked, "What made you scream?"

I turned away and looked across the dune toward the open water, not wanting to remember the image of that broken child. "When I was Millie's age, Casey, I looked a lot like her, pigtails and all. The images in my dream were grotesque manifestations of the abuse that both Millie and I have endured." I paused a moment, shaking my head as though to wipe out the memory. The tone of my voice hardened. "Casey, I've made up my mind that if her father touches her again, I'm going to talk to the local police. I just pray he hasn't done anything to her since yesterday."

"Well, we can take a walk over there and find out, if you'd like."

The time needed to walk along the beach to the park helped me clear away the dread generated by the nightmares. We walked slowly, stopping now and then to pick up a piece of sea glass or a colorful rock. Casey talked about the production plans for the movie he would be filming in Ontario. The change of subject changed my perspective and my mood. By the time we reached the park, I was laughing at his silly antics, as he demonstrated how he learned to be a fast-draw gunslinger for one of his westerns. When we entered the Carter's campsite, we found Millie sitting at the picnic table next to the tent. Her mother was sitting across from her. They were playing checkers. Mr. Carter was nowhere in sight.

"Hello, there!" I called to them.

"Hi, Annie!" Millie exclaimed. She jumped up to greet us, grabbing me around the waist in a one-armed bear hug.

"How's your arm, Millie?" Casey asked, as he responded to a similar hug.

"It feels much better today," she said, patting her wounded arm. "The cast is a little heavy, but this sling helps a lot." Her mother had braided her hair and tied each braid with a pink ribbon.

I looked around trying to determine whether Mr. Carter was in the tent or somewhere nearby.

"My Daddy has gone over to the harbor to see if he can get us some lobsters," Millie said, answering my unasked question. "I told him how we cooked them the other day, and he said that maybe we could try it ourselves." Millie nervously tugged at the sling.

"That's wonderful." I looked over at Mrs. Carter who was smiling at her child. "Who would ever believe that there was any problem here?" I thought silently.

Millie's mother had placed a large pot on the Coleman stove, ready to steam the lobsters when they arrived. "Millie was so excited about all that you taught her," she said, her arm over Millie's shoulders, "that we thought she could teach us. I'm very pleased that Bob was willing to go along with this."

"And how are all of you doing?" I asked.

Mrs. Carter knew what I meant. "We're okay, Annie, honestly. Bob has agreed to stay here for the rest of our vacation. I think the cast is a reminder of his temper. That seems to be having a positive affect on his behavior around Millie." She looked down at her daughter and smiled. Millie shrugged her mother's arm off her shoulders and sat down at the picnic table. Her mother continued, "The doctor told me that he wanted me to bring Millie to the hospital in a couple of days, so he could check her cast. I think that has scared Bob a little as well." She returned to the picnic table to clear away the game.

"Good!" I was relieved to hear that Mr. Carter had backed off a little, but I wasn't impressed that he was doing it because he was afraid of being caught.

"Mrs. Carter," Casey said walking toward her, "Annie and I normally do not intrude into other people's affairs, but we're genuinely concerned for both Millie and you. I hope when you return home, you can persuade your husband to seek help. In the meantime, if either one of you needs any help while you're here, please call us. We'll do whatever we can." He reached into his pocket and gave her a card. "This card has Annie's cottage number on it."

Casey spoke slowly and with great emotion. Millie's eyes shone with emotion as well as she watched him walk around the picnic table. He stopped and put one foot up on the bench where Mrs. Carter sat. He leaned over his knee and looked directly into her eyes. "Annie and I are involved now. That fact isn't going to change. I just want you to know that we love Millie and want only the best for her. If you need us, we're just a phone call away."

His gesture was meant to convey his deep concern for Millie, but I was worried that Mrs. Carter would read it differently.

"I appreciate that, Mr. MacDonald," she said, shifting her weight away from him. "We're taking it day by day, but I can assure you that I'm committed to the best interests of my daughter." Her face was flushed, and her hands trembled as she stacked the checkers in the box.

"Millie, come over to visit tomorrow if you can. Okay?" I looked toward Mrs. Carter for agreement. She smiled, but didn't respond verbally.

"Okay, Annie." Since Millie had been straddling the bench seat connected to the picnic table, when she jumped up to say good-bye, she hopped away from the bench on one leg until the other leg was clear. She hugged me first, her arms wrapped around my waist and her head buried in my stomach. I could feel the hard surface of her cast against the small of my back. When she hugged Casey, she raised her sunburned face to him and smiled. I wished that I had my camera to capture the raw emotion on the face of a six foot four man as he looked down upon the half-pint child squinting up at him. The hot-pink cast, resting on the back pocket of his jeans, matched the ribbons tied on the end of her pigtails.

Casey and I walked out of the park along a trail that led to the beach. Our trek back to the cottage was long and silent. Like two sleepwalkers, we poured ourselves a cool drink and settled heavily into the chairs on the deck. The frosty glass of lemonade was refreshing; the air was summer warm. Once my heartbeat had returned to normal, I looked at Casey and asked, "Are you all right?"

A deep furrow creased the skin between his eyebrows. "I think so. I hope I didn't scare Millie, but I wanted Mrs. Carter to understand that she can count on us if she needs help."

"You know, I think Millie's cast has scared her mother, too." The sound of two gulls squawking over a crab that had washed up on the shore called my attention to the world around the cottage. "Casey, look out there," I said, sweeping my arm toward the ocean in an attempt to change the mood. "There's a beautiful world out there to explore. Let's go for a ride on that two-seater bicycle that you repaired. I want to see what kind of handyman you really are."

"That sounds great, Annie. We definitely need a change of perspective. Let's ride up to Miminegash for lunch and some of that seaweed pie." At the mention of seaweed pie, he screwed up his face as though he had tasted something horrible.

When we wheeled the two-seater out of the shed, I noticed that Casey had spray painted the front fender a deep, burgundy red, and had attached a basket to the front handlebars. We lined the bottom of the basket with a light blanket, then anchored it down with a small cooler I filled with bottles of cold water, apples and a few of Linda's peanut butter cookies.

"Annie, we're going to have lunch in a couple of hours," Casey laughed.

"I know, but I never like to go anywhere without some 'just in case' food," I said, remembering a time long ago when I was stranded by the side of the road in a wintry blizzard for six hours with no food or water.

"Come on," he urged, "let's head up the coast. We've got a beautiful day. I don't want to waste a minute of it."

The bicycle built for two was old, but Casey had fixed all the important parts and had installed comfortable, new seats. We walked beside it until we reached the main road before we attempted to get on. Riding a two-seater isn't all that difficult, but getting started can be. Our first attempt was shaky, and we both put a foot out to stop our forward motion. Our second and third attempts were terribly uncoordinated as each of us tried to over-correct the forward motion of the bicycle. Our shouts of frustration and contradictory movements reminded me of a scene from a Laurel and Hardy movie, and I began to laugh so hard that I wasn't sure whether or not I would be able to continue.

Our last attempt was successful, however, and in a few minutes we were sailing along quite well. Casey rode on the front seat and I on the back. As cars passed us, we waved and they blew their horns. At one point I put my feet up on the handlebars and let Casey do all the work. The people in the cars that passed by honked and waved and pointed at us, but Casey just smiled and waved back not realizing that I was loafing. As we started up a hill he looked back and said, "The pedaling is getting harder, Annie, how are you holding out?"

"Great!" I exclaimed, but before I could get my feet down to help him, he caught me.

"Hey, what are you doing back there?" he said, pedaling even harder.

"Getting a free ride for once in my life." I laughed.

Climbing that hill was nearly impossible. My laughter became infectious, and as a result, we lost our concentration. The bicycle started to wobble, but Casey's strength kept us upright as we crested the hill.

The panorama before us stretched hundreds of miles to the north across the cobalt blue waters of the Straight to the New Brunswick shore, and far up the famous red sand beaches of Prince Edward Island. As we traveled toward Miminegash, the red sandstone bluffs lining the shore rose higher. The land between the road and the sea was a flat terrace of freshly mown barley fields. Acres that had not been mown were full of clover and honeybees. At the edge of the bluff there was a border of tall grass peppered with purple vetch, Queen Anne's lace, brown eyed Susans and daisies. The confusion of color was magnificent.

"Wow," Casey said, as he breathed in a lung full of air. "The air is so much clearer and fresher here."

As we passed by a long, wooden fence, one of the cows on the other side looked up at us and mooed. Casey laughed and said, "Hi there. How ya' doin'?"

The bicycle held up well as we crested hills, coasted down the other sides and over bridges that crossed streambeds fed by saltwater tides. When we arrived in Miminegash, we decided to ride down into the harbor to look around before lunch. Miminegash Harbor was larger than the harbor at West Point with many more boats. Here an inlet had been cut through the dune and a harbor about three acres in size had been dredged out behind it. A wharf, similar to the one at West Point, was built around the harbor forming a square with an opening out to sea. A bridge had been built over a small stream so the trucks could carry supplies to the boats on the other side.

Before the season opens, the wharf is covered with lobster traps and brightly colored buoys that are used to mark where the traps are set in the sea. Each fisherman chooses a different color scheme to distinguish his buoys from another's. When they are all piled up on the wharf, the day-glow colors of orange, red, yellow and lime green are dazzling.

After wandering around the wharf, Casey and I peddled back to the main road to the Seaweed Pie Café. The building had been renovated by a group of fishermen's wives to house a small interpretive center about Irish moss, a gift shop and the cafe. They call themselves Women in Support of Fishing and are dedicated to educating Islanders and tourists about the Irish moss industry.

We found a table already set up for two near a window. No one seemed to know Casey there so we were free to relax and enjoy our lunch.

"What'll you have, Annie?" he asked, looking at the menu.

"The food is very good here. Let's see, I think I'll have the seafood chowder and a biscuit."

"Let's make it two! And we'll top it off with seaweed pie?" Casey wrinkled up his nose again when he said seaweed pie. I laughed and assured him that it tasted a lot better than it sounded.

The chowder was rich and creamy, full of haddock, scallops, crab, clams and lobster meat. When we had finished our meal, the waitress brought us the pie, a light pudding-custard confection thickened with the carragheenan derived from the Irish moss. The pudding-custard, poured into a flaky pie shell, was topped with a choice of raspberry or blueberry syrup. A couple of small dobs of whipped cream completed a lovely dessert. Casey laughed out loud. "*This* is seaweed pie?"

"Taste it," I said laughing.

With his first tenuous bite, Casey's expression reminded me of my two-year-old nephew when he tasted a candy cane for the first time. His look of surprise was precious. "I envisioned a mass of gooey seaweed mixed up with raisins or something. Truthfully, I wasn't really looking forward to this part of our lunch, but this is delicious!"

"It's good to know that taking a risk can be fun once in a while, isn't it?"

Our light-hearted mood evaporated in an instant with the unintentional impact of my words. The smile drained from his face, as Casey took my hand and looked out the window, lost in that moment of time to his life back in California. After a few moments, I squeezed his hand to bring him back.

"I'm sorry, Annie." He put his fork down on the table and leaned back in his chair.

"I know. Come on, let's go look around the museum. They've got a wonderful slide presentation that will fill you in on the Irish moss industry."

We found our way to a small auditorium where four rows of chairs faced a movie screen. Casey leaned back in the wooden chair, crossed his legs and put his arm around me all in one smooth motion. The slides of men on horseback riding in the surf reminded us of our first trip together to North Cape. The guide, who spoke with a distinctive and lovely colloquial accent, told us about the families who harvest the Irish moss in the area. "When the Northwest wind comes in, people pack their gear in their trucks, put up a lunch in the refrigerator and wait. The harvesters know where to go and have named various spots where the moss is the thickest after a good wind: The Point, White's Cove, MacDonald Shore, North Cape.

"Whole families go to the shore to gather the moss. Some use horses that have been specially trained for this. Some use gloms that they throw into the waves. This method is called 'gloming' and takes a strong man, or a good woman, to do it because the waves want to pull the glom out of their hands.

"Raked moss is really clean. The harvesters take the moss home and spread it out on lawns and driveways and even in some cases right in the road. The whole community works. The children pick out the kelp and put it on the gardens. Where the moss has been on the lawns, the grass grows faster and greener.

"We have been told that the moss from PEI is a better quality and has a better life span. It is baled in the plant and shipped to companies that make jello, ice cream, medicines, cosmetics and many other products."

Casey and I listened to the entire presentation, thanked the woman for the information, and then checked out the gift shop. I found a couple of books about Island women and their families that looked interesting. Casey picked up some children's books for his kids.

"Annie, look at this. Do you think Millie would like it?" He held a small, framed painting of the West Point Lighthouse. The artist had painted the distinctive black and white striped landmark with the dunes and the beach in the foreground.

"Oh, Casey, she'll love it!" I said, remembering the dancing leprechaun on the beach the first time I saw her.

After thanking the guide who was doing double duty as the gift shop proprietor, we packed our treasures into the basket on the front of the bicycle, climbed aboard and pushed off. We were getting better at synchronizing our balance on the two-seated contraption. About five miles down the coast, we found a dirt road that led to the water. Because the road was bumpy and seemed to disappear at the bluff's edge, Casey suggested that we park the bicycle in the tall grass behind a fence. He retrieved the blanket and cooler from the basket, then reached for my hand as we walked toward the top of the bluff.

"Annie, I can't get over how beautiful this Island is." His head was in perpetual motion as he looked from side to side at the great expanse of water in front of us. The New Brunswick shore, ever-changing in perspective, was a thin ribbon of land floating on the far-away horizon. When we reached the spot where the road veered off to the left and disappeared down under the bluff, we stopped. "Suppose this is one of the places where the mossers come to gather moss?" I wondered.

"Could be. Let's spread the blanket out over here. Look at this view!" The point of land where we stood jutted into the Straight in such a way that we could see the red sandstone cliffs on either side of us. Below, on the left, a red sand beach curled around the base of a bluff. Ocean waves, breaking thirty feet offshore in jagged lines of white foam, gently flowed inland. On the right those same waves broke with great energy over layers of a sandstone reef that made up just off shore.

We had to tramp around in the tall grass and wildflowers to make a place to spread the blanket. As a result, our rest area was soft and inviting, and the sweet smell of the grass and flowers was intoxicating. We lay down on the blanket on our backs and stared at the sky.

"You know, Annie, I feel as though I've been transported to another planet."

"I know," I sighed, feeling my shoulders and hips relax into nature's spongy bedding.

Casey reached for my hand. We lay there like that for a long time, holding hands, connected each to the other and to the vastness around us with an intimacy that defies expression. He caressed my fingers with his thumb and said, "I love you, Annie."

I let the words float up into the sky and then turned to reply when I noticed the tears running down the side of his face onto the blanket. I put my arm across his chest, moved my body closer to him, and kissed that favorite spot under his chin.

"Annie, I think I'm losing it. I've cried more in the last couple of days than I have in my entire life." He wiped his eyes with the back of his hand.

"We're both ready for this, Casey. We've been ready for this since the first time someone hit us. We've swallowed an awful lot of hurt and denied it was even there." I paused a moment to think about what I was saying. "And now that we have touched it and exposed it, that hurt has to get out. It's like a big boil that needs to be lanced. It hurts like the devil when you squeeze the poison out, but until you do, it can't heal. It just keeps hurting."

"It's so sad, Annie. Think of the countless number of kids who are enduring that kind of pain right now." He had pulled his arm out from beneath me and draped it across my back. As he talked, he gently kneaded my shoulder.

"I can't, Casey. If I did, I *would* go crazy. All I can do is to try to deal with what's right here. Loving Millie is hard enough. Her situation triggers all the old memories, even some that were buried deep. That's what's happening to you, too. She's triggered all those raw sores that you thought were scarred over years ago."

"Yes, scars. Too many scars." He sighed deeply.

I held him and kissed his face and eyes. When I tasted his tears, I cried too. He rolled me over onto my back and kissed me with a passion that reached down into my soul. We made love, passionately at first, and then slowly and deliberately as though each of us were memorizing every movement. When we were finished, we wrapped ourselves in the blanket and relaxed. I spoke first and giggled. Casey kissed me on the neck and said, "What are you giggling about?"

"I was just thinking that it's a good thing we haven't had a strong Northwest wind in the last day or so. We might have been interrupted by a whole family of mossers standing over us wondering if we were dead or alive."

Casey laughed harder than I had ever heard him laugh before. "I guess we had better get dressed before someone catches us."

He held me in his arms. His kiss was soft and warm, his touch tender. "Careful, Cowboy, we'll end up staying here all night."

"Sounds good to me, but you're right. We probably ought to think about getting back to the cottage." We dressed hurriedly. Casey fished in the cooler for the bottles of water. "Let's take advantage of this peaceful spot for a few more minutes, Annie." We sat on the blanket facing the water, arms around our knees, each holding a water bottle in one hand. As the silence settled over us, the sounds of boats working on the New Brunswick shore drifted toward us over the watery expanse.

"Gosh, I miss my kids," Casey whispered into the silence. "Millie is so much like Amanda. Vibrant. Full of questions and full of love. Dennis is only four, but he's all boy. Gets into everything."

A small, orange butterfly landed on my knee. "I wondered when you would tell me about them," I said, fascinated by the intricate beauty of the creature.

Unaware of my visitor, Casey continued to pour out his thoughts. "Annie, I didn't want to talk with you about them, because it puts the reality of our situation right out there. I guess I just don't want to face it, but now that I've got to go home next week, the reality is pretty obvious, isn't it?" As if to emphasize his last remark, he tossed the empty water bottle into the cooler. The butterfly flew away.

"Yes, it is." I watched the tiny butterfly drop onto a daisy next to the cooler, its wings continuing to move slowly. "But, Casey, you need to understand that I'm trying not to have any expectations. I think we've discovered something pretty wonderful in each other, but our lives are so different. This Island is giving us a place in time where we can get to know each other and love each other. When we leave here and return to the real world, all of this is going to look very different."

"I know," he said, leaning back on his elbows. "Your friends are going to tell you that I was taking advantage of you, and my friends are going to tell me that I was lucky no one found out about us because they'll be worried about publicity and my career."

"Well, your friends will have a point," I said, as I looked down at him. "I hope no one does find out about us! The publicity won't help either one of us. Don't get me wrong," I responded quickly to his pained expression, "I would be proud to stand in front of a camera with you, but what they would print would be a lie."

"I don't think anyone would believe me if I told them that I love you. Maybe that's because I've never let any of them see as far into my soul as you have. But, Annie, I do love you." He relaxed onto the blanket, reached for my arm and pulled me toward him.

"And I love you, Casey." I caught my breath as I said those words to him for the first time. My eyes glistened from the emotion.

He smiled, looked at me and said, "Annie, I'm sorry. I never should have gotten you mixed up with the likes of me."

"Casey, these few weeks that we're spending together are wonderful. I would never give them back." I leaned back, kissed him and put my head on his chest, relaxing into the warmth of his body.

"But I wish things could be different for us, Annie," he said, taking my hand.

"I wonder how many others have said the same thing?" I sighed as I wrestled with thoughts of watching him leave to return to the reality that waited in California.

A warm breeze blew over the bluff. The daisies and wild mustard flowers danced beside us in the sunlight, lobster boats worked offshore taking on their precious cargo, one trap at a time, and our conversation floated in the air, carried across the meadow behind us on a northwest gust of wind. This was a memory for my mental scrapbook.

"You're right," he said, putting one hand beneath his head. "It's an old, old story, isn't it? The movie studios have made millions telling it thousands of ways. I just wish we could have a happy ending."

"You know, Casey, we just might have a happy ending in one way. Even though we may never be able to be together, perhaps we'll each have the resolve now to let go of the past and get on with our lives. You have a lot of work to do at home, and I have memories to sort through in Maine. The ending that we get might not be our choice, but let's pray that it's at least a good one for each of us."

"You're being awfully brave," he said, squeezing my shoulder.

"Mmmm," I responded. "I can do that with you right here holding me, knowing that we still have another week together. I wish things were different for us as well. I've lost so much already, and losing you is going to be a lot to deal with."

"You're not going to lose me, Annie," he said, the tone of his voice deepening.

"You can say that now, but Casey you have a family and all the issues that go with it to resolve before you can make any decisions, or any promises." I sat up and looked away from him toward the sea. "And what about your career? Your life is totally foreign to me, a life that I wouldn't enjoy and couldn't really appreciate. This time that we're having together is a fantasy, a moment in time that has been given to us to live to its fullest and to give us some real answers for the rest of our lives. You'll forget about me in time."

He grasped my arm to direct my attention back to him. "Don't bet on it, Annie. I wish I could say something to you that doesn't sound like a line from a B movie. Good grief," he said shaking his head, "this really is a classic dilemma, isn't it?"

"Yes, it is. Except that our classic dilemma involves Millie. And I think that just might be why we're together. She feels safe with us, Casey. She relaxes with us and is transformed from a wary, abused child just trying to stay out of harm's way, into a giggling, little girl who embraces her life." I smiled, remembering Millie squealing with happiness while standing on tiptoes as she peered down into the lobster pot. "She's an intuitive child, Casey, amazing really. She senses our love for each other and our love for her." His hand brushed the back of my arm. "From what I've seen, it doesn't seem that she experiences love like that at home. If nothing else, maybe we've given her a glimpse of what can be possible for her."

"I hope so. When I return to California, I'm going to check on the child abuse laws in New York. My studio has enough high priced lawyers sitting around getting rich that they can spare a little time for this."

"Don't forget her, Casey. She's grown to love you just like I have."

"I won't forget her, Annie, or you either. Do you realize that today is the first time you've told me that you love me?" He jumped up suddenly, turned toward the water and yelled, "Annie says she loves me!" When I laughed at his antics, he turned back to me, extended his hand and pulled me to my feet. As he hugged me, he said, "I think we should do something to celebrate. Let's go to Tyne Valley tonight for dinner."

"I'd love it! But first we've got to get ourselves back to West Point." I bent over to pick the daisy blossom where the butterfly had made its temporary home, and tucked it into my pocket intending to press it into my journal later. With the blanket tucked under his arm and the cooler in his hand, Casey paused, looked toward the water, and took my hand. We strolled along the dusty, dirt road to find our transportation. No one had disturbed it.

"Can you imagine leaving a bicycle by the road back home?" Casey asked.

"Would they even know what this thing is in California?" I teased.

"Probably not. Come on, hop on and we'll head back," he said, tossing the blanket and cooler into the basket.

I started to climb on the back seat when Casey said, "Wait a minute! Maybe you should ride on the front on the way back, Annie." Casey laughed, remembering my trick earlier that morning.

"Okay, but you have to promise to pedal!" The bicycle wobbled as we adjusted to the new arrangement, but soon we were gliding along the side of the road singing a round of 'Row, Row, Row Your Boat.' We stashed the bicycle in the shed at Casey's, then drove to my cottage where we found a note pinned on the door. It was an invitation to dinner from Linda and Barry.

"We can say no, Casey," I said, disappointed at the prospect of canceling our plans.

"Nonsense. Let's spend the evening with them. I'd really like to get to know them. We can go to Tyne Valley tomorrow night." When he noticed the look on my face, he added quickly, "Or, we could just say no and go to Tyne Valley tonight."

I laughed. "No, you're right. Linda and Barry are great. This will be fun."

Linda answered my call on the first ring. She told me that the boys had gone to Cavendish with a neighbor, and the girls were over at the Browns. "Come over around six, Annie."

"Are you sure you guys don't want to spend a relaxing evening alone?" I asked, still thinking about Casey's initial plan.

"Don't be silly, Annie. We thought this would be a perfect night to have you and Casey to dinner. We'd like to get to know him, too!" she exclaimed.

"Okay. We'll see you at six." When I turned to tell Casey the plan, he had disappeared. I found him in the bathroom rummaging in the closet for bath towels. "I need to wash off the road dust, Annie. What do say, want to climb in this old shower with me?"

Casey was singing "Ol' Solo Mio" when I eased into the phonebooth-sized shower stall. The "Mio," bouncing around inside the tin box, sounded like the howl of a wolf.

"I never would have believed that we could both fit in here, Casey, but this is fun!" We were tucked into the cramped enclosure in such a way that we really couldn't move around. About all we could do was wash each other's back. However, Casey's offer to wash my hair turned out to be a very sensual experience. As he gently rubbed the sweet smelling shampoo into my scalp, I closed my eyes and wrapped my arms around his waist. The lather from the shampoo washed down over our bodies making them slick. We tried to fool around, but it was impossible and only resulted in our laughing hysterically as we banged into the sides of the thin metal shower stall putting a big dent in the back wall. We rinsed off, stepped out, wrapped ourselves in two large terry cloth bath sheets, and padded into the bedroom to get dressed.

Casey sat on the side of the bed, his jeans pulled up but not zipped, tugging on a sock. "You look awfully good, Annie," he said, watching as I towel dried my hair.

"So do you, but if we're going to get to Linda's before dessert, we need to get a move on." I hurriedly brushed my hair, thankful for once for the natural curl.

When we arrived at the farmhouse, Barry greeted us at the back door, hugged me, and shook hands with Casey. "Come on in," Barry offered, holding the door for us. We brushed past him and walked through the entryway cluttered with sandy sneakers and flip-flops. Linda greeted us from the kitchen table where she was frosting a couple dozen cupcakes. "Hi, guys. Glad you could make it," she said looking up, a cupcake in one hand, the chocolate covered knife in the other.

"Linda, do you ever get out of this kitchen? Every time I come over here you've got something cooking in that oven!" Casey carefully hugged her, then sat down on the bench across from her.

"You're right, Casey. But we need to feed all those folks who are coming over tomorrow to help clean out the barn." She swirled a spoonful of chocolate frosting over the last cupcake, put a cherry on top, and placed the tempting confection on the plate with the others.

"Need more help?" Casey asked, watching her cross the kitchen to the pantry where she added the cupcakes to the pies, breads and cookies she had been baking all day.

"Yes, we do!" Linda poked her head out of the pantry door. "Can the two of you come over early in the morning to help us set up?"

"Sure! What time do you want us?" Casey asked, looking at me for agreement. I nodded my consent, then turned my attention back to Barry who was trying to remove a dry cork from a bottle of Merlot. He had successfully pulled the cork, but a few pieces had broken off and were floating in the bottle. As he poured four glasses of wine, I spooned out the debris.

"I expect everyone else some time around seven-thirty or eight. That will give them time to get their morning chores done and have their breakfast." Linda was in perpetual motion as she reached in a cupboard for a box of crackers, found a tub of cheese in the refrigerator and a small knife in a drawer. She put everything on a tray and suggested with a nod of her head that we follow her into the living room.

"Sounds like a long day for them," I said, joining Casey on the well-padded sofa. Barry had already made himself comfortable in one of the matching chairs.

"Not any longer than any other day, Annie," she replied, placing the tray on the wicker coffee table in front of us. "These people up here work hard for what they have. They're wonderful folks. They've all made arrangements to have others bring their cows in late tomorrow afternoon. After we eat supper, they'll go home and pick up right where they left off the next morning. They're doing all their field work today so they can have tomorrow to help with the barn."

"They sound like good neighbors, Linda," Casey said impressed with the generosity of so many.

"They are, Casey. Best in the world. There are times when I wish we could just stay here forever. But Barry's business is in Ottawa and we've got to get back." She took a sip of wine and gazed at her husband. They smiled at one another, exchanging past conversations in a glance.

Casey turned to him then. "Are you planning to retire here, Barry?"

"Yes, we are. And you're welcome here any time you want to visit. Annie knows that, too. We'll be moving here in two years." When he said two years, he lifted his glass to Linda.

Waiting for them to enjoy the moment before I spoke, I cleared my throat and said, "I appreciate your kindness, Barry, but I've got some news for the two of you. I'm going to buy the 'Lady Ann' so I'll be your neighbor for a long time."

"Oh Annie, that's wonderful!" Linda exclaimed.

"Yes, it is. I made the offer when Susan was here, but I haven't said anything for fear the offer wouldn't be accepted. They called me yesterday to tell me they had accepted. There's some legal stuff to work out, but I'll own it before I go home."

"Well, then, we need to make an official toast." Barry's deep voice resonated in the large room. "Here's to the 'Lady Ann.' Long may she ride the dunes."

The four of us stood in the middle of the room, clinked our glasses, and took a sip of the wine. Casey put his arm around me, looked down at me and smiled. He started to say something to me, but hesitated.

"What?" I said.

"Nothing." He kissed my forehead. "You know I should have called the boys out West when I was at your house, Annie." He turned to Barry. "Mind if I use your phone, Barry? There's a little business deal brewing back home that needs some attention."

Barry showed Casey to a small office at the back of the house where he could speak with his business partners in private.

Linda sat down next to me on the sofa, looked at me with concern and said, "What's going on with you two?"

"I have no idea, Linda, but whatever this is, it's wonderful! For the first time, in a very long time, I feel whole…complete." I sighed and leaned back into the soft cushions.

"What do you mean, Annie?" she asked.

"For years I've believed that there was something missing in my life. I've never really known what it was, but there's always been an anxiety about me to achieve, to be the best, to strive for the top. For over twenty years the work at that damned company has been stressful and hard. And while I've had some success, the missing piece has always eluded me. I've searched my entire life for it, and must have believed in myself to achieve what I have, but never really believed I deserved happiness or love. I guess I always thought you had to work for that, too, to take care of others, to give yourself away."

"To be happy is to live a self-less existence?" Linda said, affirming my thoughts. She took a last sip of wine, placed the glass on the table, and sat back into the corner of the sofa.

"Exactly. I've taken care of everyone else all my life. Coming up here to spend two months away from family and friends was a giant leap for me, Linda. You know that."

"I sure do. We've asked you a dozen times over the last few years to spend more time on the Island." She reached toward me to touch my arm, a gesture that was meant to convey her understanding of the past. She was a good and thoughtful friend, who had written letters and called every week after my husband had died.

"That's right. Even this summer, I felt guilty coming here. Especially this summer, Linda. How did I have the right to just close up the house when there was so much to do?" Thankfully, my wineglass was empty, because I was unaware that I had been waving it in circles to emphasize my point.

"I'm glad you got over that!" she laughed, taking the glass and placing it beside her own on the table.

"So am I. I never would have met Casey." Relaxing once more, I leaned back into the soft comfort of the furniture and closed my eyes. "He's given me a wonderful gift, Linda. He's allowed me to see into my own soul. Through his eyes I've seen beauty there and discovered that I'm a good, whole and passionate being." I started to cry.

Linda responded immediately. She moved closer to me and took my hands in hers. "Annie, I'm so pleased for you," she said, lowering her head so that she could look into my eyes. "But, honey, we've all known you're a special person ever since we met you. It really surprises me that you've lived with that kind of emptiness for so long."

I hugged her. "Thank you for that. You've been a wonderful friend." We sat there in silence absorbing the emotion before speaking again.

Linda broke the silence. "Annie, have you seen that little girl since her adventure in Casey's shed?"

I had been dreading the moment when I would have to tell Linda about Millie. "Yes, we have. She and her folks went over to Cavendish for a couple of days and when they came back she appeared at the cottage. That was the day Casey wanted to buy lobsters off the boat and cook them, so we asked her to ride over to the harbor and then eat lunch with us. Evidently her father was fishing somewhere and her mother was enjoying the time alone."

"From what you've said, I can't say as I blame her." Linda sat back against the cushions.

"We had a wonderful afternoon with her, Linda, laughing and joking and squirting each other with lobster juice, but then everything got pretty serious when she told us her right arm hurt because her father had hurt her again."

"No!" The word blew out of Linda's mouth like a bullet.

"I'm afraid so. We persuaded her to go to the hospital for an x-ray. We picked up her mother at the park and drove into Summerside. The doctor was suspicious right away and took Millie's mother into his office. When she came out she asked if Millie could stay at the cottage for the night." I paused and poured myself another glass of wine."

"Why do you suppose she let her do that?" Linda asked.

"This is the part that's so awful. Millie's arm was fractured in two places so they had to put a cast on it. The doctor wanted her to sleep in a real bed away from her father."

"My God! Annie, somebody's got to do something before he kills her." Linda's face had turned white with shock.

"I know. Both Casey and I are frustrated and terribly worried about her. We went over there this morning and were surprised to find a happy little family. I guess after an episode such as this Millie's father is nice to her for a while. I can't imagine what her mother must be going through."

"Do you know how much longer they're staying on the Island?"

"No, not really, but Casey is going to check with a lawyer to see what can be done for Millie once she's back in New York."

"I hope there's a good solution for that little girl."

"So do I, Linda." My face was hot, flushed from concern and frustration.

Just then Barry returned from the kitchen announcing that the grill was ready for the burgers. A bear of a man, nearly six three, he resembled a linebacker on a professional football team. Because his thick, sandy hair was cut in the style of a Dutch boy, he looked younger than his fifty years. A round face, rosy cheeks and blue eyes accentuated the boyish look.

"Hey, you two, what's going on? You okay, Annie?" He put his hand on my shoulder as a sign of concern.

"Yes, Barry, thanks," I said smiling up at him.

"Great." He turned to Linda. "Want me to start cooking?"

She smiled at the man who stood before her wearing a chef's apron with "Kiss the Cook" printed in red letters on the front of it. She stood up, kissed him, and said, "Yes, by all means, before you starve to death."

"Barry, do you still play cribbage?" I asked before he disappeared.

"Sure do. Does Casey?"

"I'm not sure, but if he does let's play after supper."

"Good idea, Annie. Be good to get Linda out of the kitchen for a few hours. All she's done on this vacation is cook!" He patted Linda's backside as he hurried away to cook the burgers.

"Men really are all alike aren't they? Just little boys all grown up," Linda laughed. She tidied up the coffee table, putting the wine bottle and glasses on a tray and taking them into the kitchen. I followed her with the empty box of crackers that Barry had left beside his chair. Chuckling, I thought about the man with a young child's appetite, not only for food, but for anything that resulted in fun.

Linda asked me to set the table while she prepared a salad. "Linda, what's the story with the barn? Why are so many of the neighbors coming over to help get it ready?"

"The back side of the roof took an awful beating from the winter winds, so we'll be needing to replace a good part of it. We had hoped we could get away with waiting until after the reunion, but the storm the other day did more damage. Now there's a pretty big hole back there, and if it should rain next Saturday, we'll all get drenched." She chopped celery, cucumbers and carrots as she talked. "And because we've had a leak, all that stuff that Barry has been storing in the hayloft got wet, so we've got to sort through it and take a good part of it to the dump, before it rots from the dampness. It's quite a mess, Annie," she sighed. "I couldn't believe it. He's tucked odds and ends up there for five years. I don't have a clue where he got it all, but we're 'Going to need it some day' he says." She laughed as she tossed the salad.

"Tell me about it. I've still got a two-story garage to clean out when I get home," I groaned. Thoughts of my husband flickered in my subconscious for the first time that day. The pain of grief was subsiding, but I still missed his laughter and teasing.

Linda noticed the change in my face. "Annie, you've been grieving for him long enough. You grieved for two years before he died and now another nine months. Let go of it soon, honey." She placed the large salad bowl in the middle of the table and returned to the counter for the dressings.

Changing the subject, Linda said, "Why don't you go see what's keeping Casey and I'll check on our boy-chef."

Casey was just finishing his conversation when I tapped lightly on the door. "Food's on the table, Casey," I said, poking my head into the room.

"Good. I'm starved!" He lifted me off the floor in a bear hug, kissed me quickly, and put me down. "These are nice folks, Annie. I'm glad they asked us for dinner." He put his hand on the small of my back, nudging me back into the living room.

"Do you play cribbage, Casey?" I asked, as we neared the kitchen.

"Yes, but I haven't played for years. Are we...?" Before he could finish his question, Barry burst through the back door with a plate of burgers. While I had been talking with Casey, Linda had added potato salad and a basket of hot, butterfly yeast rolls to the table.

"Come and sit down. Nothing fancy tonight," Linda announced.

"What do you mean, Linda?" Casey asked. "This looks like a meal fit for a king!" he exclaimed, as he waited for Barry to join us at the kitchen table. He held the chair for me and then sat down beside me.

Barry opened another bottle of wine, poured four glasses and then stood up for a toast. "To good friends," he said, smiling.

"Here, here," Casey cheered as he clinked his glass against mine.

We thoroughly enjoyed the meal and the conversation. Linda served her special lemon meringue pie for dessert, and then Barry and Casey disappeared into the living room to play cribbage. I didn't leave the table right away to join them, but instead remained there, remembering the hundreds of meals we shared with my husband's family who had come from this place. The butterfly yeast rolls seemed to be the mark of a good Island cook. My husband's mother made them for every meal, even though her hands were terribly crippled with arthritis.

"Annie, are you going to join us?" Linda had put away the leftovers and was taking off her apron. I had been staring out of the big picture window next to the table longer than I had realized.

"What?" I said, as though awakening from a deep sleep.

"Where have you been?" Linda asked.

"Oh, just thinking how good it feels to let go of some of the old stresses."

Linda hugged me and gently pushed me toward the living room. "Okay," she announced, "how about the women against the men. What do you say, Annie, let's beat the pants off them!"

"A figure of speech, I hope," Casey laughed.

We all laughed. The evening was relaxing and very enjoyable. About eight thirty the boys arrived home full of news about their day in Cavendish. Linda escorted them upstairs. When she returned, we played a few more rounds of cribbage and then Casey said, "We should go home, Annie, and let these people get to bed."

I retrieved my sweater from the back of the chair. "Yes. It's going to be a long day tomorrow," I agreed. "Linda, thanks so much for a delicious dinner. I really enjoyed the evening," I said, hugging her.

"So did I, Linda. You must be the best cook in Canada," Casey said, as he leaned over and kissed her cheek.

"Well, Casey, you just have to look at me to figure that out!" Barry laughed as they shook hands.

They stood on their porch, arm and arm, waving goodbye, as we drove out of their driveway. Just as we turned onto the road, I looked back and saw Barry lean down and kiss Linda on the cheek.

"They're nice people, Annie, who have a nice life," Casey said, a note of wistfulness in his voice.

"Yes they are," I sighed.

He put his arm around me and pulled me to him. "Let's go back to your place and watch the sun come up."

"Casey, the sun won't be coming up for hours!"

"Exactly!"

Part Three

Hearing
The New Song

Chapter 11

August – 1993

The sky is streaked with milky white clouds again this morning. The air is balmy, warm and heavy with an unusual humidity. There is a strange silence, as though everyone has slept in.

Something has been removed from me. Perhaps I have unconsciously shed the protective crust that has covered the scars of the past. New life is under there, vulnerable and tenuous, but whole. Truth is under there, too, exposed to the light, perhaps for the first time in my life.

I am frightened but stronger.

♪♪♪

Our lovemaking was intimate and almost sacred. Gentle and caring, Casey explored my body with his hands and his mouth. When I finally relaxed into the rhythm of our passion, we complemented each other's movements like fine musicians playing a symphony. At the crescendo, my mind and body soared into the deep, blue sky, flying higher and higher through white, puffy clouds. We loved each other until late into the night. When the music slowed, he brought me gently back to earth and whispered, "You're wonderful, Annie." We woke up just as the sun began to warm the bedroom.

"Hey, Beautiful, we've got to get up. Linda is expecting us early, remember?" Casey eased his arm from under my neck and rolled out of bed.

"Mmmm. Can't I just lie here for five more minutes?" I pulled the sheet up to my ears and covered my face to block out the sunlight.

"Okay, but just five minutes. I'll make coffee," he said, as he left the room, "but you better be up and at 'em before I get back in here." Just before I fell back to sleep, I heard him whistling as he poured water into the coffeemaker.

Early morning is not my best time of day. Since being on the Island, I've often awakened early and thoroughly enjoyed it, but my internal clock has never allowed a permanent adjustment to sunrise. When Casey called to me again from the kitchen, I dragged myself out of bed and into the bathroom for a quick, warm shower. The force of the water against my body helped to wash away the sleepiness, but I was still groggy from sleep deprivation. I looked in the mirror, laughed, and said to my reflection, "Face it, girl, no one is going to feel sorry for you today. Besides you really can't tell them why you didn't get much sleep last night, now can you?"

"Annie, who are you talking to?" Casey asked appearing in the doorway holding two mugs of coffee.

"You're a lifesaver!" I exclaimed. The caffeine went to work almost instantly. "Mmmm, thanks."

"So, who *were* you talking to?" He leaned against the door and sipped his coffee.

"Huh? Oh," I laughed, "I was talking to myself. Do it often. Runs in the family, too. An old family curse, they say."

Now Casey was laughing at me. "And what did yourself say to yourself?"

"I'm sleepy, but I wouldn't change a thing." I hugged him and kissed him and said, "You're quite a lover, Cowboy."

Casey sat on the edge of the bed while I sorted through a few old t-shirts, choosing one that had paint stains on it. Working in Linda's barn was going to be dirty business. Casey leaned forward, his elbows on his knees, his hands cupping the mug. "You know, Annie," he said, staring into the coffee mug, "we really are living a fantasy. Before I met you, I wouldn't have looked at a script with this kind of storyline."

"Why?" I asked, as my head popped through the opening of the t-shirt.

As though he had found the answer to my question floating in the mug, he looked up, smiled, and replied, "Because the people and the dialogue never sound real. At least not to me, anyway."

"Cynic! Your industry has made millions telling this story, hundreds, no, thousands of times!" I leaned over him to kiss his ear and whispered, "I love our story, Casey."

"Mmmm. Guess I'll have to take another look at some of those scripts. You're certainly real, and what I feel for you is real. God, I love you." He put his hand on the small of my back and pressed gently guiding me onto the bed. His lips were soft, covering mine as though he wished to share every breath. Soon we were lying on the bed lost in the desire to love and be loved.

A car door slammed somewhere behind the cottage. "Casey?" I said, thinking someone was about to knock on the back door.

"Hmmm?" he groaned.

"Lying here with you feels awfully good, but we've really got to get up now. We promised Linda we would be there early to help." No one had knocked on the door, but, to be sure, I tiptoed to the window to check for visitors. Children, dogs and adults had just spilled out of a van in our neighbor's yard. Their enthusiastic shouts of greeting and laughter floated across the road and in through the window.

"We're all right. I set the alarm an hour early just for this possibility." He grinned, obviously proud of his trick.

"I don't believe you!" Before I could grab him, he ducked into the bathroom and shut the door.

I poured myself another cup of coffee and stepped onto the deck to enjoy the morning air and write in my journal. The breeze was warm, more humid than usual. Working at Linda's was going to be uncomfortable unless the wind changed. Just as I closed the journal, I heard the screen door slide open.

"Okay! Let's get going." Casey, handsome as usual, was dressed in a pair of old jeans and a yellow t-shirt that showed off his tan. He gulped down a cup of coffee and hurried me out the door.

"That's not much of a breakfast," I complained.

"Don't worry. Remember all that food Linda has been cooking over the last few days? There will be enough to eat over there to make up for a hundred missed breakfasts."

"Wait," I shouted after him. "I better leave a note for Millie, just in case she stops by."

"Better yet, let's go get her. There'll be lots of kids her age over there. Linda won't mind, will she?" he asked, looking back at me over the roof of the Jeep.

Sure that Linda would be the first person to encourage Millie's participation in the day's activities, I agreed.

When Casey and I arrived at their campsite, Millie and her mother were just returning from an early morning walk on the beach.

"Annie!" Millie cried, running to me. "I was hoping I'd see you today." She wrapped her arms around my waist, burying her head against my stomach. I instinctively bent over her and hugged her.

"Millie, dear, Casey and I are on our way over to my friend Linda's farm. She's having a big gathering today to clean out her barn, and lots of kids your age are going to be there." I looked up and directed my next statement to Mrs. Carter. "They're getting ready for a family reunion this weekend. We'd love to have all of you come with us." I turned my attention toward the tent expecting to see Millie's father step out.

"Bob has gone to O'Leary for gas, Annie," Mrs. Carter responded to my unasked question. "But I don't see why Millie can't go with you. Would do her good to spend some time with other children."

"Yea," Millie shouted as she ran to her mother.

"Mrs. Carter, you're more than welcome to come along." Casey opened the door of the Jeep, and Millie hopped into the back seat.

"Thanks anyway, but I'd better wait here for Bob." She opened a small jar and added a few pieces of sea glass to it.

"When your husband gets back, why don't you folks come over for lunch? Linda has cooked plenty of food. There's more than enough to go around." I found an envelope in my pocket, scribbled the directions on it and handed it to her.

"Thanks. We'll see." She sounded doubtful. "Millie, have a good time, honey." She waved and disappeared behind the tent flap.

Millie chattered non-stop all the way to Linda's, telling us about their success in cooking the lobsters, about stargazing on the beach with her mother, and about a special piece of blue sea-glass she had found that morning. She reached into her pocket and handed it to me.

"Millie," I exclaimed, "this is beautiful." The deep, cobalt blue piece of glass was the size of a fifty-cent piece with ridges on one side. "You should keep this treasure for yourself."

I handed it back to her, but she put her hand over mine and said, "Oh, Annie, I was going to bring it to you as a special surprise this afternoon. This is the best present I could find for you." She leaned forward over the seat, put her arms around my neck and kissed my cheek. "Thank you, Annie."

As I turned toward her to acknowledge the gift, I put my arm over the seat and hugged her. "I'll treasure this gift forever, Millie. Thank you." Her eyes glistened with excitement and pride.

Clearing his throat, Casey asked, "How's that arm, Millie?"

"Great! Mommy taped a plastic bag over it last night so I could wash up. The doctor told me to be sure to keep it dry." She held up the bright pink cast so Casey could see it in the rear view mirror. "What are we going to do today, Annie?" she asked, sitting back in the seat.

"I'm not exactly sure. Linda's barn needs to be cleaned out first. Then I have a special project that's going to be lots of fun. You'll like it."

When we arrived at the farmhouse, Linda was busy removing folding tables from the back of a truck. "I'm sure glad to see you guys. Barry had to go in to O'Leary to see if he could find a few more planks for the staging. I need some help with these tables," she groaned. "They aren't heavy but they're awkward and hard to handle alone. Let's put them out of the way along that wall," she directed, pointing to a wall inside the barn. Focused on pulling the tables out of the truck, Linda had not seen Millie standing next to me. When she turned to speak to me, she smiled. "Well, now, you must be Millie. I'm delighted to meet you."

"Thanks," Millie replied, moving closer to me.

"We thought Millie might enjoy playing with some of the kids," I explained.

"I'm glad you thought of her, Annie. I should have mentioned that last night." With Casey's help, she continued to unload the tables while she talked. She told Millie that there would be lots of kids her age arriving any minute. A master of organization, Linda had arranged the day's schedule around everyone's chores. After the local farmers had sent their cows to pasture and cleaned out their barns, they would help clean and repair this one.

We heard them before we saw them. Horns blared from trucks and cars overflowed with men and women, children and dogs, all full of energy and life. Everyone who had been asked had agreed to help. The atmosphere was charged with the spirit of an old-fashioned barn raising.

Linda took the time to introduce Millie to four young girls her age, suggesting that they play on the beach and look for treasures to make centerpieces for the tables. She created a scavenger hunt for them by writing out a list of items to search for along the shore. Millie's cast created an instant topic of discussion for the five new friends. As they walked toward the beach, I heard them giggling and squealing, and whispering questions as she pointed out Casey's signature.

Linda's hand clasped my elbow as she approached me from behind. "She'll be fine, Annie," she reassured. "Those kids will love her and she them." We turned and walked into the barn.

None of the volunteers had any idea what was in store for them. Linda had kept geese in the barn after last year's reunion. The filthy mess they had made covered a good portion of the ground floor. In addition to the hodgepodge of junk that Barry had stored in the loft, there were also forty or fifty bales of hay water-logged by the leak in the roof. The weight of the saturated bales had weakened the loft's floor. Support beams were needed under the loft's cross-timbers before anyone could safely remove the mess of junk tucked into every corner.

By the time we were ready for lunch, we had made significant progress. The loft was empty and swept clean. Items of value had been piled outside and to one side of the barn doors. Everything else was loaded into several pickup trucks and hauled off to the dump: old tires, an over-used washing machine, two pieces of veneer furniture, the veneer curled up from the dampness, several rusted deck chairs, and boxes and boxes of unidentified junk.

On the ground floor, the men found an old tractor pushed back in one corner. The engine wouldn't start, so Casey backed Barry's pickup into the barn, hooked a chain to the front of the antique machine, and carefully pulled it out into the light. It was a forty-year-old Arrow, a little rusty here and there, but in fairly decent shape considering its age. As soon as it broke free of the barn into the daylight, one of the men on the roof yelled down to Linda asking what she wanted for it. They all knew that Barry wasn't the farmer here, but that Linda did most of the yard work.

She squinted into the sun, put her hand over eyes, and yelled up to him. "Not going to sell her, Albert. We're going to take her out to Dale's to be overhauled. Next year I want to mow all the fields myself."

Albert owned an 800-acre dairy farm just up the road with several hundred acres put to potatoes and barley. He had only the best farm equipment, but he enjoyed tinkering with old machinery, restoring antiques for fun and in some cases for use around the yard. His wife, Betty, mowed their three acres of lawn with an old riding mower he had purchased on a trip to Charlottetown. He had repaired it and repainted it, carefully detailing her name and racing stripes along both sides. She loved it.

"But Albert, you can come over and paint racing stripes on her any time." Everyone laughed.

Albert and several other men had been working from the staging all morning. The roof timber that had rotted, starting the deterioration process, had been replaced. The new roof had been nailed in place and was ready for the shingles.

The barn floor had been hosed down where the geese had made their mess. The children attacked the cement floor with push brooms working six across. The doors were open on both ends of the building. With a slight breeze at their backs they pushed dirt and hay down the middle and out the back door onto a large tarp. The older children pulled the tarp to an area that needed fill and dumped it. With a truckload of soil to cover it, the area would be perfect for Linda's herb garden.

Fresh hay had been placed in the stalls for decoration purposes only. Old farming tools and wagon wheels had been cleaned and hung on the walls and against the stalls. Linda had cleaned the saddle she had found in the cellar and had draped it over a sawhorse. Some of the children were already climbing on it, riding the wind and chasing buffalo across the plains. Millie and her new friends had returned from the beach, their pails full of the treasures Linda requested.

At the sound of a dinner bell, we all gathered outside for lunch. Linda had told the families who had volunteered that she would provide the meals. She had been cooking for days, the fruit of her labor laid out buffet style for the hungry workers. There were hearty sandwiches made on homemade bread and two large watermelon shells filled with fresh fruit. She added pickles, olives, chips, and several of her blueberry and apple pies to the fare. Most of us sat cross-legged on the grass forming a large circle. As we ate Linda's delicious offering, we exchanged stories about the morning work.

"Barry, how on earth did you get that old washing machine up in that loft?" Fred, the local electrician, sat on the only sawhorse, his plate carefully balanced on one knee.

"The same way you guys got that hay out. I tied a rope on it and hoisted it up through the hay door." Barry popped an olive into his mouth.

"But why did you put it there in the first place?" Fred asked.

Barry leaned back on the grass and rubbed his stomach. "Saving it for parts, Fred."

With that comment, there was an uproar of laughter from the entire work crew, for most of us knew that Barry was a pack rat not a handyman.

Everyone there had recognized Casey, but they were sensitive to his privacy and avoided asking him a lot of questions about Hollywood life. He appreciated it, enjoying their company and friendship.

Millie forfeited her new friends to join Casey and me for lunch. She sat cross-legged in front of us, her plate of food on the ground, and animatedly explained where they had gone and what they had found on the beach. "Linda is going to show us how to make the decorations after lunch. She's going to put them on the tables tonight and save them for the reunion. Isn't that great?" She picked up a potato chip and crunched it into her mouth. The sun had highlighted her hair and darkened her freckles.

The Carters evidently had decided to stay away. I hoped that Mr. Carter wasn't upset about Millie being with us. Given the broken arm, my rational self believed that Millie's mother would never have let her go with us if she thought there would be a problem. My concerned self wondered.

Soon people were standing up, brushing the red PEI dirt off the back of their pants, and going back to work. Casey and Barry teamed up at one end of the barn to build a platform for the band. Several men climbed onto the staging and began to nail the shingles to the roof. The roofing crew worked swiftly, hoping to finish before dark.

Millie and her friends helped Linda clean up after lunch, collecting the paper plates in a garbage bag and putting the leftover sandwiches in a large cooler. In case someone wanted more to eat during the afternoon, everything was placed on one table tucked just inside the barn out of the sun.

With that task completed, Linda told the girls to gather up their treasure pails and join her on the porch. There she had placed a plastic tub filled with arts and crafts supplies: yarn, ribbon, glue, scissors, pipe cleaners, buttons, string, paint and much more. With the shells, rocks, feathers and driftwood gathered from the beach, the girls were left to create centerpieces for the supper tables. I watched them from the barn door, making sure Millie was comfortable. Before Linda had stepped off the last board on the porch, the girls were laughing easily and exclaiming over the new treasures in the tub.

One of the boys ran out of the barn yelling for Linda. "Fred wants to know where you want the new electrical outlets." Linda hurried off to show him.

I had my own special project to tackle. Now that the ground floor of the barn was clean, we planned to paint a huge checkerboard on one end. Linda, who had a gift for devising innovative fun, had created a human checker game. The area that needed painting was located below and in front of the loft so that two players or teams could sit above the game board to direct the movement of their human checkers. At home in Ottawa the previous winter, Linda had found enough black and red hats for the checkers. She also made crowns to indicate when someone became king. This would be a game that intentionally involved a lot of people and promised to be lots of fun.

Several of the older children volunteered to help. We tied strings across the barn for guides so we could paint straight lines, making a checkerboard large enough for the human game pieces. We painted the game board in the traditional black and white pattern, and as a surprise for Linda, we added a big, red L right in the middle. Standing as a group, arm in arm, we surveyed our handiwork. "That's cool," one of the boys said, affirming our creativity.

The afternoon passed quickly. The young people joined the others who had gathered in the field beside the barn to play softball. The roofing crew worked as a team and finished the project that had seemed overwhelming at the beginning of the day. Casey and Barry continued their carpentry in the barn creating a new railing along the loft so the children could play safely during the dance. Fred and his brother pulled wires through the wall for the new light fixtures that would hang over the refreshment area.

When I approached the porch, I discovered Millie and her friends laughing hysterically. They had made six centerpieces using driftwood for each base and adding bits and pieces from their treasure pails and Linda's tub. I was impressed with their creativity in complementing the natural objects with colorful ribbons and buttons. Now they were making a joke centerpiece to fool Linda. The confusion of color, shapes and objects grew into a grotesque structure that covered the middle of the table. When I stepped onto the porch, they jumped. The laughing stopped instantly.

"Whew, Annie," Millie said, putting her hand over her heart. "We thought you were Linda." They all giggled.

"What is that?" I asked, smiling at the thought of their conspiracy.

"That's our masterpiece!" one of the girls exclaimed. "Do you like it?" She grinned.

"I love it," I said, wrinkling my nose. They burst out laughing once again.

"I hate to break up this creative energy, but Millie we have to go back to the park. I promised your mother I would bring you back by five if they didn't show up for lunch." I could see that she was disappointed, but she quickly said her goodbyes to the girls. They gathered around her and, one by one, hugged her, promising to remain friends forever. The drama surrounding the hugs and tears and goodbyes was palpable.

When Millie slid into the seat beside me, she said, "Thanks, Annie. This has been the best day ever. I'll never forget them." As though to memorize their names, she spoke them aloud, looking down at her cast at their signatures and well wishes. "Sadie, Elizabeth, Kelsey and Sarah. Gosh they were nice."

I took her back to the park, parked at the entrance, and walked to the campsite with her. Mrs. Carter was sitting at the table making sandwiches for their supper. Mr. Carter was resting in the tent. Millie sat down next to her mother and handed her a shell with a blue ribbon tied through a small hole in the top. "Here, Mommy. I made this for you."

"Thank you, honey. Did you have a good time?" her mother asked.

"The best. I wish you and Daddy had come over for lunch. You would have liked all the people there." Millie patted her mother's arm.

Mrs. Carter looked up at me, smiled and said, "Thanks. This was good for her."

"You're welcome. And yes, it was. Millie made four new friends today," I said, proudly. "Well, I've got to get back over there. See you tomorrow, Millie?" She hopped off the picnic bench and ran to me. We hugged our goodbyes, then I turned and walked back to the Jeep.

When I returned to the farmhouse, the work crew had packed away their tools and were gathering in front of the barn. The afternoon had been hot and muggy. Most of them were covered with sweat and grime. Without warning, Casey opened fire with the garden hose. He had most of us soaked before Albert and Fred got the hose away from him and returned the favor. The water was cold, but it felt good. The men cocked back the spray handle and hooked the hose over the old rose arbor. The children ran back and forth under it squealing with surprise and shock as the cold water sprayed over them.

The barn was ready for Linda's reunion. "Oh, Annie, this can't be my barn. It's so clean and neat. And look what you've done with that checker board!" As we looked around, I noticed the six centerpieces prominently displayed on the tables. They added a touch of whimsy to the festivities. The joke centerpiece, covered with one of the red and white tablecloths, had been placed on the stage, a curiosity to be sure. The four girls pulled at Linda's arms to encourage her to unveil their masterpiece. She screamed, everyone laughed, and the girls giggled. The monster centerpiece was a resounding success. I wish Millie had been there for the unveiling.

Linda's excitement was contagious as people gathered around us to appreciate the day's hard work. Betty took her hand and soon the entire group had formed a large circle around the checkerboard. Ed, being a lay minister at his church, said a prayer of thanksgiving and blessing for the day's work, the safety of the crew, and for Linda's good food. Soon chairs were scraping on the cement floor as everyone sat down to enjoy a delicious supper of cold fried chicken, fresh bread, potato salad, cole slaw, and the best three-bean salad I've ever eaten. The meal was simple, but good, and over forty hungry, tired and wet volunteers consumed every last bite. We topped our meal off with large, juicy slices of watermelon. Not to be outdone by his wife, Barry organized a watermelon seed-spitting contest along the side of the barn. One of the boys who had helped paint the checkerboard won.

The tired but happy volunteers piled into their trucks and were gone by eight. I helped Linda clean up while Casey and Barry washed off the tables and closed up the barn for the night. Casey and I said good night to them and drove back to the cottage. As the beam from the Jeep's headlights swept across the back of the cottage, I noticed a white piece of paper stuck in the corner of the screen door. It fluttered in the breeze like a heartbeat.

"This is strange," I said, tugging the note away from the door and wondering who had left it there. "Millie has been here. I wonder what's up." Fearing the worst, I hurried into the cottage, turned on a light, and sat down to read her note.

Dear Annie and Casey, Daddy has decided to go home tomorrow morning. I wish I could see you. I'll miss you. I love you. Millie

"Oh, Casey, they're leaving!" I cried.

"I was afraid of that. I bet they were supposed to go back to the hospital tomorrow and Millie's father doesn't want to risk it. Let's go over there right now. We can at least see Millie and say good-bye to her." When we arrived, Millie's father was packing their car.

"Hello there," Casey called to him.

Mr. Carter looked up and seemed quite surprised to see us. "Millie and her mother are over at the bathhouse. They should be back in about half an hour."

"So you're leaving tomorrow?" I asked hesitantly.

"That's right." He ducked his head beneath the open trunk lid. The car rocked back and forth as he pulled and tugged on the boxes and suitcases, making them fit the available space like giant pieces of a puzzle. "It will take us a couple of days to get home. I want to be there by Sunday so I can get a few things done around the house before I have to go back to work." He straightened up and slammed the lid shut.

I jumped involuntarily. "We'll miss her," I said, backing away from him.

Casey grasped my arm and whispered in my ear. "Annie, in our rush to get here, I forgot that little gift from the café at Miminegash."

"Mr. Carter, we'll be right back," I called over my shoulder. He didn't seem to care one way or the other.

When we returned to the campsite, Millie ran to me and hugged me. She was trembling. "Oh, Annie, I was so afraid that I would never see you again!" Her hair, still damp from the shower, curled around her face and hung down her back. She was wearing short-sleeved pajamas with little red and pink hearts all over them. Her pink cast, autographed in various colors by her new friends, no longer seemed out of place.

"Millie, I'm sorry you have to leave so soon," I said. Casey and I sat on the bench, our backs to the picnic table. Millie stood between my legs, hugging my neck with her good arm.

"I know," she whined softly. "I hoped we could stay for the barn dance, but Daddy wants to go home." She looked over her shoulder to determine whether her father could hear our conversation.

"Did your mother take you back to the hospital for your check up?" Casey asked in hushed tones.

"No. We were supposed to go tomorrow, but Daddy changed our plans. He said it could wait until we got home." She put her head on my shoulder. "Gosh, I'm going to miss you, Annie."

I hugged her to me and said, "Me, too, Millie."

Casey looked at me with an 'I told you so' look. Anger raged within my chest cutting off my breath for an instant.

Casey looked away, cleared his throat, then turned back to us and said, "Millie, Annie and I have written our phone numbers on the back of this card. Will you call us when you get home?" She moved toward him, her hand outstretched. He reached for her, wrapping his long arms around her in a bear hug. Millie giggled. Casey looked at me over her head and smiled. She had instantly lightened the mood with a little girl's response to genuine affection.

"Promise me, Millie, that you will call when you get home," I insisted.

"I will, Annie," she said, leaning into Casey as if to store the love she felt for him.

"I'm looking forward to seeing you and Annie in Ontario when we come up to make the movie. Okay?" Casey reached behind him to retrieve the gift he had bought for her at the café. He had wrapped it up in tissue and tied it with a piece of bright pink ribbon he had begged off Linda. Millie's eyes opened wide with surprise. Her hands trembled as she carefully slid the ribbon off the package.

"Oh, Casey, I love it! It's the Lighthouse!" Unable to contain her excitement, she ran to her mother who graciously had allowed Casey and me a private moment with her daughter. "Look, Mommy, at what Casey and Annie gave me!" Mrs. Carter smiled as Millie took her hand, urging her to join us.

"Thank you, Casey," Millie said, hugging the picture against her chest. "Now I'll have something to remember you by." She looked down at the ground and started to cry.

I leaned toward her, gently embraced her, and whispered, "Millie, honey, you'll see us both again, and soon." I nudged her closer to me, put my hand under her chin, and lifted her head so I could look into her face. "We love you, and we want you to know that if you ever need us, we'll be there. Okay?" Millie's large blue eyes were brimming with tears. My heart was breaking, too.

"I love you, Annie," she whimpered, falling against me, my arms wrapping her in a protective cocoon, but only for that brief moment.

Casey and I drove back to the cottage in silence. He grabbed the blanket from the back seat of the Jeep and said, "Annie, let's walk down to the beach and watch the stars for a while."

We spread the blanket out on the sand and lay down. Casey held me while I cried. "It just keeps hurting, Casey. She's so little. I'm really afraid for her."

"I know, Annie. So am I. When we were at Linda's yesterday, I called Keith Hamilton, my lawyer in New York, and asked him to help us. I'll bet there's a file on old Mr. Carter sitting in some Human Services office in New York. Maybe someone has reported him back there. If so, perhaps we can set up some protection for Millie. Let's go back to the hospital in Summerside tomorrow and talk with Dr. Green. Maybe he'll have some suggestions."

"That's a good idea," I sighed, relaxing with the thought that there actually might be something we could do to keep Millie out of harm's way.

As we lay there cuddled together watching the night sky, Casey pointed out many of the constellations, and I pointed out a couple of satellites passing overhead. The night was warm. The beach was comfortable. Both exhausted from the long day of hard work, we rolled up in the blanket and relaxed under the ebony canopy.

Chapter 12

August – 1993

These past few days have been intense…filled with raw emotion…calling up all the old memories and yet, strangely, planting a seed of hope. No one helped Casey or me as children, but both Casey and I can help Millie. God has given her love and her trust to us…precious gifts that must be protected.

As if to affirm my thoughts, a horn beeped on the road behind the cottage. The Island is waking, its early morning sounds comforting and familiar. Neighbor's screen doors bang like gunshots, as the children rush to the beach. Dogs bark and traffic rushes by on a distant road taking Island workers and early risers to their destinations. Gulls cry at one another as they fight for food, and motors hum rhythmically across the waves as trap-laden boats head for the bright-colored buoys that mark their fishing territory.

I wonder where Millie and her parents are right now. Have they left the park? Are they already crossing to New Brunswick? They will need at least two days to get home, maybe three. Then what? I can't go there. And yet, I must.

Breathe deeply, I remind myself. Oh God, protect that child. Protect that child. Protect that child.

♪♪♪

I had mindlessly covered two pages of my journal with the words 'Protect that child,' when Casey poked his head through the open door. The journal slipped from my lap and fell onto the deck, its pages spread-eagled beneath the hard cover.

"Good morning, Beautiful," he said, thick tongued and not fully awake.

"Good afternoon. Ready to start a new day?" I laughed. We had fallen asleep on the beach, waking around four and stumbling back to the cottage. Exhausted from our long day at Linda's, Casey had slept until late morning.

"Sure. Got any barns that need repair?" He yawned, as he stepped through the door, then stretched and groaned. He bent down to retrieve the journal and handed it to me as he leaned over the chair and kissed my forehead. "Sleep okay?" he asked, straightening and stretching again.

"Yes. Even my nightmares were exhausted," I chuckled.

"Me, too. Did you make coffee?" he asked, turning and looking through the door toward the coffee-maker. Still groggy from sleep, he put his hand on the top of the picnic table and dropped onto the bench next to it. He looked like a little boy: his hair tousled, his cheeks flushed, and his eyes big and wide. He was not aware that I had stepped into the kitchen to pour him a cup of caffeine. When I handed it to him, he smiled like a drunk man and patted my fanny. "Thanks, Annie. I hope this helps me wake up." He sipped the hot liquid carefully and looked out across the water.

Turning back, he said, "Let's take a ride later and explore some other parts of the Island. I'll call Keith when I'm more awake to see if he's found out anything."

"Let's drive into Summerside to see the doctor first," I suggested. "I don't suppose Mrs. Carter called him and told him they weren't coming in today." I sat down next to him on the bench, my arm resting on the tabletop.

He yawned and leaned back against the table. "You're probably right." Rubbing the sleep from his eyes, he frowned. "Suppose they left early?"

"I was just thinking about that. I'm sure of it. Mr. Carter probably wanted to catch the first ferry." I looked toward the New Brunswick shore. "I miss her already, Casey."

"I know, honey. So do I." He took my hand, pulling me close enough to kiss me. "What do you say, let's get breakfast at the Lighthouse and then head for Summerside."

"I'm for that," I agreed, picking up the two empty mugs and following him into the cottage.

Casey called his friend Keith just before we left for the Lighthouse. I read his scribbled notes over what turned out to be brunch. Keith had managed to get the name and address of Millie's doctor in New York and suggested that we have the Island doctor send his findings. "This is good, Casey. Maybe we really can help Millie," I said, sounding more hopeful than I felt. Other parts of his notes revealed that Human Services had been called twice, but no complaints were ever filed against Mr. Carter.

When we arrived at the hospital, Dr. Green was with a patient. The nurse at the desk remembered us. She asked us to take a seat and disappeared through a door marked 'Examining Rooms.' A short time later, Dr. Green opened the door and ushered out a pregnant woman carrying a toddler in her arms.

"Mrs. York? Mr. MacDonald?" he said, acknowledging both of us.

"Yes," I replied, jumping to my feet.

Casey and I followed him into an examining room. Casey leaned against the examining table, and I took one of the chairs. The doctor sat down on a rolling stool and opened Millie's file on the examining table.

"When Millie Carter was in here the other day, she told me how much she thinks of both of you. Nevertheless, I am limited as to what I can discuss with you." He looked at the file again, then asked, "Do you know how she received her injuries?"

"Yes, we do doctor," I replied confidently. "She told us that her father hurt her. We were very concerned about her arm and that's why we brought her here with her mother."

He leaned back in his chair and closed the file. "They were supposed to come in today for a follow up, but I haven't seen them yet."

"And you won't," Casey said, moving away from the examining table. "Mr. Carter packed them up last night. As far as we know they headed back to New York early this morning."

"Really?" he said, looking up at Casey over the top of his glasses. "Well, that's disappointing." He took off the reading glasses and placed them on the closed file. "That's not good. This type of abuse rarely just stops." The doctor absent-mindedly tapped the file with his glasses.

"Casey has friends in New York where they live, Dr. Green," I said, hoping to gain his confidence. "We've found out this morning that Mr. Carter has been investigated by Human Services twice. Unfortunately, though, there's never been a witness to corroborate their suspicions and I guess Millie wouldn't talk to the case worker."

"That's not unusual. She probably doesn't trust anyone, especially if they haven't been able to help her." He exhaled loudly with the frustration of the situation.

"We've also got Millie's doctor's name and phone number," Casey added. "We were hoping that you would send her your report complete with your observations. With that, perhaps she can talk with Human Services and ask them to pay a visit to the Carters when they get home."

Dr. Green placed his glasses back on his nose and opened the file. "I had planned to send my report after seeing them today. Mrs. Carter gave me the doctor's name, but I don't remember that it was a woman. Let's see, I wrote it down here somewhere," he said, running his finger down the page of notes. "Yes, here it is. Dr. David Bowen."

"Uh, no. The doctor's name is Dr. Karen Wade. And this is her telephone number." Casey handed him the information.

"Interesting," he said, as he wrote the information on Millie's chart. "Evidently Mrs. Carter is protecting her husband. That's not good news. I'll dictate my report this afternoon and ask my secretary to call and get their fax number. Maybe the doctor in New York can get something started even before the Carters get home. I don't like the fact that she lied to me about this." He took his glasses off and slipped them into his lab coat pocket. "Millie is a fortunate little girl to have your help."

"Thank you, Dr. Green. We really appreciate your care and concern for her," Casey said, shaking his hand.

"You're very welcome. This is an overwhelming problem, both in your country and in mine, that isn't going to go away. All I can do is handle each case as it comes to me. I wish more people who see abuse would do what you're doing." He stood up, signaling the end of our visit.

"We plan to stay in touch with Millie, Dr. Green," Casey added. "I hope the road ahead isn't a terribly bumpy one, but both Annie and I are committed to protecting her whatever happens."

"Well, I'll certainly do my part. And I would appreciate hearing from you when you do see Millie again. I can't divulge what we found in her x-rays, but I can tell you that all of us should be concerned." He held open the door to the waiting room, as we passed through.

"Will your concerns be in your report?" I whispered, remembering the bruises and the pain reflected in Millie's eyes.

"Yes. They may be taking her to several doctors. If none of them have done extensive x-rays, then there may be no one doctor who has the total picture. I'll send copies of our x-rays to Dr. Wade. If I had my way, those x-rays would put Mr. Carter behind bars for the rest of his life." Realizing he had revealed more information than he should have, Dr. Green added quickly, " Sorry. I never should have said that."

"We understand," I said, putting my hand on his arm. "I don't know how to thank you for what you've done."

"No thanks necessary, Mrs. York." Dr. Green turned abruptly and vanished behind the door.

We left the hospital in shock. Our plans to explore other parts of the Island were abandoned. Casey drove around Summerside because we just couldn't bear to go back to the cottage. Finally he stopped the car in the parking lot of a popular restaurant by the water.

"I'm not sure I can eat anything, Casey. I have this horrible mental image of Millie's x-rays revealing all those broken bones."

"I know. The abuse seems to be far worse than we imagined, Annie." Casey slumped in the seat, his hands draped over the steering wheel at the six o'clock position.

"It's no wonder that she was so afraid of her father," I added, trembling with rage and fear.

"Annie, this whole thing scares the hell out of me," he said, shifting restlessly in his seat. "When I think about what I said to Millie's mother, trying to help that kid, I'm sure I only made everything worse."

"Do you remember what she said to you?" I asked, recalling the conversation between Casey and Mrs. Carter.

"Yes. 'I'm committed to the best interests of my daughter.' Evidently that includes lying."

"Maybe she thinks that by protecting her husband from the authorities, she is protecting Millie. I don't know," I said, throwing my hands in the air in frustration. "I can't even begin to understand any of this."

"Come on," Casey said, taking my hand. "Let's go inside and relax."

The waitress took our order for a light supper. The coffee was fresh, the atmosphere was pleasant, and the lighting was subdued. We ate our meal saying little, but speaking volumes each time we looked at each other.

"I'm sorry, Annie," Casey sighed. "I promised you a romantic night on the town, but it seems that neither one of us is up for that now."

I folded my napkin and laid it beside the plate. "You're right. Let's go back to West Point, Casey. I'm exhausted."

We spent a quiet evening watching an old movie with Cary Grant and Catherine Hepburn. The comedic banter between the two helped us laugh, and the laughter helped us cry. When the movie ended, we went to bed, holding each other most of the night. Wanting to be close, we cuddled together like two spoons nestled in a drawer. Tucked under his body like that, I felt warm and safe. When he rolled away from me later in the night, I woke up instantly, vulnerable, cold and feeling abandoned.

I tried to sleep after that but couldn't. Each time I closed my eyes, I dreamed about Millie. I could see her with bruises all over her, broken arms and broken legs…just broken. Casey must have sensed my uneasiness because he turned back to me, put his arms around me and pulled me closer to him. He was back to sleep instantly.

After a few moments, the warmth of his body helped me to relax. I slept, but the dreams continued.

♪♪♪

The city was crowded, noisy. People were screaming and running. The buildings seemed hundreds of stories high, towering, looming over my head. Everyone around me was a giant. Their long legs and big feet threatened to trample me. I called out but their bodies were so tall that they couldn't hear me. I began to scream. "Mommy! Mommy! Where are you? Help me, Mommy!"

A hand reached out of the crowd and grabbed me and shook me.

♪♪♪

"Annie. Annie." Casey's voice called to me from some place far away. "Annie, honey, wake up." He rubbed my shoulder, trying to wake me. When I opened my eyes, all the images of big feet and tall buildings vanished. Casey was there, speaking to me, holding me.

"I must have been dreaming," I said, bewildered.

"I'll say! But that was more than just a dream. Do you remember it?" He stuck his elbow into the pillow and propped his head with his hand so he could look down at my face.

I rested on my back and closed my eyes recalling the dream's images. "I was lost in a big city. Everything was huge." I opened my eyes to verify that he was still there. "The people were giants, and the buildings were hundreds of stories high. There was a lot of noise and a lot of confusion. Then someone grabbed me and I screamed."

"If you were feeling that small, honey, maybe your dream was about something that happened to you when you were a child. What do you think?"

We shifted our bodies at the same time. Casey put his arm under my neck as I rolled toward him. When I rested my head on his chest, I said, "You're probably right. Maybe I'll remember later."

Unable to relax, I slipped into a robe and padded into the kitchen to make a cup of tea, hoping that the aroma of the herbs and the warmth of the honey-gold liquid would help me relax so I could sleep. Casey had moved to the sofa and was wrapped in my grandmother's quilt. I sat down beside him, shivering, holding the cup with both hands. The warmth of the medicinal brew restored my soul. Casey took the teacup from me and placed it on the table by the sofa. He raised one arm taking the quilt up with it in a gesture that invited me to lie down beside him.

He touched me as though he were still holding the fragile teacup. He kissed my lips and my eyes and my neck with soft, quick kisses. His hands were gentle as well, slowly rubbing my back and shoulders as we slid further beneath the quilt into the embrace of the old sofa. Our lovemaking was passionate, but not the hurried, heavy breathing passion born of high energy. We made love slowly, intimately, touching each other with the gentleness of a child, feeling the wonder of each other's love. Some time before sunrise, the sofa claimed us, wrapping us in the comfort of its soft cushions.

Sleep was peaceful and renewing.

Chapter 13

August – 1993

Last night's dream has triggered the feeling of homesickness that lives deep in my soul…the manifestation of my childhood grief and the fear born of abandonment.

My dream was a horrible memory about abandonment on the day when I got lost in the five and ten cent store. I was only four. The store seemed awfully big, especially when I turned around and everyone around me was a stranger. I remember the feeling of panic as I ran down an aisle, the counters towering over my head like skyscrapers. She wasn't there. I turned and ran down another aisle. She wasn't there either. There were people everywhere, tall people, who reached out for me to try to help me. But as they reached out for me, they scared me because I didn't know them. Finally, the babysitter grabbed me and pulled me out of the store, yelling at me for getting lost. I had been terribly frightened, and cried all the way home. Instead of holding me and comforting me, she yelled at me and threatened to tell my mother that I had been a bad little girl. Evidently, I have suppressed these memories until experiencing the trauma of discovering the extent of Millie's abuse. Now the frightening experience of a four-year-old has been manifested as a horrible nightmare.

How will Millie manifest her awful days? Is she swallowing the pain, forgetting it, only to have to deal with it forty years from now? I hope not. But who is helping her deal with it? Who is working to put an end to her awful experiences of abuse and abandonment? And what is she doing with her anger and fear?

A thunderstorm in the night has cleared out the humidity leaving the air crisp and much cooler. The high surf has stirred up the beach sand, turning the water a bloody red along the shore and out as far as I can see. The morning rays of the sun cast a golden glow over the fields and farmhouses.

Change is everywhere this morning. O God, help me to release these terrible memories so that I might truly embrace the joys of this new day.

♪♪♪

"Annie?" Casey called from inside the cottage. I closed my journal and put it on the kitchen table as I walked into the living room.

"Well, good morning, Cowboy." I leaned over him and kissed him. He reached up and pulled me down on top of him, tickling me in the ribs until I cried out for mercy.

"You're in a good mood this morning," I said, wiggling down beside him.

"You put me in a good mood. I love you, girl." He opened my robe and put his hands under the terry cloth to caress my back. I snuggled into him enjoying his touch, feeling his passion kindle my own. We loved each other with an intimacy I had forgotten.

"You feel good, Annie," he said, breathing the words into my ear.

We lay there, warm and silent, for a long while. The panic and grief of the dream had been abated by Casey's tenderness. The homesickness was gone. The sun shining through the bedroom door into the living room brought with it both warmth and light.

"What would you like to do today?" Casey whispered as he kissed my neck.

"This feels pretty good," I laughed.

"Let's relax today, Annie. Maybe we can take a walk on the beach later and have lunch over at the Lighthouse. What do you say?"

"I say, yes." I kissed him and jumped up to get him a cup of coffee. "Do you want to take a shower first?" I asked as I rummaged in the refrigerator for some milk.

"No. I'll run over to my cottage for a change of clothes and shower there. And while I'm at it, I'll stop at Linda's on the way back to see how things are going there and call Keith. I left all my business papers in that neat little office Barry has at the back of the house." As he pulled on his shirt, he walked to the opened door and breathed in a lung full of fresh air. "Wow, what a day! Say, Annie, when I tell Keith about our conversation with Dr. Green yesterday, maybe he'll be able to put a little pressure on Human Services."

As Casey finished buttoning his shirt, I handed him the cup of coffee. "Here's one for the road."

He took a swallow and said, "Mmmm, that's a good cup of coffee. Now give me another one for the road!" With that he kissed me and was gone.

"Don't be long! I'll have pancakes when you get back!" I called after him just as the screen door banged against the frame.

As I finished brushing my hair, the phone rang. Hoping to hear Millie's voice, I rushed to answer the call.

"Hello?" I said, expectantly.

"Hi, Beautiful."

"Casey! Is something wrong?"

"No," he laughed. "I'm at Linda's. She wants you to come over and have breakfast here."

"She does? They usually eat earlier than this." I said, curling the receiver cord around my finger.

"Oh, they have. But when I told her I was headed back there for pancakes, she insisted I call you to come over here." He was chuckling. I knew then that Linda had told him about the pancake fiasco of two years ago when I invited her whole family to breakfast and burned every pancake I cooked. They ate them anyway, smiling through it all, telling me the pancakes were delicious. Realizing that arguing about this change in plans was fruitless, I said, "Okay. I'll be right there!"

When I walked in, Casey and Linda were having an animated conversation at her kitchen table. "What's up?" I asked.

"The band that I hired for Saturday night has had some terrible luck," Linda replied. "Someone broke into their van and stole their audio equipment and all their instruments. Looks like we won't be having a barn dance after all."

"Oh, no!" I cried. "How awful!"

"All is not lost yet," Casey said. "Let me make some phone calls and see what we can do to fix this."

Linda stared at him in disbelief. "Fix this?"

"Sure. I know this must be devastating for you, Linda, but things like this happen all the time in my business." He whistled as he walked through the living room to what had become his makeshift office on the Island.

"If he gets me out of this mess, I'll never forget him," Linda said, shaking her head.

"Join the club!" I said, as I sat down at her kitchen table.

Linda put a dish of fresh fruit and a homemade pineapple muffin in front of me. "Want some coffee?"

"Yes, please. Thanks for the breakfast, but I think I really have mastered the art of cooking pancakes." I laughed, remembering the look of horror on Kevin's face when he saw the burned stack.

Casey suddenly appeared in the doorway with a big Cheshire cat grin. "That fruit and muffin look good, Linda. Got any more?"

"You bet. Coming right up." She hurried into the pantry. We laughed as we heard the noise of cupboard doors opening and closing. In a panic to get back to the table, Linda returned with a plate of muffins and a plate of cookies. Saying nothing, Casey smiled and sat down.

"So? Are you going to tell us what you've been able to arrange so quickly for Saturday night?" I asked impatiently.

"Patience, my dear," he said as he took a bite of the muffin.

Linda poured a cup of coffee for Casey and sat down next to me. "Casey, were you able to find someone?" Her face was flushed with anticipation.

"Yes. You're not going to believe our good luck. Cal Harper is a good friend of mine, and…"

"Cal Harper?" we cried in unison, interrupting him. "Casey, he's one of the most popular country western singers in both the USA and Canada," I continued, looking at Linda.

"Yup. I called his office and found out that he's in Canada this week. Over in Toronto. And, as luck would have it, he doesn't have a scheduled performance for Saturday night. His agent is going to get in touch with him later this morning to see if they can get up here for your barn dance."

"They?" Linda asked, instinctively filling his empty coffee cup.

"Yes. Cal and his band. They'll all come if they can." There was a hint of pride in the tone of Casey's voice.

"My God, Casey, I can't afford a band like that!" Linda's face had turned stone white.

Casey laughed. "Linda, don't worry about the cost. If Cal can get up here, he'll come as a favor to me. We really are very good friends. And I suspect that he'll enjoy the break. They said his next stop is in Maine some time later next week."

"I can't believe this." I had never seen Linda so flustered. "Will he be calling you here?"

"No. I told them to call me over at Annie's. We'll let you know as soon as he does." Casey grinned and leaned back in his chair. "Linda, this is really okay. Both Cal and I are in the business. Our schedules get changed all the time. This type of schedule change will be fun for him. Believe me, he'll love it. Why before it's over, I bet he'll thank you for inviting him here."

"You're not serious!" Linda gasped.

"Yes, I really am. I'll bet you a home-cooked dinner." He wiped his mouth with a napkin, stood up and stuck out his hand to shake on it.

"You've got a bet!" she said, pumping his arm enthusiastically.

Casey and I left Linda sitting at her table, still stunned by her apparent good luck. As we neared the back steps of The Lady Ann, we could hear the phone ringing. Still hoping to hear from Millie, I hurried to answer it.

"Hello?" I said, breathlessly.

"Hello there. Is Casey MacDonald there somewhere?" The man's soft, southern drawl was lyrical.

"Just a minute." I blushed as I looked up at Casey and covered the receiver with my hand. "I think this is Cal Harper," I whispered.

Casey just laughed, kissed me and said, "That's how you looked when you first met me, remember?" He turned his attention to the phone. "Hi there, pardner! How the heck are you?" Casey's voice resonated with the happiness of talking with an old friend.

Although I heard only half of the conversation, I could tell that they were, indeed, good friends. Cal told him that they should arrive early Saturday morning. Casey told him that there was plenty of room in Linda's yard for the tour buses. Of course, tour buses would mean that we would have to call Fred to make arrangements for additional electrical requirements. Casey hung up the phone and let out a loud, rebel yell. "Annie, honey," he said, picking me up and carrying me out to the deck, "this barn dance is going to be a humdinger!"

"I'll say! I guess the big surprise is on Linda this year," I chuckled, holding him around the neck as he carried me to the railing and put me down.

"We're going to have a good time, Annie," Casey said, looking down the beach toward the Lighthouse. "Cal is a super guy who really enjoys a family gathering like this. I just wish his family could be here with him."

"I think you're pretty wonderful to do this for Linda. She'll never forget you for it."

Suddenly he put his arms around me and lifted me off the floor, spinning me around, until I became dizzy.

"What are you doing?" I cried.

"I'm holding the woman I'm going to love forever! World, do you hear me? This is Annie! She's the best thing that's ever happened to me! I love her!"

When a group of teenagers running along the beach below the deck heard Casey shouting, they looked up and waved. One of them yelled back, "We hear you, man! Go for it!"

Casey put me down, but didn't let go of me. We stood against the railing, holding each other, looking out over the silvery blue water of the Straight.

"Go for it, the boy says. Do you want to 'go for it', Annie?"

"You know I do," I said, standing on tiptoes to kiss him.

"You're wonderful," he whispered.

"I love you, too." I put my arms around his neck and kissed his cheek. His mouth found mine instantly. His kiss was gentle. His lips were soft and giving. I rested my head under his chin and let the warmth of his body join with mine. We stood there for a long time, it seemed, until the phone rang again.

It was Linda. "I'm going crazy over here wondering if you've heard anything."

"Oh, Linda, yes," I giggled shamelessly. "Cal Harper called us a few minutes ago and said he should arrive Saturday morning. They've got two tour buses and a large truck. The tour buses will need electricity."

"Tell Casey I'll love him forever, Annie. We'll take care of the hookups for the buses. Thanks, honey. Thanks so much!" She hung up before I could say another word.

"Linda says thanks, and she'll love you forever. She'll probably hook up the electricity herself!" I laughed, imagining Linda talking animatedly with Fred as she described the need for more electrical outlets.

"Fred's got a full-time job over there this summer," Casey chuckled. "Let's go get the two-seater and ride over to the harbor. Maybe we'll see Ernest."

"What a good idea." I was pleased that Casey had suggested finding Ernest. The man was a special friend, and I had missed seeing him. "I want to make sure he saves a dance for me," I added playfully.

"Just be sure to save the last dance for me. Okay?" He grinned

"Hmmm. I can see mischief in that grin, Cowboy. What are you up to now?"

"Let's get a move on," he said, changing the subject, "before the day has passed us by."

We rode over to the harbor on the two-seater bicycle, waving at everyone who honked and yelled at us. Ernest was nowhere to be found. One of the fellows at the red lobster shack said he thought he had gone to Charlottetown for the day. Disappointed, we turned the bicycle around and headed for the Lighthouse. After a wobbly start, we successfully controlled the two-wheeled contraption. We were surprised when a group of adults, watching us from the porch of the Community Center, clapped and cheered our achievement.

The Lighthouse restaurant was crowded, but there was an unoccupied table-for-two near the windows. Varied shades of rose and green on the walls, draperies and tablecloths provided an elegant splash of color in the Victorian-style eatery. A piano, often played by a guest of the inn, graced one corner.

The young woman who had waited on us during our last visit beckoned us to our seats. "Sit down right here, and I'll get you some menus." She hurried off returning with the menus in one hand and a pitcher of ice water in the other. "I'll be back in a few minutes for your order," she said, quickly filling our water glasses and leaving the menus on the table.

Because I was concerned about Ernest, I asked about him when the waitress returned to our table. "Jill, do you happen to know if Ernest MacDonald is okay? Someone said he went in to Charlottetown this morning."

"He's okay. Just had to have a test at the hospital down there. Nothing serious, though."

We ordered lobster salad club sandwiches and iced tea. She hurried off to the kitchen.

"How does she happen to know about Ernest?" Casey asked.

"Ernest's granddaughter runs this place. But even if she didn't, everyone around here knows him and keeps an eye on him. Island folks really do respect the elders of the community. There's a lot more interaction between generations than we tend to see back home."

Casey moved his chair away from the table so he could lean back and cross his long legs. "Tell me more, Annie."

"You know how it is back home. The elders of the community often live alone or in boarding homes. They seldom see young people, except for an occasional visit from their grandchildren. But up here, the elders still live with their families, usually in the family homestead. Many times a son or daughter will build a new house right next door to the homestead. And if the elders do live alone, like Ernest, the young folks in the community drop in now and then to visit. They understand that the elders are interesting and have wonderful stories to tell. Ernest has taught a whole generation how to knit heads for lobster traps. The young men who work on the boats talk with him about fishing. The respect is there, Casey. Both generations learn a lot. But the best part is that the Island folklore is being passed along to another generation. It's a grand thing to see."

Jill delivered our sandwiches and tea, asked if we needed anything else, and left us to wait on another couple who had just sat down at a vacant table near us. I recognized them as the folks with the black lab. They looked over at me and nodded. I smiled at them and then looked back at Casey.

"We'll have to make sure to save some time to visit with Ernest before I leave," Casey said, handing me the pepper.

"Ugh. There's that word," I groaned.

"What?" Casey asked, as he took a big bite of his sandwich.

"Leave. I get an awful feeling in the pit of my stomach every time you talk about leaving."

"I know, honey, but I really do have to get back to work." He put the sandwich down, wiped his hands on a napkin and reached across the table. Taking my hand, he said, "I'm sorry, Annie. With all the excitement these past few days, this is the subject we've been able to avoid completely. I guess it's pay-up time."

We finished our meal, paid the bill, and stepped out into the sunshine. "Let's take a walk on the beach," Casey suggested, sensing my uneasiness.

As we stepped off the boardwalk onto the red sand, I thought about everything that had happened this past week. And as we strolled silently along the beach, I thought how quickly Millie, Casey and I had fallen in love, weaving our lives together with the threads of childhood trauma and a heightened sense of compassion that comes with understanding the cause of the deep scars. I thought how both joy and pain had been such intense players in our game of love and discovery, overshadowing thoughts of those who waited for us at home. I thought how Linda and Barry's love for one another had become an example of what could be, clouding our conscience to the reality of life as it truly is. The Island had become a perfect metaphor for the relationship that had developed between Casey, Millie and me. Like our relationship, the Island is complete and self-sustaining, detached from distant influences, and yet protected by that very separation from all that exists beyond its shores. I dreaded the realities that faced us when we connected once again to the life all of us had left behind.

Casey and I walked for miles - past The Lady Ann, past Casey's cottage. We held hands, walking slowly, each contemplating the responsibilities and difficult decisions waiting for us at home.

"Annie, my wife has filed for a divorce," Casey declared into the silence. I barely heard him. "I'm not surprised," he continued, needing to tell me everything before he no longer could. "This has been coming on for a long time, but I had hoped she might wait until I got back. Typical man, I guess, expecting everyone to schedule their life around me. Anyway, I'm concerned about the kids."

"Don't you think they know what's been happening between the two of you?" I asked.

"Yes, they probably do. Kate is very good with them. She believes in telling them the truth. They trust her." He bent down to pick up a rock and side-handed it into the ocean.

"She sounds like a good person, Casey."

"She is, Annie, but our dreams for our life together just haven't matched. I've been too busy making movies, being a star. Kate enjoys the freedom the money gives her, but she resents the demands on my time. Oh, I don't want to make it sound like she's a shallow person. She isn't. She just can't cope with the limelight. Over the last several years, we haven't slept under the same roof more than six or seven times. My production company in California takes up most of my time, and Kate has refused to move there. The kids fly in on the corporate jet every other weekend, but she stays in Montana at the ranch. You can't make a marriage work under those circumstances." He threw another rock, this one skipping over the water three or four times before it sank.

"No, you can't." I thought about life in California. Could I just pick up and move there, stand the constant scrutiny of the media, live with the demands placed on him, and lose my own identity in his shadow?

Casey stopped and turned to me, his face ashen white. "Are you thinking that my lifestyle isn't something you would want to share either?"

"I don't know, Casey. My life so far has been pretty simple compared to yours. I can go anywhere I want to without fear that some reporter is going to embarrass me in front of my friends or some photographer is going to take a picture of me picking through the fruit at the local supermarket. I've worked hard at understanding who I am and what I really do want out of life. Being Annie York is important to me."

"And it's important to me. That's part of why I love you so much. You're strong, Annie. You've survived on that strength. There isn't any way I would want to overshadow you or let my career control you. I know you've got wonderful things ahead for you, things you want to create and support. You need the space and freedom to do that."

We stood facing each other, holding hands, as we anguished over the disparity of our life styles. The familiar sounds of the beach went unheard as I listened for every nuance and inflection in Casey's voice. This is the reality Linda warned me about, I thought.

"What are we saying, Casey?" I asked, dreading his answer.

"We're saying that there's a chance for us, Annie. That's all. There's a chance for us. The answer is there, just like you said. We've just got to take our time and be patient until we find it."

"Oh," I sighed with relief, leaning against him.

"What?" he laughed, gently pushing me away from him so he could look into my eyes. "You weren't expecting that answer, were you?"

"Not really. But it was a beautiful answer, Casey. If you can live with it, so can I." I looked up at him and smiled.

He pressed his hand against my back and bent his head to kiss me. "I love you, Annie."

"And I love you," I said, throwing my arms around his neck. As he hugged me, my feet left the ground. I threw my head back and my arms out as though I were flying. When he lowered me back to the sand, he said, "You know, we're one hell of a long way down the beach. But like the song says, Annie. 'I'd walk a million miles for one of your smiles.'"

As we walked back to the Lighthouse to retrieve the bicycle, Casey talked about the timing of the movie to be filmed in Ontario. With luck, he thought we might be able to spend part of the Christmas holidays with Millie. By the time we returned to the cottage, it was nearly five. "There's a note on door, Casey," I said, remembering the message Millie had left for us earlier. My hands trembled as I opened it, fearing bad news. "Good. It's from Linda," I sighed. "She wants us to come to dinner at six. Want to go?"

"Sure, why not. Maybe Barry and I can beat you women at a couple games of cribbage." He followed me into the kitchen, took a beer out of the refrigerator and stepped out onto the deck. "Let's sit out here until its time to go. What do you say, Annie?"

Barry was busy in the kitchen when we knocked on the back door. "Barry! What are you doing in here?" I laughed.

"I told Linda that she had done enough cooking over the last few weeks, so I'm getting supper for us tonight. Hope you folks like steak cooked on the grill." He was wearing his 'Kiss the Cook' apron over a short sleeved shirt and shorts in such a way that the apron looked like a skirt. His hairy legs were bare and tanned.

"Nice outfit," I said, tugging at the apron. "Where's Linda?"

"She's in the living room waiting for you, Annie. Go on in and join her." He turned back to the platter of steaks, shook seasoning over them, and headed for the grill located on the side deck. Casey went with him offering to help. I found Linda sitting with her feet up drinking a glass of wine.

"Hi, Annie. Would you like some wine?" she asked, leaning over to pour a glass of zinfandel from a bottle sitting in a large dish of ice.

"I would love it. What's going on here?" I asked, taking the glass and making myself comfortable in the chair next to the sofa.

"Barry insisted on cooking tonight. And to tell you the truth, I'm exhausted. I got so excited over the fact that Cal Harper is coming that I've spent the entire day in the barn trying to make it look better than it is." She wiped up a pool of water that had dripped off the wine bottle onto the floor.

"You're kidding! Cal Harper is a country boy who isn't expecting anything more than a family farm. He probably knows better than anyone the simplicity and value of a beautiful barn like that one out there."

"Well, I gave up anyway. We did a good job the other day. Fred met the electric company out here early this afternoon, and they've got enough power lines installed now to start a campground. They even put in a couple of poles and installed outlets on them. Fred didn't believe it at first when I told him about Cal Harper."

"Everyone is going to be blown away," I said, sipping the wine.

"I'll say. Casey certainly saved the day. Speaking of Casey, what have you guys been doing today?" She leaned back against the cushions and sighed.

"We rode that old two-seater over to the harbor looking for Ernest, but I guess he's gone to the Charlottetown hospital for the day for some tests. Jill, that cute waitress over at the Lighthouse, told us the tests weren't serious though."

"That's good." Her eyes closed as she relaxed and listened.

"I'll find out more from Ernest when he gets back. Anyway, Casey and I took a long walk on the beach, not really talking that much, just walking. We were nearly to West Cape before we realized how far we had gone."

"Annie, that's miles down the beach!" she exclaimed, sitting forward.

"I know. But the walk was easy and, honestly, time passed by all too quickly. We stopped down there to talk for a while, and that's when Casey told me that his wife has filed for a divorce. She doesn't want any part of his public life, I guess."

"Well, I can understand that, can't you?" Linda scooped a handful of peanuts out of a dish on the table in front of her. She passed the dish to me.

I leaned forward. "Yes, I can. I've been thinking about it all day."

Before we had time to take our discussion further, Barry and Casey called to us from the kitchen. They had set the table and dished up all the food. The steaks were still sizzling.

Casey beamed with pride. "Linda, I don't think you need to worry about cooking ever again. Look at this meal!"

"Now wait just a minute!" Barry complained, sounding like Jack Benny. We all laughed.

Linda and Barry were good company. The four of us ate as though we hadn't seen food for three weeks. The cribbage games were fun. Linda and I won every game but one. Some time later in the evening Casey began to tell them a funny story about one of his movies. He dramatized the story using different accents and imitating other famous stars that we knew. By the time he had finished, Linda, Barry and I were laughing so hysterically, we cried. The release of the emotion all of us had experienced over the last few days was cathartic.

"Do you need any help on Saturday, Linda?" I asked, as we got ready to leave.

"You folks have done enough," she said, hugging me. "Several of my cousins will be here to help with the food. Casey, I haven't forgotten that you agreed to call a square dance."

"I haven't forgotten either, Linda. It should be fun, especially with Cal's band. I'm really looking forward to it."

"So are we," Linda agreed. "I can't begin to thank you for what you've done."

"It's the least I can do," he said, kissing her on the cheek. "Remember, you introduced Annie and me. For that, I will be eternally grateful. I really mean it."

"Thanks for supper, Barry. It was elegant." I hugged him and followed Casey out the door. Casey took my hand as we walked back to the cottage. We decided to sit on the deck and enjoy the sounds of the night. Our up-back neighbors were gathered around a campfire on the beach singing camp songs. The distinctive smell of the wood smoke and the sweet harmony of their voices floated over the deck on the warm southern breeze.

Casey stood at the railing, a silhouette against the light of the passing day. "What a great day," he said.

When the last song was sung and the campfire had been extinguished, we let go of the night and went to bed.

Chapter 14

August – 1993

The morning is new...radiant. My heart, my whole being is refreshed, as though every breath bears new life. The Island has given me the gift of time...time to heal, not only from the grief of losing my husband, but from the shame and ugliness of so long ago.

Scars of the past have littered my soul. The crust of those scars covered the answers to so many of the questions that have plagued me for a lifetime. Why homesickness? What is the common thread that ties the real feelings of homesickness to that deep, empty hole in my soul that consumed me when I least expected it? Now I know. Abandonment, manifested in so many terrible ways.

Physical scars are visible reminders that something dreadful happened there. But emotional scars are much different...lying unseen, hidden deep, confusing and terribly, terribly painful. For years I had no idea that the pain existed, only that I reacted with confusing and often irrational behavior, often to otherwise benign situations.

God has waited until I was in the right context to reveal the source and depth of those feelings. This Island, just different enough from the familiar to allow a new perspective, is the context. With that perspective I have looked once again at the past and seen there a child who was not shameful or ugly, but a child full of life, strong and resourceful

♪♪♪

The contract for the sale of the Lady Ann was ready for my signature. Since the real estate company handling the negotiations was located in Kensington, Casey and I decided to make a day of it and explore Malpeque Bay just north of there. We left early, stopping at a small café along the way for breakfast. The road wound through quaint villages and over terrain that was peppered with hills and vales and backwater marshes.

"This Island is magnificent, Annie. Look over there." Casey pointed to a narrow harbor, much like the ones we had visited on the West Shore. A dozen small sheds, built side by side along the length of the wharf like the little houses in a Monopoly game, were all designed from the same pattern and painted the same muddy brown color. Each one contained the fishermen's gear stored there between seasons. The small harbor was home to only a few small boats, some unloading oysters as we watched from the highway. Behind us was a backwater sea marsh filled with great blue herons.

"Have you ever seen so many herons in one place?" I asked, reaching for my camera.

"Annie, honey, I'm not really a bird watcher," Casey chuckled.

"Would you mind if I get out and take a few pictures? Susan loves great blue herons and perhaps I can create a lovely birthday present for her," I said, as I rummaged in my camera case for the telephoto lens.

Casey waited in the Jeep while I walked along the road to find the right angle for the perfect picture. It took about five minutes of walking back and forth, getting down on my hands and knees and even lying on the ground before I found the best shot. When the telephoto lens brought the scene into focus, the image of a majestic male robed in his regal plumage sat on the end of my nose.

"Wow! There must be over thirty of them out there," I exclaimed, as I jumped back into the Jeep. "Susan will love these pictures." Casey was laughing.

"Okay. What's so funny?" I said, as I replaced the lens cap and stored the camera in its case.

"You are, Annie," he said, moving his sunglasses to the top of his head. "I can't think of one person I know who would be as excited as you are about great blue herons, much less get down on her belly to take a picture of them." He reached for my hand and pulled it to his lips.

"It's fun! Don't you love being spontaneous, Casey? Finding fun and pleasure in simple things? I've been taking myself way too seriously for way too long."

"Annie, when you get those pictures developed, send me one, will you? I want to remember this moment forever." He pulled me to him and kissed me, softly, and then looked at me. His curious expression seemed a mixture of awe and sadness.

"What?" I asked.

"Nothing. We better head back to Kensington." He started the engine, looked over his shoulder and made a u-turn across the road.

Casey was quiet as we retraced our route along the same shore. I sensed that he was thinking about leaving the Island for home and about the consequences of the decisions he had been making or trying to make over the last week. After a long silence, I said, "Taking yourself too seriously?"

"Yeah, I guess I am right now." His grip on the steering wheel tightened.

"Then we need to talk," I said, reaching out to touch his shoulder. "Let's pull over. There's a good spot just ahead."

He turned onto a short dirt road leading down to a saltwater cove hiding in the bend of the main road. One lone storage shed sat sentinel along a wharf that was only long enough for two boats. The tide was low, the boats moored so that just the top of their wheelhouses were visible to us as we coasted in beside them. Casey turned off the ignition and turned to me.

"Casey, this Island may be the only place we'll ever be free enough to love each other. If we really do want to look at our relationship seriously, neither one of us would be comfortable in the other's world for very long," I said, taking his hand.

"Do you really believe that, Annie?" He looked down at our hands.

"Yes, I'm afraid I do. You're good at what you do. I think I've seen most of your movies, and I see a man who is passionate about his craft and puts his whole being into a role. You wouldn't be happy without that part of your life. And I know that I couldn't be there with you, watching you with other women, seeing you make love to them even if it's only for a movie. That may sound shallow, but...."

Before I could complete my thought, he sighed and sat back against the door. "Annie, honey, that's what my wife has been dealing with for years. That's part of her reasoning for living at the ranch."

"I think I understand that. Whether you're guilty or not of whatever it is she's accused you of, being there in the midst of your other love is just too hard to take."

"I have *never* been in love with another woman, Annie, at least not until now," he said adamantly.

"That's not what I meant. It's your work that's the other love. Your wife knows too much about that other love. She knows the games you play with it, the compromises you make, the thought you give it, perhaps even more thought than you give her. It hurts, Casey." I had turned to face him, my left leg pulled up on the seat.

Casey didn't reply. His eyes had misted over. His face was flushed. He reached up and rubbed his eyes with both hands. "God, Annie, I don't want to hurt you like that." His eyes filled with tears as he shifted in his seat and reached for me. With his arm around me, he stared, stone-faced, at the little cove that widened to the sea beyond. Lost in thought, he rubbed my shoulder then slid his hand under my arm and softly caressed my breast. Every once in a while he pulled me closer as though afraid to let go. Like me, Casey responded to the intimate touch of another. Denied that kind of love as a child, he craved it, needed it. Unfortunately, that need had directed a good part of his life, as it had mine. Both of us had been searching for a lost part of our soul for too long.

The quiet of the place was like the awesome silence in an empty church. Once in a while a car would pass by on the road that rose above our heads. The tide had turned and brought with it a warm, fragrant breeze that blew over us through the open window. A few seagulls, perched on the pilings, guarded the boats. Casey relaxed. "Why is life so complicated, Annie?" His finger traced the emblem in the middle of the steering wheel. "The divorce is going to be hard for the kids."

"Are you sure that a divorce is the right decision to make right now?" I asked trying to feel as sincere as I sounded.

"Yes, I do. My wife and I have been separated for too long now. She's made a life for herself in Montana. She tells me it's the life she needs." He paused, still focused on the emblem. "I know the kids love it there as well, and I guess it's hard to admit that they'll all be okay without me."

"Will you be okay?" I asked.

"Yup," he said, clearing his throat. "I've got that new movie to make, and that will keep me plenty busy over the next six to eight months." He stretched, kissed me tenderly, and then abruptly changed the subject. "Let's get this show on the road so we can take care of your closing and head back to West Point."

We arrived at the lawyer's office right on time. The closing took only half an hour. When we got back in the Jeep I hugged Casey and said, "The Lady Ann is all mine now. Wouldn't it be nice to think we could spend a couple months there every summer…together?"

"Best idea you've had all day," he said, starting the engine.

Our trip back to West Point took most of the afternoon, so we decided to stop at a local wholesaler to buy mussels for our supper. "PEI mussels are some of the best in the world. I think they'll pack them in ice for us to keep them fresh until we get back to the cottage," I said, as we pulled into the parking lot.

We stopped in O'Leary for wine and fresh yeast rolls. While I was in the Co-op, Casey went to a local florist and bought a bouquet of summer flowers. We were ready to celebrate the acquisition of the Lady Ann.

By the time we reached the shore road from West Cape to West Point, the sun was low in the western sky. The cottage, closed up all day, had efficiently stored the afternoon heat.

"Wow, it's hot in here," Casey said, as he busied about opening doors and windows. Soon the fresh evening air had cooled the rooms to an agreeable temperature. The mussels were steaming by then and the picnic table was set. Casey had found an old lantern under the kitchen cupboard that he lighted and placed in the center of the table right next to the vase of flowers.

"Ambiance!" he exclaimed. He poured two glasses of wine, handed one to me and said, "To the Lady Ann. Our life. Our home." He kissed me and then tapped my glass. "Here's to you, Beautiful."

We sat side-by-side on the bench facing the water. The evening air was pleasant and comfortable. The steamed mussels, cooked with wine and dipped in butter, were deliciously sweet and satisfying after a long day on the road. The beach below was strangely quiet for a Friday night. As we enjoyed our lovely meal, we talked about Linda's reunion.

"Do you have any idea what time Cal Harper is arriving tomorrow?" I asked, popping a mussel dripping with butter into my mouth.

"They'll probably get here early in the morning. Most of the people won't be arriving for the reunion until after lunch tomorrow, so that will give Cal and the band a chance to rest before they have to set up the sound system. I hope we get a chance to visit with him before then."

"Really?" The word sounded like the squeak of a schoolgirl.

"Yes, really. Now don't go getting all starry eyed on me, girl." He poured each of us another glass of wine.

"Those singin' cowboys are really somethin'," I drawled, teasing him just a little.

"Cal's going to like you, Annie," he laughed.

Just as we were clearing away the dishes, the phone rang. The annoying sound of the worn bell instantly changed the mood of the moment.

"Hello?" I said, thinking the caller might be Linda in need of some last minute help.

"Annie? Is that you?" The voice sounded frail and far away.

"Millie! I'm so glad to hear from you, honey. Are you okay?" I looked up at Casey who had frozen in place, a dinner plate in both hands.

"Yes. We just got home. You asked me to call you when we got here, remember?" I could hear her mother talking in the background telling Millie not to be too long.

"Yes, I do." I sat down at the desk and listened to Millie recount the adventures of her long trip back to New York. She described in adolescent detail the sleazy hotel they stayed in where the police came at three in the morning to arrest someone, a great restaurant where they got huge hamburgers, and a highway rest stop where they saw a bus belonging to a teenage boy band I had never heard of but she absolutely loved. Her voice grew animated and strong as she chattered about her trip, adding that they had seen lots of deer feeding in the woods along the way.

"Is Casey still there?" she asked.

"Yes, he is. Do you want to talk to him?" As I stood up to pass the phone to Casey, I heard her say, "Sure!"

Casey, who had been standing next to me, eagerly took the receiver. "Hi, Millie!"

"Hi. I'm so glad you're still there, Casey. I wanted to thank you again for the beautiful little picture of the Lighthouse. I'm going to hang it up in my room right over my desk so I can look at it when I do my homework," she giggled.

"I'm glad you like it, honey. Was your trip home okay?" Casey held the telephone with one hand while the other was around my waist.

Millie, sensing that Casey really wanted to know if her father had hurt her again, replied quickly. "Yes, Casey. Everything is okay. Mom is going to take me to the doctor tomorrow to check on my arm. How much longer are you going to be up there?"

"I'm leaving on Sunday, and Annie is going home a week from tomorrow. Have you got our home numbers in a safe place?" he asked, holding his breath, waiting for her answer.

"Yes, but don't worry. Everything is cool." When she answered him, Casey looked at me, nodded and exhaled.

I motioned to him that I wanted to talk to her before he hung up.

"Millie, Annie wants to talk to you again. You take care of yourself now, and don't forget me."

"Don't worry about that, Casey. I love you."

"I love you, too, sweetheart. Here's Annie." He passed the phone to me and reached into his back pocket for a handkerchief. He sat on the couch and wiped his eyes.

"Hi, Millie. Gosh, I miss you." As I talked with her, I pictured the dancing leprechaun, pigtails flying in the breeze.

"I miss you too, Annie. When are you coming to see Casey's movie?" she asked wistfully.

"I'm not sure, honey. Probably some time in December when you have your school vacation. I'll write to you next week," I promised.

There was a shuffling noise as though she were covering the receiver with her hand. "I've got to hang up now. Mommy says I've talked long enough. Have fun at the barn dance and say hi to the girls for me."

"We will, Millie. I love you," I said, hurriedly.

"I love you, too, Annie. Bye." The click was deafening. She had hung up before I could say good-bye. As I placed the receiver in the cradle, I felt both elated that we had heard from her and scared that she was now home in familiar surroundings where so many of the beatings must have occurred.

"Oh, she sounded so wonderful and so happy," I exclaimed, clapping my hands as I turned to look at Casey. "Wouldn't it be great if he really has changed?"

"Yes, Annie, but we both know that probably isn't the case. Keith is going to let us know if he's been able to talk to Dr. Wade and make some arrangements for Human Services to look into this situation. We'll probably hear from him tomorrow. On second thought, though," he said, standing up, "maybe I should call him right now. Millie said her mother was taking her to the doctor tomorrow. Maybe Keith should give the doctor a call today." He looked through his wallet for Keith's card.

"I bet this is the point where most people back out of a situation like this," I said. "You know what's going on, but everything looks okay for the moment, so you don't do anything. And then, well, I just don't want to think about what might happen to that kid if her father beats her again."

"That's it. You've convinced me, Annie. I'm going to call Keith right now." The thought that he might be able to do something to protect Millie filled Casey with purpose and energy. While he made the call, I returned to the deck and finished clearing the table. The sun was setting in a clear sky casting a golden pathway across the water. Terns flew in and out of the sun's reflection, diving into the molten gold as though looking for hidden treasure.

"We're all looking for hidden treasures," I thought.

"What was that?" Casey stood in the door.

"Oh, I was just thinking out loud." When I turned toward him, he was frowning. "What's wrong?"

Casey sat down on the bench facing me. "Keith hasn't been able to talk to the doctor. It seems that she's away on vacation and isn't expected back until Sunday. He doesn't really want to get anyone else involved right now, since the x-rays from Canada have been sent directly to Dr. Wade. He thinks we should wait until she gets back to coordinate the next move."

"I wonder where Millie's mother is taking her tomorrow. Probably yet another pediatrician, telling them that Millie fractured her arm accidentally on vacation." I wiped my hands on the dishtowel I had been holding, threw it on the table, and sat down next to him.

"Well, if that lie works, Millie's father probably won't get upset. Hopefully nothing will happen over the weekend." Casey put his arm around me as a gesture of comfort.

"God, this is frustrating! I'm not looking to break up a family, but if that man hurts her again, well, I just couldn't take it, Casey." My anger fueled a flood of tears.

"Annie, we've got to be careful," he said, hugging me and kissing the top of my head. "Our first priority is to protect Millie. If we start calling doctors all over that city, or send Human Services in there before there's a legal way for them to remove her father, we could set Millie up for a terrible beating. When the time comes, he needs to be removed from her presence quickly and for a long time and given some help to stop this horrible behavior."

"I'm so frightened for her, Casey," I said pulling away from him to look into his face.

"I am, too, Annie. But we'll just have to pray that everything will be okay until Monday when Dr. Wade returns from her vacation. I'll be back in California by then and will make sure Keith stays on top of this."

"And Monday is only a few days away," I sighed.

"That's true," Casey said, putting his arms around me again, holding me close to him. "That's true."

Both of us wanted these next few days to last forever for ourselves, and yet they needed to pass quickly for Millie.

"Why is life so complicated, Casey?"

"I don't know, Annie. I asked that question earlier today, remember?"

We picked up the bottle of wine and the glasses and went into the living room to relax. We had had another long day and were both physically and emotionally spent. The old sofa claimed us quickly. Some time in the night, Casey carried me into the bedroom where he removed my clothes and put me to bed. The wind woke me around four. Casey and I were turned toward each other holding hands.

Life was not going to be the same after Sunday.

Chapter 15

August – 1993

The sky is dark, blackened by clouds made heavy with rain. The wind tears at the cottage, throwing sheets of water against the north wall. In all the years I have visited here, I have never experienced this kind of energy from Mother Nature. And yet, Casey continues to sleep like a baby.

I fear this storm is a portend of things to come. Blowing sand and seawater whirl around and against the side of the cottage. The forces of nature are out of control.

But where is the control? Who has it? At times like this I see so clearly that I certainly have no control. All I can do is hide in the safest spot possible and wait out the storm…let whatever happens, happen. Just let go. And pray.

My chest is tight. Adrenalin pumps and bursts through my entire body every time a gale force gust threatens to blow the doors off their hinges. The old feelings of panic are back, aggravating the immense sense of loss that has been building over the last few days, as I worry about Millie and prepare to say good-bye to Casey.

The familiar comfort of the sofa, placed too close to the windows, has been forsaken for the matching armchair usually cluttered with magazines, beach towels and old throw pillows. Pushed against the inside wall, the chair seems the safest spot in the room. A candle glows beside me, fluttering madly every time a gust of wind rips at the shingles.

Chaos. Is this storm a reminder? Have I become too relaxed, too removed from the realities of life? My home, my friends and family, all that I have known for the past forty plus years wait for me back in Maine. Is this storm preparing me to leave the Island, literally blowing me back into the rest of the world that I have been able to forget for the past few weeks?

Calm down, Annie, my inner voice offers. Home doesn't have to be chaotic. Everyone there loves you and misses you. They'll be happy to welcome you back.

Yes, but without meaning to they'll put pressure on me with their expectations of time: time visiting and running their errands and listening to their problems and, and, AND! Back to the same old way of life…care giving. I've been a caregiver since I was five and sat in my mother's lap protecting her from my father's wrath...taking care of her when I was seven because she had scarlet fever...putting her to bed when I was thirteen because she scared us to death when she took a sleeping pill and didn't tell us...watching over her when I was thirty as she recovered from her last nervous breakdown. I don't begrudge her that care. I loved her deeply, but I'm tired. The early socialization to that kind of caregiving has influenced my entire life. All of the relationships that I've ever had have been anchored in that same responsibility.

Being here has been a wonderful opportunity to let go of all that responsibility...to take care of myself. Maybe this storm isn't so much a symbol of chaos, as it's a symbol that there is much more in the universe to discover, much more in my life, much more in everyone's life.

Wisdom is born of stuff like this. In the brief instant when a new awareness emerges, wisdom sparkles like a fine jewel in the sun, sometimes blinding those who dare to look for the treasure behind the glow, sometimes spotlighting the new discovery.

Do I dare look? What wondrous treasure waits there for me?

Annie, the treasure isn't back home. It's right here on this Island. You have been living within it these past weeks. The clean, crisp air...the vibrant colors...the freshness and beauty of the wildflowers...the discovery of another soul...the love and trust of a broken child. What more do you want? And even though you've cared for them, they've given back something you've never had before.

Trust. A child's trust. That same trust that you lost so early in your own childhood. She put it right out there for you. As you looked into her eyes and saw there a beautiful, innocent child, you looked at yourself. And for the first time, you reached out to and loved that awkward, ugly, shameful nine-year-old that has lived in your soul all these years. Don't let go of her, Annie. Keep loving her and you'll both heal.

Casey has shared his trust as well and in doing so allowed you to be vulnerable. The two of you discovered the common ground of childhood pain. You've been able to touch that pain with one hand while holding on to someone who understands it with the other. Healing has begun for both of you. What a special gift!

Remember the book, <u>Don't Push the River</u>? Well, don't push the river right now...it flows along quite nicely all by itself. Don't expect solutions and answers. Don't expect chaos-free days. And don't expect that Casey is going to disappear. Neither one of you knows what the future holds. Give it a chance.

The wind continues to howl.

♪♪♪

"Annie, where are you?" Casey called to me as he appeared in the bedroom doorway.

"I'm out here hiding in this big, old chair!" I shouted, over the noise of the wind.

"What are you doing out here?" he asked, hunched over and shivering.

"Trying to calm down by talking to myself in my journal." I laughed.

Ignoring the lightning, he sat on the sofa, quickly wrapping the quilt around him. "And did you discover any nuggets of wisdom?" His voice was muffled as he snuggled into the quilt.

"Funny you should mention that. Yes, I did. Now all I have to do is remember them." I closed the journal and placed it on the lampstand. The candle had burned itself out dripping globs of wax onto the base of the candlestick. We continued to talk in the dark. An occasional bolt of lightening brightened the room for a milli-second as though angels were taking our picture.

"How long have you been out here?" he asked, jumping at a particularly loud crash of thunder. Not fully awake, his speech was slow and slurred. An errant cowlick of hair shooting straight up reminded me of Dennis the Menace.

"A couple of hours. The storm has let up a lot over the last half hour. I was beginning to wonder if you were still alive in there."

"When I was a kid, I could sleep through anything. But I haven't slept like that in years. You've worn me all out, beautiful."

"I doubt that!" I jumped out of the chair, took his hands in mine, and pulled him up. The quilt fell back onto the sofa. Dressed only in boxer shorts, he started to shiver once again.

"Let's go back to bed and warm up, Annie," he said, as he picked me up and whisked me into the bedroom. I felt his warmth still in the bed as he pulled me to him. He quickly fell asleep. I followed soon after.

The alarm woke us around seven. Casey stretched, hugged me quickly and bounced out of bed. "What a beautiful day for a reunion!" he said, as he looked out the window. The rain the night before had washed everything like new. The morning sun was drying up the moisture, creating a soft mist over the fields. "You know, Annie, I've been thinking. What would you say if we drove down to Maine together? I could stay with you at your camp there tomorrow night and take a plane out west on Monday."

"I'd love it!" I shouted from the bathroom. "You can leave from the Bangor Airport."

"Great. I'll call the airline right now, then I've got to hustle because I told Cal I'd meet him at the ferry at ten."

He poked his head through the door within minutes it seemed. "Good news, Annie. There's a flight out of Bangor at two in the afternoon on Monday that connects in Chicago for the west coast." He picked me up in a great bear hug, spun around, and kissed me as he put me down. "I'm glad we can do this. This way I'll have a picture in my mind of where you are and what you're doing."

"I'm glad we can do this, too," I said, thinking about what had to be done to close up the cottage sooner than I had planned. "Having you stay with me at camp will be very special…something I can remember forever."

"It won't be the last time, Annie. I promise." He kissed my cheek.

"Let's rustle up some breakfast, and then you've got to get on the road if you plan to catch up with Cal. Are you sure you're really up for the long drive back to Maine? It's going to be a late night tonight and then a long day tomorrow." The toaster popped. The fresh smell of warm whole wheat would forever remind me of this moment.

"I can sleep on the plane Monday. I want to spend as much time as possible with you before I leave. And, during that long drive, we can fantasize about the future. Sound good?" he asked, as he picked up our mugs and the coffee pot and eased sideways through the door to the deck.

We ate a hurried breakfast, enjoying the early morning sounds and smells blown about by a gentle sea breeze. The Irwin's had let their cows out of the barn for the day to graze among the wildflowers and rich green clover. We could hear their barn dog, Katie, barking as she chased them across the road to the pasture below. Ed MacLeod was working some heavy machinery in front of his barn. One of our summer neighbors was repairing a deck, the sound of the pounding hammer echoing off the side of his cottage.

A few people were making their way toward us as they took their morning stroll. The vivid splash of color from the red and yellow hues of their clothing complemented the deep blue backdrop of the sea. They waved as they passed by on the beach.

Casey gulped down the last of the coffee and said, "Gotta go, Beautiful. I'll be back with the band as soon as I can."

I rushed to follow him to the back door tripping over a wayward sneaker. "I'm going over to visit with Ernest and find out about those tests, then I'll come back here to pack. I'm sure Ed will do what needs to be done to close up the place after we leave."

Casey stopped on the bottom step and looked back at me through the closed screen door. "Is this bright idea of mine putting too much pressure on you? I didn't even stop to think that you had planned to stay here another week. Would you rather do that?"

"No!" I jumped at the force of my objection and then laughed. "Don't you know that I want to spend every minute we can together? Barry and Linda are leaving earlier than they planned, and I was thinking of leaving too. This is perfect."

"You're sure?" he asked, as he opened the door to kiss me.

"I'm sure. Now go get that band!"

After Casey left, I drove over to Ernest's home to find out about his tests. I entered the house through the back door and found him in the kitchen making fudge. He told me that the tests were nothing serious, obviously not wanting to talk about something that private. I was glad to know he was okay and left with a hug and a bag full of fudge for our trip home. The rest would be added to the dessert table at Linda's reunion.

A quick trip to the Crawford farm was the next move on my agenda to tell Linda that Casey and I were leaving the next morning. She was in a panic because Barry had forgotten to get ice. He had just been directed to drive into O'Leary and buy out the ice supply at the Co-op. As he pulled out of the drive, the four huge coolers in the back of the truck slid sideways, thumping and bumping against the tailgate until he was out of sight.

"He's in a hurry," I exclaimed.

"He's forgetful, but I love him," Linda laughed.

Linda wasn't surprised to hear that my plans to leave for Maine had changed. She was pleased that Casey was driving back with me. "To be honest, Annie, when we found out we had to go home earlier than planned, I was worried about leaving you here alone."

"I know, Linda, and I love you for it, but I had already decided to leave early too."

"Casey is going to love your camp at the lake. Perhaps he'll be able to get up there after he finishes that movie in Ontario." Linda talked with me as she wrapped cookies, a half dozen at a time, in brightly colored tissue paper tied with raffia twine.

"I hope so. Gosh, look at the time. Casey should be back before lunch with the band. I've got a lot to do back at the cottage," I said, as I took the bundle of cookies she handed to me. "These will be a great treat on our long drive home. Thanks."

By the time Casey returned with Cal and the band, I had packed what I needed to take home and had moved all the furniture from the porch to its winter sanctuary. Linda had said she would clean out the refrigerator and Ed would turn off the water and do whatever else needed to be done to close things up until October, when I would make my annual trek to the Island to close the cottage for the winter.

"Annie! Where are you?" Casey called from the back door.

"In here. I was just getting dressed for the reunion," I said, still in my underwear, hoping he didn't have Cal with him. I reached for my robe.

"There you are," he grinned, as he hugged me and kissed my neck.

"Where are Cal and the band?" I asked timidly, as I looked out into the living room.

"They're over at Linda's getting the buses and truck situated for the night." Then he laughed as he noticed the worried look on my face. "What? Did you think I had them tagging along behind me after being gone all morning?" he teased. "Actually they have a lot to do before tonight, so Cal said there would be plenty of time to meet you then. He'll probably eat with us."

"What did you find out about Ernest?" he asked, as he sat on the bed and watched as I combed my hair and put on a little makeup.

"Not much. He didn't really want to talk about it. Said it was nothing serious. I hope not. He was making fudge," I said, packing shampoo and other toiletries in a canvas bag. "He gave us some for the trip home."

Casey didn't respond to the comment about the fudge, so I poked my head out of the bathroom door to see if he had left. He was still sitting on the bed looking at a small piece of yellow paper. He quickly stuffed it in his shirt pocket when he realized I was standing there. "Listen," he said suddenly, "I've got some things to pack before tomorrow. Why don't I go do that now? I'll put everything in the car and come back in about an hour. That way we can get an early start in the morning."

"While you're gone, I'll call my neighbor at the lake and ask him to open the windows at camp to air it out. And I probably ought to call Susan to let her know about my change of plans." I rummaged through another canvas bag searching for my address book that I had packed just twenty minutes earlier.

"I'll be back as quickly as I can." Casey kissed me and was gone before I could say another word. He seemed nervous about something, but I dismissed that thinking he was probably just glad to see his friend Cal.

True to his word, Casey was back in an hour. I heard him hollering to me as he came through the back door. "Time to go, Beautiful. You can hear the band from here." When he burst into the bedroom, he stopped quickly and whistled. "Wow, Annie, you look great!"

Each of us had put together a western outfit for the occasion. Casey was dressed in blue jeans and a light blue western shirt with mother of pearl snaps. An oval silver belt buckle and a black bolo with a silver fastener completed his look. I wore a pair of blue jean shorts with a pink and white checked short-sleeved shirt and a white neckerchief knotted at my throat. I had tied my dark, brown hair back into a ponytail with a pink ribbon leaving bangs over my forehead.

Casey packed my bags in the car before we walked over to join the crowd at the reunion. "Cal has a wonderful time planned for all of us," Casey said, taking my hand. "I'm really glad he's going to get a chance to meet you, Annie."

As we approached the sprawling yard of the old farmhouse, our senses were overwhelmed with motion, color and noise. In the field beside the barn, the softball game was well underway to the cheers of family and friends. Shouts of laughter could be heard coming from the barn as a group of teenagers had found the checkerboard. Linda had filled hundreds of primary colored balloons with helium and had tied them to everything.

Most of Linda's family had arrived, and a few of the neighbors were there as well. There were excited voices everywhere: children laughing and squealing, mothers calling to them to be careful or to take care of the dog, various friends and family members exclaiming over how long it had been since they had last seen each other.

Elders were seated in lawn chairs, some with large straw hats to keep the sun off their heads and out of their eyes. Their chairs were positioned in such a way that they could see nearly every activity happening nearby. As each new carload of family and friends arrived, the folks in the cars went directly to the elders to greet them first. It was a lovely tradition.

Nearly everyone had received the message about the western wear. Friends, neighbors and relatives milled about in a sea of colorful shirts, hats and neckerchiefs. Most of the children arrived adorned with cowboy hats, toting six-guns on their hips, and scuffing cowboy boots through the red PEI dirt. One little girl, Emily, was dressed like a Navajo princess. Her mother told me that the costume was Emily's idea. She wanted to represent the entire west she said.

When Casey heard the band playing again in the barn, he said, "Annie, I've got to talk to Cal about the square dance. I'll see you later." He hurried away through the group of teenagers that had finished their checker game and were now eager to join the softball game.

"You two look mighty handsome, ma'am," Barry said, as he walked up behind me.

"Wow, Barry!" I said, turning to face him. "That's a gorgeous shirt!" He had on a cherry red western shirt with mother of pearl snap buttons.

"Linda picked it up for me a couple of years ago when she took that trip to Colorado. This is the first time I've had a chance to wear it to something *western*." As he said the word western, he crooked his fingers as though he were drawing quote marks in the air.

"Now don't make fun. Linda loves doing special things like this and so do you," I scolded good-naturedly. We walked arm and arm toward Linda, who was busy handing out cold sodas and ice cream bars to a family with three young children, all with the same strawberry blonde hair. She, too, was dressed for the occasion, wearing a white short-sleeved cotton shirt with yellow polka dots, blue jean shorts, and a yellow bandana tied at her throat.

"She's all yours, Annie," Barry said, heading for the barn.

"Hi, Annie. How about helping me out here. These kids can eat ice cream faster than I can get it out of the coolers." She handed two more ice-cream bars to a woman pushing a stroller with two young boys in it. "There you go, Edna. Those boys look just like their father."

"Did you get the beans put down in the bean-hole?" I asked, as I handed sodas to a group of teenagers.

"Yes, Barry and Ed dug the hole this morning. They put enough beans in there to feed an army. And the chicken has just been put on the big barbecue." Linda's face radiated with excitement.

"Judging by what I see here, you've *got* an army to feed. Do you think there'll be more coming later?" I smiled at a little boy about four whose six-gun holster had just dropped to the ground. As he bent over to pull it back up, his hat fell off. I knelt down to help him. "Thancths," he lisped, through a gap in his teeth.

Unaware of the wardrobe malfunction that I was attending to, Linda kept right on talking. "Oh yes. There are at least thirty neighbors who aren't here yet. Most of the family has arrived, though. By the time we sit down for supper, I expect we'll have about a hundred and twenty-five." She laughed.

"Laugh if you will. If I had that many people to feed I'd be a nervous wreck!"

With a lull in the action, Linda and I sat in lawn chairs behind the soda and ice-cream stand. She wiped her face with a paper towel. "I'm used to it. Some weekends at home during snowmobile season, we feed several hundred in one morning."

"And you love it!" I exclaimed, waving at Betty who was tying the last of the balloons to the rose arbor.

"Yes, I do. So does Barry, even though he moans and groans for days beforehand about all the work we'll have when it comes time to clean up. This year, I've hired the group of teenagers that gather over at the Brown's to help me, including my own. They arrived right after you left this morning dressed in red and white shirts and blue jean shorts. One of them made special armbands to identify them as 'Ranch-hands.' I got quite a kick out of their enthusiasm." Linda was obviously delighted that everyone had gotten into the western spirit.

"The band sounds wonderful, Linda." I said, reaching for a cold bottle of water.

"Cal is a great guy, Annie. I must admit that I owe Casey a home-cooked dinner. The first thing Cal did was thank me for inviting him here. He said he hasn't played at a family gathering for quite a while and he misses it."

"Wonderful!" I laughed. "Casey will be thrilled to know he was right."

"I was right about what, Annie?" Casey had walked up behind me, put his hands on the arms of the chair and his head down next to mine so his chin was resting on my shoulder.

"The first thing Cal did when he got here was to thank Linda for inviting him here. Said he missed this kind of family get-together," I repeated.

"I knew it!" Casey exclaimed, as he stood up and started toward Linda. "Cal really is a family man. I wish we had known soon enough so we could have arranged to have his family here too. That would have been a wonderful surprise for him. So, Linda, guess you owe me that home-cooked dinner." Casey pulled her out of the chair and lifted her off the ground twirling her around in circles.

"Put me down, Casey!" Linda was as flustered as I've ever seen her. Everyone around us was chuckling. "Now listen, you'll just have to come to Smith Falls to collect on that dinner."

"You've got a deal!" Casey exclaimed.

"Isn't this just a perfect day?" I was feeling on top of the world, surrounded by good friends, laughing with the man I loved and standing on ground that seemed sacred and safe. This had to be the closest I had been in a very long time to a state of grace. God's gift was good, and I was glad to be recognizing it now as I experienced it instead of looking back and naming it later.

"By the way, what was that tune Cal was playing a few minutes ago?" I asked Casey. "I don't recall ever hearing it on any of his albums."

"I don't know, Annie. Perhaps he's got some new material to try out on this crowd," Casey replied.

"Why don't you two go mingle with the folks, Annie," Linda said as she motioned us along with her hands.

"Are you sure?" I protested.

"Yes! I'm all set here for now." She sat down again and crossed her legs.

"Barry has organized the annual tug of war over there," Casey said, as he pointed toward a large group of people who were screaming, "Go! Go! Go!"

Linda moaned, "I don't know who is the biggest kid around here, but Barry sure is in the running!"

Barry had gathered all the children, split them up so there were young and old on both teams, and then gave them a rope that crossed over a large red mud hole. When we arrived, one team was just about to pull the other into the oozing muck.

"Pull! Everyone, pull!" shouted a slim but muscular young man at the front of the line, as he leaned precariously over the mud hole. The losing team gave a mighty pull, saving him from the red muck. But in another five minutes, he was perched over the same spot. This time all of his yelling, and that of the crowd, didn't help. First, he went sliding into the mucky mess and then, one by one, his team was pulled in on top of him.

The last two or three members of the losing team, seeing that they had lost, jumped into the mud hole as well. The crowd cheered as mothers and fathers helped their slippery, slimy children out of the mire. Soon, even more people were covered with the red PEI mud that sticks to everything like thick red paint.

Barry directed the dirty but happy crew to the rose arbor where he had hung a long garden hose. He turned it on and each person stepped under it to get cleaned off. They were then ushered to the back of the barn to change their clothes.

When everyone returned, Barry made a big production about presenting the winning team with a trophy. It was an old gold cup he had received when he was younger for being the most valuable player on his high school hockey team. The inscription on the cup had long since been forgotten, as the cup was now the official winner's trophy at the Crawford Games.

In addition to the trophy, which would eventually be placed back on the mantel in the farm house and a notation made in a special book as to which team won, every child on both teams received a special button that Barry had created several years ago. The button was PEI red with the word 'winner' printed in green. He told them every year that they were all winners. This gesture especially pleased the youngest children.

After the presentations and picture-taking frenzy, Linda rang a huge cowbell signaling that it was time for supper. The elders were ushered to tables well inside the barn and were served by their grandchildren. Everyone else lined up on both sides of two long tables where the food had been spread out buffet style.

In addition to the bean-hole beans and the barbecue chicken, neighbors and family members had brought along their favorite casseroles and salads. Linda's ranch hands were busy delivering baskets of hot rolls to each table and serving pitchers of iced-tea, lemonade, water or milk along with carafes of hot coffee or tea. She had thought of everything.

Casey and I sat with Ed MacLeod and his wife Doris and their three children. Cal joined us. "Annie, Casey tells me you live in Maine. We're playing in Bangor next week. How far is that from here?" Cal asked, as he took a bite of a barbecued chicken leg.

"Bangor is about 400 miles from here," I offered. "But there's usually construction on the hundred miles of Route 9 between Calais and Bangor, so you should plan on at least two hours for that part of your trip."

"We'll probably leave here in the morning and spend some time playing golf in a little place called St. Andrew. Ever heard of it?" he asked, nibbling every bit of chicken off that drumstick.

"I sure have. It's a beautiful spot, Cal. You'll love it! St. Andrew isn't very far from the border at St. Stephens, and it's a great place to shop for a gift for your wife." I looked at Casey, and he was laughing.

"She's got you there, pardner," Casey chuckled.

"Yes," Ed MacLeod offered as he winked at me, "we have cousins who own a beautiful gift shop there. They sell hand knit wool sweaters and the like. You could probably find something for the whole family!"

"And you would be helping Ed's family, too, Cal," Casey said still laughing. "Why they could put up a big sign that says 'Cal Harper, that USA singing cowboy, shops here'."

By now we were all laughing, including Cal. 'Okay. Okay," he said. "I'll stop in. What's their name, anyway, Ed?"

"Vi and Gordon MacLeod!" Ed offered proudly. "Just tell them it was me that sent you."

The rest of the meal was spent telling stories about the Island and listening to Casey and Cal describe the action in a movie they had made together. Soon people from other tables had pulled their chairs around to listen to the two of them swap stories about horse riding and the many tricks that they had played on each other on the set of a movie filmed in Colorado.

"Well now," Cal said, "I'm full and happy. Guess it's time that I gathered up the band and started to play for the crowd."

Chairs all over the barn scraped the floor as everyone moved about so they could see the stage. Cal and the other members of the band jumped onto the stage and began tuning their guitars. Soon they were playing some of their famous songs that everyone knew. I looked around and could see people singing along with Cal as he sang one of his popular ballads.

When he had finished, someone three tables over yelled, "Can you play 'Sugar in the Gourd'?"

Before Cal could answer, his fiddle player struck up a swinging little number and within a few bars the rest of the band was accompanying him. It ended quickly with a flourish.

"Well," Cal said as he walked to the microphone, "I guess we *can* play 'Sugar in the Gourd'." Everyone laughed.

"How about 'Waltzing Through the Leaves'?" someone shouted.

Cal looked at the fiddler and shrugged. "Guess you've got us there! Is there anyone here who brought a fiddle along and is willing to help us with that one?" Cal asked.

Three men immediately stood up. The barn erupted with laughter. The three men jumped up on the stage and began to play the waltz. Soon the band joined right in playing the lovely melody through several times as each fiddler took the lead while the others harmonized. The tune was beautiful and by the time the band finished couples throughout the barn had made their way to the dance floor. As the music faded into the rafters, the dancers cheered and clapped their hands. The barn dance was off to a successful start.

Cal was thrilled. "Wow!" he said. "I better think about coming back up here and recording an album with some of you folks." Just then someone called out, "Play 'Dougals' Special!'"

The three PEI fiddlers said something to the band members, and soon they were playing a catchy tune with fiddles blazing. They kept this up for over an hour as people called out their favorite tunes. Soon someone asked for 'The Virginia Reel.'

"That's my cue," Casey said as he stood up. "I promised Linda I would call a square dance, and this is it." He bent over, kissed me on the cheek, and walked to the stage. Everyone in the place applauded as he did so. I think this embarrassed him a little as he was beginning to feel like just another neighbor instead of a movie star.

The area under the hayloft, where we had painted the big checkerboard, had been cleared of tables and chairs so people could form their squares. Soon the band and the three extra fiddlers were playing as Casey called the dance. He and Cal had rehearsed a little earlier in the afternoon, so everything worked out perfectly. The dancers loved it and were soon asking for more. Casey knew two other square dances as a result of the movie he had made with Cal, so they played both tunes. By the time they were done, the dancers were tired, and so was Casey. He stepped down off the platform and shook everyone's hand.

Then Cal stepped to the microphone to make an announcement. "Now that Casey has called the dances he promised, I have a special treat for a special lady in the audience. A few days ago when Casey called me and invited me up here, he asked if I was working on any new songs. As it turned out, I was right in the middle of putting some thoughts together about something that had been on my mind for quite a while. I asked Casey what he had in mind, and it seems his ideas were pretty close to mine. So I finished up the song, just last night as a matter of fact, and we're going to play it now for a special lady. Annie, this song is for you. It's called 'If I Hadn't Met You.' Annie and Casey, please come up here to start the dancing."

I was shocked and speechless. Casey was at my side almost instantly, helping me to stand up. I looked up at him with tears in my eyes.

"I love you, Annie," he said. "Can I have this dance?"

"Yes. Oh, yes," I said, as I took his hand and followed him out to the checkerboard dance floor. Just as we turned to hold each other, Cal began to sing his new song. Casey must have heard the words earlier in the afternoon, because he sang them softly in my ear as we moved to the rhythm of the music. The words expressed all the emotions that we had felt over these last two weeks.

By the time Cal finished his new song, the dance floor was filled with couples singing the chorus along with him. I was in tears, as the meaning of the words washed over me. Casey hugged and kissed me. Everyone around us applauded. Then the crowd asked Cal to play the song again.

This time Casey held me at arm's length, so he could look into my eyes as he sang along with Cal. No woman on the face of the earth could have been as happy as I was at that moment. Saying 'I love you' wasn't enough to tell him how much that moment meant to me. When Cal finished singing, he asked me how I liked the song. "Annie, what do you think?"

I could hardly talk, so I just gave him two thumbs up. Casey put his arm around me as he looked up at Cal and mouthed a silent "Thank you, buddy." We walked out through the front door of the barn into the light of a perfect sunset.

"Casey, thank you for that song. No one has ever done anything like that for me. Thank you, thank you, thank you," I said over and over as I kissed his cheek and his neck and finally his lips.

"Annie, I meant every word. If I hadn't met you, I would be a terribly lonely man. Come on, let's go sit over there under the tree."

As we sat down on a bench that Barry had built at the base of the tree, Casey reached into his pocket and pulled out a jeweler's box. "I hope you like this, Annie."

The box contained a ring with a half-carat square cut emerald surrounded on both sides by small diamonds. As Casey slipped the ring on my finger, he told me that he had ordered this ring from a local jeweler in Summerside, and had picked it up on his way to the ferry to meet Cal.

"Casey, it's a perfect fit! And emerald is my birthstone!" I said, holding my hand out before me to admire the ring.

"I know, Annie," he said, as he wrapped his arms around me and kissed me tenderly "I love you."

"I'm glad you do, Casey. I love you, too." The ring sparkled in the colored lights Linda had draped through the trees. "Let's go say our goodbyes to these good folks and head on back to the cottage," I suggested.

"What are we waiting for?" He pulled me to my feet, grabbed my hand and ran toward the barn, pulling me along behind him. I was completely out of breath by the time we came to an abrupt stop at the doors, and walked in as though we were just strolling by.

"Here they are!" someone shouted.

Linda was at the microphone thanking everyone who had helped clean out the barn. She had just asked if anyone knew where we were.

"It's a good thing we came back when we did," I whispered to Casey. He laughed and waved to Linda.

"And I want to thank Casey MacDonald for arranging to have Cal Harper and his band play for us this year. I don't know how the rest of you feel, but wouldn't it be great if they came back next year?" Linda was on a roll. Everyone clapped and hollered their approval. "I hope you all come back next year with your families as our guests for a week!" she continued, directing her remarks to the band members. "There's plenty of room in our front yard for your buses and trucks and because of Fred's handiwork we know there's enough electricity out there for a motor home park!" She was laughing as she thanked Fred for his help.

"We'll put your reunion on our schedule, Linda," Cal said, stepping up to the microphone next to her. "I hope it all works out. We've had a wonderful time with you folks, and I was serious about coming back to record some of your down home favorites with you fiddle players. Perhaps we can do all of that at the same time next year." Cal was serious about his music and serious about what he was saying to the fiddlers.

"Well, Annie, looks like you and I have started something," Casey said, as everyone in the barn started clapping and stomping their feet for one more song. "Will you join me here again next year?"

"Yes, but I hope we find a way to get together long before then." With my arm around his waist, I leaned into him.

"Don't worry about that," he said, looking down at me. "We will. Now let's say goodbye to these kind folks and get on home for a good night's sleep."

As people had their last dance to Cal's music, Casey and I waved goodbye to him and then found Linda and Barry.

"Linda, we've got to get up early tomorrow morning, so we're going to say good night," Casey said as he hugged her. "Thanks for everything and thanks again for introducing me to the greatest woman on earth."

Linda smiled at him and said, "Take good care of her, Casey. She's been through too much to get hurt again."

Casey hugged her again and shook hands with Barry. He took my hand as we walked out of the barn and across the meadow to the cottage.

We made love on the old sofa in the light of the fading sunset reflecting in the front windows. The passion overtook us quickly and carried us to a wondrous place far, far away. We were together and would be forever. Somehow. Somewhere.

Part Four

The New Song

Chapter 16

August –1993

The irritating sound of crows calling to one another woke me just after five. A fine mist had settled over the Island during the night creating a cool, muggy atmosphere. I cannot see the New Brunswick shoreline because of the foggy veil between here and there. The cottage is damp. The fire in the woodstove crackles and snaps happily warming the room and my heart.

Casey is still sleeping soundly. Some time in the night Casey had carried me into the bedroom where he could stretch out and sleep more comfortably. This vacation has been good for him…a time to release the stress of a frenzied career…a time to see what life has to offer from a different perspective. This time has been good for me as well for many of the same reasons.

My ring shines in the lamplight. I love it. That he gave it so much thought is very special. And Cal's song, a beautiful lyrical melody, plays in my head. Cal told me that he had written most of the words, but was looking for a particular line for the chorus when Casey called and gave him the idea. Evidently Casey said, "If I hadn't met Annie, Cal, I don't know what I would do." That was the phrase Cal had needed. They were both happy with it…Cal expecting it to be a hit, and Casey, glad he could give something back to him for making the trip. Of course, that song is already a big hit for me.

What am I going to do when Casey's plane leaves on Monday? Will that awful feeling of emptiness that threatens to pull me back into the dark pit of depression return?

No! Not this time! God truly has put a new song in my mouth, both the one Cal and Casey wrote, and my own. I've been singing that new song for the last two weeks…a song of wholeness and well-being. Somehow, I'll find the courage to sing it back home where friends and family can hear it too.

♪♪♪

I jumped when I heard the telephone ring and automatically looked at the clock. It was six-thirty.

"Who on earth could be calling here this early?" I whispered, as I picked up the receiver. "Hello?"

"Hello. Is Annie York there, please?" A strong, female voice spoke to me over the din of distant sirens and closing doors.

"This is she," I said, beginning to tremble. Who was this strange woman who knew my name and yet was calling so early in the morning? I looked into the bedroom and saw Casey coming toward me, a puzzled expression on his face. He had jumped out of bed at the sound of the early morning alarm and brought a blanket to me, wrapping it around my shoulders to warm me. It didn't help. I knew something was terribly wrong.

"Miss York, this is Dr. Wade in New York. Your name was given to me by Millie Carter."

The rush of adrenalin propelled me off of the sofa. "Millie? Is she all right?" I asked. The blanket dropped to the floor.

"No, Miss York, she isn't. Her father lost his temper with her last night, and I'm afraid she's badly hurt. Her mother tried to intervene. She was hurt as well. We don't expect her to live."

"You don't expect *who* to live?" I asked, beginning to panic. By now Casey was pacing back and forth trying to understand what I was hearing on the other end of the line.

"We don't expect Mrs. Carter to live, Miss York." But before I heard her words, my knees buckled, and I dropped to the floor. Casey helped me to the sofa and took the phone from me.

"Hello. This is Casey MacDonald. I'm a friend of Miss York's and a friend to Millie. What has happened?" Casey's voice was deep and stern. He continued to pace back and forth as he talked, looking down at me with great concern. His eyes had turned a dark shade of blue.

"Millie is going to be all right, Mr. MacDonald, but she's badly hurt," the doctor explained. Casey said later that it was the professional tone in the doctor's voice that had calmed his rage.

"How bad is it?" he asked, his voice now a mere whisper. He slumped down onto the sofa next to me, tears marking his cheeks.

"She has a broken collar bone, a broken arm and severe bruises to her head and back. He threw her down a flight of stairs," the doctor replied.

Casey took a quick, deep breath and said, "Oh, my God!" Of course, this reaction to what he was hearing from the doctor caused me to panic even more. I put my head down between my knees and breathed as deeply and slowly as possible, while I tried to concentrate on what I was hearing.

"I am most concerned, however, about her mental health. Her mother is here at the hospital as well, in a deep coma. We don't expect her to live."

"No!" Casey exploded off the sofa to a standing position. "Is her father in jail?"

"Yes, he is, Mr. MacDonald. I'm calling you and Miss York because there doesn't seem to be anyone else who can help this child. We found your names and numbers in a little pouch she carried in her pocket. I was sure you would want to know about this."

"You're damned right we would want to know," he yelled into the phone. Then he composed himself saying, "I'm sorry to yell, Dr. Wade. We both love that little girl like she was our own. You tell Millie that we'll be there just as soon as we can get there."

"It's okay, Mr. MacDonald, I understand completely. Come as soon as you can. Millie needs all the support you can give her right now."

"Thank you. But wait! Can we talk to Millie now?" Casey was calming down and beginning to think more clearly.

"No, I'm afraid not. She's still in recovery. She had a slight concussion, so we're monitoring her carefully. I expect she'll be taken to her room some time later this morning."

The doctor gave Casey the name and address of the hospital and her phone number so we could call back when we knew our traveling plans.

"Thank you, Dr. Wade. We'll be there just as soon as we arrange transportation."

Casey hung up the phone and then sat down next to me on the sofa. I was crying hysterically and saying over and over, "She's going to die. She's going to die. That bastard killed them both."

"Annie, honey, Millie will be okay." He held me close to him and whispered in my ear. "Millie is alive, Annie. She's going to be okay." He talked very slowly, as he held me out away from him and looked directly into my eyes. "Do you hear me, Annie? Millie is okay. She's going to be okay."

"She is? Are you sure? The doctor said that she wasn't expected to live." I shivered.

"No, honey, her mother isn't expected to live. Millie is going to be okay." Casey held me again as we both cried with outrage at the brutal act, and with relief that Millie was alive. "Annie," he said calmly, "we've got to leave right now. The doctor said that she has Millie heavily sedated, but she'll need us with her when she wakes up."

"Will you call Linda?" I asked, pulling the blanket around me. "I don't think I could tell her without getting hysterical again."

"I'll do better than that. I'll run over there to tell them and while I'm at it I'll check in with Cal. I think he'll be able to help us."

Still buttoning his shirt, Casey kissed me, urged me to get ready to leave, and hurried out the back door. The warm shower felt good, washing away both the tears of anguish and the sweet smell of our lovemaking. My heart ached for Millie. I couldn't stop trembling. By the time I got dressed, Linda was pounding on the back door.

"Annie! Annie! Are you all right?" She came in and hugged me, great sobs coming from deep within her. "I'm so sorry, honey."

Casey was right behind her, going directly to the bedroom to pick up the last of our suitcases. He took everything out to the back door where Barry was waiting to carry the bags to the car.

"Linda, I can't bear to think about how much she hurts. My heart is breaking," I said as I cried in her arms.

"I know, Annie. I'm just sick about all this." She reached out to Casey and took his hand as she kept her other arm around me. "Now I don't want either of you to worry about anything. Barry and I will take care of closing your cottage. Casey, just leave your car at the airport, and we'll see to it that it gets back to the rental agency in Charlottetown. I had no idea what she was talking about, but then Cal arrived.

"Annie, I'm awfully sorry about your little girl," he said, hugging me. I was touched by his words. Still holding me, Cal turned to Casey and said, "Everything is all arranged, Casey. Your flight will be at Summerside in a couple of hours."

Casey shook his hand and hugged him. "Thanks, bro, for being there for us." I didn't know it at the time, but Cal had called New York where he kept his private jet while he was traveling in the northeast. The band had needed some additional equipment for the Bangor performance, so with great luck the plane had already arrived in Maine. The pilot thought he could get to the Island airport in just a few hours.

When I understood what was happening, I couldn't speak. With one arm over my shoulder, Cal hugged me and whispered, "I know, Annie. Our children are God's best gift to us. Go on now, and love her back to health." I kissed him and turned toward Linda who took my hand and walked with me to the car.

She embraced me, letting my body slump against hers, and rubbed my back as she breathed words of encouragement into my aching soul. "It's going to be okay, honey. It's just got to be okay." She fished a handkerchief out of her pocket and gently wiped the tears from my cheeks.

"Give the kids a hug, okay?" I croaked, blowing my nose.

She held my arm, as I settled into the front seat beside Casey, kissed me on the cheek and closed the door. Casey nodded to Linda as he put the car in gear and drove us out of our dream into the nightmare of our life.

As I looked back through the rear window to wave, I saw the basket on the back seat. Linda had made sandwiches for us, filled a thermos with coffee, and added a half dozen of her doughnuts. There was a fresh-picked pink rose tied to the handle.

"We're lucky to have such good friends, Casey," I said, as he put his arm around me and pulled me closer to him.

"Yes, we are, Annie. And we're lucky to have each other." He pressed his cheek against the top of my head, then straightened himself as he concentrated on the road ahead.

"I love you," I said in response.

The road from West Point to the major highway that crosses the Island twists and turns around cow pastures and potato fields for fifteen miles or more. When we finally turned south on the main highway, I asked about Millie's injuries. "Casey, did the doctor tell you anything about her bruises?"

He tightened his grip and took a deep breath. "She has a broken collar bone, Annie. That's awfully painful."

"Oh, God," I sobbed.

"There's more." He was silent for a few moments before he continued. "She has a broken arm and bruises on her head and back. The doctor didn't explain any further than that, but I think we had better be prepared to see a badly bruised little girl." He remained silent for a moment, and then added, "I hope they put her father away for a very long time."

"I'm going to try to get temporary custody, Casey." The words were barely audible, but Casey heard them.

"If Mrs. Carter dies, Millie is certainly going to need someone she can trust. And she surely does trust and love you, honey. I'll help you any way I can."

"Thank you," I whispered, as I rested my head on his shoulder. "I'm so tired right now. I wish I could just crawl back into bed and sleep for three days. Maybe when I woke up all this would have been just a bad dream."

When we arrived at the airport, a messenger told us that the pilot of Cal's plane had radioed ahead that he would be landing in about an hour. We piled our luggage near a door that faced the tarmac and gave the car keys to the messenger. Barry and Ed were driving out later in the day to take the rental car to Charlottetown.

We sat down to wait. "Is the fog going to keep them from landing here, Casey?" I asked, looking toward the airfield. The glow of the morning sun penetrated the bank of low clouds that hung over the far end of the runway.

"No, I don't think so. Cal's plane is equipped with the latest gear," he said, looking out the window, "and the fog doesn't seem to be too bad here anyway." He continued to pace back and forth in front of the large plate glass windows.

The minute hand on my watch seemed to stop, but then I checked it every twenty seconds or so while we waited for the plane. The airport was quiet on an early Sunday morning, with little activity to captivate our interest. We both jumped when the door suddenly opened, and the pilot stood there asking if we were the couple going to Albany.

"Yes, we are. I'm Casey MacDonald, and this is Annie York."

"Hi, Casey, Mike Hulsey," the pilot said, as he extended his hand. "The plane is being refueled right now, but we'll be ready to go in about twenty minutes. Why don't you two follow me, and I'll get you on board and comfortable." He picked up some of our bags and headed out the door. Casey picked up the remaining bags, and I carried Linda's basket of love.

We made ourselves comfortable in large, padded chairs and buckled the seat belts. True to his word, just twenty minutes later, the pilot announced from the cockpit that we would be taking off.

Our flight to Albany was smooth and uneventful. I fell asleep soon after we took off and woke when Casey put his hand on mine and said, "Wake up, Annie. We're going to land in a few minutes."

"I can't believe I fell asleep," I said apologetically.

"You're emotionally drained, honey. I'm glad you could get some rest now. Once we get to the hospital, God only knows when you'll be able to relax again."

"I'm scared, Casey," I said suddenly. "I'm frightened of seeing Millie all broken and bruised. She's too young to have to go through this. I don't know if I can be strong enough for her."

"You can, Annie. I know you can." His grip on my hand was reassuring. "We'll go to her room together. I'm sure that Dr. Wade will be there as well. If there's any problem for you, just squeeze my hand, and we'll step out. Okay?"

"Thank you, Casey." Our kiss was soft and warm. "I love you."

"And I love you, Annie. We'll be all right. Millie needs our strength."

As soon as the plane landed in Albany, we taxied to a special gate. Since Cal had thought of everything, there was a car waiting for us there to take us directly to the hospital. Casey used the cellular phone stored in a case by the door to call Dr. Wade.

"I'm glad you're here this quickly, Mr. MacDonald," Dr. Wade replied. "Millie has just been taken to her room from recovery. We kept her there under sedation as long as we could. She's in room 512 now. When you get off the elevator on the fifth floor, just turn right and follow the signs. Your presence will make a significant difference." She paused, then continued,

"I'm afraid her mother died soon after I spoke with you earlier this morning."

"I'm sorry to hear that," Casey said solemnly. "We should be there in about twenty minutes."

"What?" I asked looking at the frown on Casey's face.

"Mrs. Carter died." His words hung in the air.

There were no words to express what we were feeling. Mrs. Carter had tried to be a buffer between her husband and her daughter. This time she had given her life doing it.

Millie was still semi-conscious when we opened her door. Dr. Wade was shining a small flashlight in her eyes, lifting each eyelid as she did. She looked up when we walked into the room.

"Good morning," she whispered. "Millie is waking up, but it will take a few minutes. Her speech will be slurry at first, but she'll be clear-headed in a few minutes."

Millie looked terribly small in the big bed. The hot pink cast was gone. Her upper body and right arm were immobilized in a strangely shaped cast that held her arm in front of and away from her chest. A steel rod protruded from the front of the cast connecting the upper part of the body cast to her wrist. Both her eyes were black and there was a bandage over her right ear that extended behind head.

"How long will she be in that cast?" I asked, not knowing what else to say.

"The break was a messy one, I'm afraid," she replied, making a notation on the chart. "She'll be in this cast for at least four weeks. Then we'll see how the bones have mended. We may be able to remove it, but if we do, we'll probably want to strap her arm down and wrap her up to keep everything immobile for another few weeks. We'll just have to wait and see when the time comes," the doctor said, without taking her eyes off Millie. "She'll need extensive physical therapy for her arm and shoulder, but I'm more concerned about her spirit."

"And so are we, Dr. Wade," Casey said. "We're prepared to do whatever is necessary to help her.

Millie whimpered and opened her eyes. She looked around the room, her eyes bright with fear. The doctor moved away, so I could stand near the bed. When Millie looked up and saw me, a faint smile brightened her bruised face. "Annie? Is that you?" she asked. Her voice was weak and hoarse.

"Yes, I'm right here," I whispered, wondering where I could touch her. "I love you, Millie, and I'm going to stay right here with you until you're all better." I leaned over the bed and kissed her tenderly on the forehead.

She shifted her focus, first toward the doctor, and then toward the trembling man standing at the end of her bed. "Casey? Are you here, too?" she asked, her voice gaining a little strength.

"Yes, honey, I'm right here." He went to the other side of the bed and tried to kiss her, but he couldn't negotiate past the cast. Millie's giggle broke the awful tension. Dr. Wade slipped silently out the door.

When I took Millie's hand in mine, she began to cry. "Oh, Annie, my Daddy got awfully mad at me." Her anguish came from deep within her, shaking her body and making her cough.

"Shhh, Millie. I'm right here." I leaned over her and cradled her as much as possible. I put my head down on the pillow near hers and whispered in her left ear as she continued to cry. "Shhh, honey. Shhh. You'll be okay. I'm right here."

"Don't leave me, Annie. I'm so scared." Tears rolled down her cheeks and joined with mine on the pillow.

"I'm not going to leave you, Millie. I'm going to stay right here with you. I love you, honey." I held her and told her that I loved her over and over until she calmed down. My back was breaking. Casey stood behind me, rubbing my back in an effort to help.

"We're going to have to get you a stool, Annie," he said, looking around the room.

"That would be wonderful. Perhaps they have one at the nurse's desk." I straightened up and stretched feeling the muscles ease somewhat from the tension.

Casey left for a moment. While he was gone, Millie asked me about her mother.

"Annie, is my Mommy okay?" As she asked the question, her blue eyes glistened with tears. The horrible black and green around her eyes was an all too vivid indication of the torture she must have suffered at the hands of her father. I shuddered.

I didn't know what Millie remembered or what she had seen and was concerned that telling her so soon after waking up that her mother was dead would be too much of a shock. I needed to talk to Dr. Wade before saying anything definite. "Your mother was hurt badly, too, Millie," I whispered, leaning over so that my head was near hers on the pillow. The voices in my head screamed, and yet my own voice was strangely calm. "She's in another room down the hall, so we'll have to ask Dr. Wade about her when she comes back. Okay?" I'll never know how I managed to keep my composure. The child trusted me so completely that she just whispered, "Okay," and closed her eyes.

When Casey opened the door, I put my finger to my mouth indicating his need to be quiet. He had found a stool. He placed it beside the bed, and I sat down. The relief was instant. Even though Millie was sound asleep, she had a tight grip on my hand.

"Did she say anything?" Casey asked.

"She asked about her mother," I explained quietly, trying to hold back the tears. "I didn't think I should say anything until we had a chance to talk to Dr. Wade."

Casey nodded his agreement. "I'll go find her and talk with her about it."

"Good," I whispered as I looked back at Millie. I put my head down on the bed and prayed. I continued to pray silently until Casey returned with Dr. Wade. She stood beside the bed and carefully released Millie's grip on my hand. She took Millie's pulse, wrote a note on the chart, and said, "She's asleep, Annie. Let's go outside to talk."

"No. No," I protested. "I told her I would stay with her."

"I'll get a nurse to come in. Okay?"

"No, really. I can't leave her. I promised her I would stay right here." I looked back at Millie, hoping I had not disturbed her.

"Annie," Dr. Wade said, putting her hands on my shoulders and urging me to stand, "Millie will sleep for several hours. The sedatives that we gave her this morning are still working." She looked at Casey for agreement.

Casey nodded and took my hand. "Annie, we can ask a nurse to sit with Millie for a few minutes while we talk to Dr. Wade about Mrs. Carter. It would be a lot better to do that somewhere else, don't you think?"

"You're both right, but I'm going to stay right here until the nurse arrives," I said stubbornly.

Dr. Wade smiled and left the room, returning shortly with a nurse. "Let's go down the hall, Annie," she said as we left the room. "No one wants to be very far away from their child," she continued, as she led the way, "so the hospital created an area on this floor where parents can rest and grab a quick bite to eat." Dr. Wade seemed proud of the new space, describing the various areas where parents could rest or eat or play with visiting children. I really wasn't paying much attention to her. I just wanted to know how we were going to tell Millie that her mother had died saving her life.

"Dr. Wade, how are we going to tell Millie about all this?" I asked as we sat down at a red plastic table.

"Has she asked about her yet?" she replied, removing her glasses and pinching her nose.

"Yes. It was the first thing she wanted to know," I said, looking at Casey.

"What did you tell her?" She looked concerned.

"I told her that her mother was hurt badly and that she was in another room in the hospital. That was okay, wasn't it?" I was beginning to panic.

"Yes," she said quickly, observing my agitation. She leaned forward and patted my arm to reassure me. "You did the right thing, Annie. We have to be very careful that we tell Millie the truth."

"I agree," I said, "but that was the best I could do." I sat back defensively.

"That's the best any of us could do for now, but I think we had better wait another day or two for the whole truth."

"Millie is a brave little girl, doctor," Casey said, shifting his weight in the hard plastic chair. "She's remarkably mature for her age. She's already been through more than most adults."

"Yes, I know. Still, I would like to wait at least one more day before we tell her about her mother," she said, checking her notes on Millie's chart. "She's had severe trauma to her body, and she's still got some signs of concussion. I would like to wait until she's a little more alert." She looked up at each of us. "Are you folks in agreement with this?"

"We'll do whatever you think is best for Millie," I said, looking to Casey for agreement.

He nodded, then frowned. "What's under that bandage on her ear, doctor?" he asked.

"When she fell down the stairs, she rolled down on her right side. That's why the breaks and most of the bruises are on that side. Her ear hit something on the way down and was torn away from her head." Dr. Wade took my hand, noticing that I was turning white. "Annie, are you okay?" she asked.

"I don't know. I feel awfully sick to my stomach. I think I'm going to faint." My body felt cold and clammy, and I was dizzy.

"Put your head down between your legs and breathe slowly," the doctor ordered. Once she had helped me move into that position, she prepared a cold, wet towel and put it on the back of my neck. Casey crouched in front of me, sitting on his heels, his hands on my knees.

"I'm sorry to be so blunt," she said taking my pulse, "but you two really need to know what has happened to Millie. I know how difficult it is to hear such things, and believe me, it's difficult for me as well. But we don't have anyone else who can take responsibility for the child."

"Dr Wade, how can we legally do that?" Casey asked.

"Well, honestly, you can't. We'll have to contact the Department of Human Services in the morning and ask them to give you temporary custody."

I was feeling better and sat up. Dr. Wade took my pulse once more. Casey sat down in the chair beside me. The room had stopped spinning, but I continued to feel nauseous. The terrible dream I had about Millie on PEI flashed through my mind. The image of her falling down the stairs and catching her ear on a rusty nail was just as grotesque as the image in that dream. I shivered. "I would like to take Millie back to Maine with me when she's well enough," I said. "What do you think, Dr. Wade?"

"I was hoping you could do that, Annie. The change will be good for her. If she doesn't have to go back to the scene of the violence, so much the better." Dr. Wade smiled as she talked with us. "I'll help you in any way I can."

"How much do you think she'll remember?" Casey asked.

"That's difficult to say until we have a chance to talk with her. The police told me that they believe that Millie's father beat her and threw her down the stairs. And they think that's when her mother attacked him. That's when he hit her. She fell back and hit her head on the corner of a metal case."

"My God," I moaned.

"One of our finest neurosurgeons operated, but he couldn't save her. The damage was massive." She stood, picked up Millie's chart and put it under her arm. "Annie, I would like to prescribe a cup of hot tea and something to eat." She turned to Casey. "You'll find everything you need over there," she said pointing to a kitchenette. "I need to visit another patient right now, but I'll be back in about half an hour." She saw the look of concern on my face. "Don't worry, Annie. Millie will sleep soundly for several hours. If she starts to stir at all the nurse will ring the buzzer and someone will come to find you."

Casey busied himself in the kitchenette making tea and a couple of ham and cheese sandwiches. Several overstuffed sofas and chairs were arranged living-room style at one end of the room. I moved to the more comfortable area and picked up a gardening magazine. As I mindlessly flipped through it, I thought about how quickly lives change. Just a few months ago I had thought that my life was over, and now I was hoping to take a child home with me.

"Annie, honey, try to eat something," Casey said, as he put a tray on the table in front of me. The tea was hot and nourishing. As we ate the sandwiches, we formulated more questions for Dr. Wade.

Brushing bread crumbs off his pant leg, Casey asked, "I wonder if she's seen the x-rays from Dr. Green?"

"That may be why she's been so supportive about helping me take custody," I answered.

While we waited for Dr. Wade to return, I hurried down the hall to check on Millie. When I opened the door, the nurse looked up, smiled and whispered, "She's okay, she's sleeping." Satisfied, I returned to the waiting area. Casey was thumbing through a sports magazine. "Is she okay?" he asked, tossing the magazine on the table.

"Yes, she's still sleeping." I sat down next to him. "I've never liked waiting anywhere, Casey, much less in a hospital. But I guess as long as she's sleeping, her body is mending." Casey put his arm around me, gently nudging my head onto his shoulder. That area of the large room was quiet, dimly lit, and very peaceful until an ambulance siren wailed in the distance. As it got closer I said, "I wonder if that's the same ambulance that brought Millie here."

Casey's arm tightened around me. "Annie, honey, she's going to be okay."

The waiting room door swept open, and Dr. Wade appeared. She walked briskly toward us, the corners of her lab coat fluttering with each step. "I just checked on Millie. She's doing beautifully. I expect she'll sleep another few hours."

"We've got a few more questions, doctor. Have you got time now to answer them?" Casey asked, leaning forward. Dr. Wade dragged one of the hard plastic chairs closer to us and sat down.

"Have you seen the x-rays that Dr. Green sent you from PEI?" I asked.

"Yes. I looked at them before we operated on her. Luckily my secretary remembered the name when I was called last night. As a matter of fact, all of this was very fortunate for Millie. I wasn't expected back until today, but we took an early flight Saturday morning. I called my office when we got home to ask about any emergencies. When the hospital called my secretary later, asking when I would be back, she told them that I had already arrived."

"Thank God," I said softly as I took a deep breath.

"Do you have any idea what triggered Mr. Carter's temper?" Casey asked.

"Not really. But in cases like this, the cause of the explosion could be anything, and usually something that sounds fairly trivial. He'll never be able to hurt that little girl again, though," Dr. Wade said.

"This never should have happened in the first place. Why isn't there some sort of system that identifies children who make repeat visits to a doctor?" Casey asked.

"There is, Casey. Most pediatricians are alert for this type of abuse. Unfortunately, Mrs. Carter must have taken Millie to a different doctor each time something happened. She must have lied each time as well when she was asked to fill out Millie's medical history. Unfortunately she got away with it until Dr. Green noticed something that wasn't written down and caught something in the x-rays."

We looked up as a young couple opened the door and looked around the room. They seemed bewildered and lost. Dr. Wade excused herself and went to them. She spoke to them in hushed tones and led them to the kitchenette.

When she returned to her seat, she continued her conversation as though the interruption had not occurred. "We haven't seen Millie in my office for about two years. Quite honestly, I was surprised when I was called to operate."

"When we were in Canada, I asked a friend to check on Mr. Carter through the Department of Human Services. They gave him your name." Casey had leaned forward, thoroughly engaged in conversation and eager to understand the sequence of events.

"Really? That's interesting," Dr. Wade responded. "DHS must have requested Millie's records from my office some time in the recent past. I'll have to check with my secretary about that." She frowned. "We've never treated Millie for any broken bones. If DHS was called in to investigate the Carters they would have requested a doctor's name for their records. Mrs. Carter would have felt safe giving them mine."

"What a mess," Casey said, exhaling as though he had been punched in the stomach.

"Indeed. There are safeguards built into the system to protect the children, but unfortunately, sometimes," she sighed, "sometimes something falls through the cracks. If I had been here when those x-rays came in last week, we would have put two and two together then and I would have been in touch with DHS immediately. With Dr. Green's testimony and the x-rays DHS could have gotten Mr. Carter out of there right away."

Casey turned white. "You mean we could have done something last week?" he asked as a red glow spread across his neck and face.

"Yes. But before you start blaming yourself," she added quickly, "you must know that you would have had a hard time of it without a doctor on this end. And I understand that you really had no other doctor's name but mine."

"That's right," he said. "The other doctor's name was false."

"If you had called DHS, I'm afraid they might not have done anything anyway until they called me. We'll never know," she said as she reached over to Casey and put her hand on his. "Please, just concentrate on Millie today and forevermore. There's nothing any of us can do about last night, but there's a great deal we can do about tomorrow."

"You're right, doctor," I said, patting Casey's knee.

Casey took my hand and kissed it. "God, Annie, I feel awful," he said.

"I know, but let's listen to Dr. Wade. Perhaps when all this calms down, we can make a difference in Millie's future. We both love her and she loves us. In time, I think she'll be able to adjust to living in Maine. Don't you?"

I knew that our conversation about Millie's welfare was putting stress on the future for Casey and me, but worrying about that now wasn't going to help Millie. Talking out loud about living in Maine, however, was bringing reality closer than either of us had allowed over the past two weeks.

Dr. Wade sensed the slight tension. "I think the two of you need some time to talk about all this. I'll go back to Millie's room and check on her. If she's awake, I'll come right back. Otherwise, I'll ask the nurse to stay there with her until you return."

"Thank you, Dr. Wade," we said in unison. Before she left, I hurried across the room and hugged her. "I keep saying thank you, Dr. Wade. I really don't know how to express my appreciation for all you've done for us."

"I know, Annie. I have three children of my own. This kind of trauma is horrible and truly unimaginable. I see too much of it." She paused and was about to say something else, then turned and left.

"What a wonderful doctor!" I exclaimed, as the door closed behind her.

"That she is, Annie. Millie is a fortunate little girl, in that respect anyway." He took my hand as I sat down beside him. "Annie, you talked about taking Millie back to Maine. Is that what you want to do?" he asked, looking into my eyes.

"I think it's the best course of action for her, don't you? Where would we go otherwise?"

He hesitated, still looking into my eyes. "The two of you could come out to California and live with me."

I sighed and leaned back against the cushions. "Casey, you know I would love to do that, but that would be an enormous adjustment for me let alone for Millie. I wouldn't know anyone there, and, quite frankly, I would feel terribly disconnected from my family and friends. I have a feeling that I'm going to need to be stronger than that for that little girl." I paused and looked up at him. He had laid his head back and closed his eyes. "Casey?"

"I hear you," he said, opening his eyes and staring at the ceiling. "I just don't like what you're saying."

"I'm sorry, but this is the conversation we would have had at the lake tonight."

"I know," he said. "I was looking forward to going there with you." He sat up and turned to me. "I guess I was looking forward to a lot of things."

"I'm not saying that I don't love you or that I don't want to be with you. I do. But I'm going to be much more in control in my own home and around my family and friends. I believe that Millie is going to need that stability, and I'm going to need their help."

"You're right, of course," Casey said, as he kissed me and held me close to him.

"Can we just believe that we'll find a way to see each other over the next few months and leave it at that for now?" I asked.

"Yes, you can certainly believe that," he said leaning back and looking into my eyes. "And let me tell you something else. When I leave, don't be thinking that I'm back in my own environment and have forgotten all about you. That will never happen. I love you - deeply, passionately, and forever. I know this is true, and I know it will be true tomorrow and next week and all the days thereafter." He hugged me once more. I had listened to every word trying to memorize them so I could call them back after he had left. He knew me well. I would doubt everything. "If you have any problems, and I mean *any* problems, you call me."

"Okay," I said leaning back, "but I'm not going to feel comfortable calling you, Casey. I can't really express just why, but you need to know that your calling me will be much better."

"I'm glad you told me that, Annie. When I get involved in a new project, I barely take time to eat. That was one of the problems I had with Kate. Weeks would pass and I might not talk to her or the kids. Of course, when I was immersed in the project, I had no idea that weeks had passed. Maybe she felt like you do. I never thought of that." He stopped talking a minute, lost in thought. I waited for him to continue.

He leaned forward and put his elbows on his knees. As he stared down into his hands, he spoke softly. "Annie, this has to be different'"

"What has to be different?" I asked, wanting him to name it.

"Our relationship," he said quickly, turning toward me.

"Our relationship is different. Now, we're going to have to work hard at maintaining all the aspects of it that make it different. The Island was a place that held us suspended in time. Everything up there supported us and helped us to feel good about each other and ourselves. The stress of our life back here in the states was forgotten for a short time while we had the time to get to know each other. If you think about it, we're awfully fortunate. Linda and Barry could have reacted very differently."

"If they had, would it have made a difference?" he asked.

"Truthfully? It might have. But they did support both of us. Barry really likes you," I said kissing him and chuckling as I thought about Barry and Casey whooping it up over the cribbage game.

"I like both of them, and I like what they've done with their lives," he said, relaxing.

"Linda has been a terrific friend. At first she was very worried about me, cautioning me every chance she could about falling in love with you. But it didn't take her long to realize that I had fallen in love with you. Then she worried about the time when you would leave." I looked around the room and noticed a telephone on the opposite wall. "You know, I should call her right now. I'm sure she's thinking the worst. I know I would be."

"Here," Casey said taking a card from his wallet, "use this calling card. And say hello for me."

When Linda answered the phone, I leaned against the wall for support as I told her about Millie's injuries. Both of us cried when I told her that Millie's mother had died trying to save her life. She agreed that Millie would be happy in Maine and offered to stay with us for a while if I needed her. I thanked her and told her I would call later when I had more information.

"Everything okay?" Casey asked, looking up at me.

"I guess. She's just as shaken by this as we are. I told her I'd call her later when we've got more information." I curled up next to him hoping the warmth of his body would help me relax.

"I've been thinking about our conversation while you were talking to Linda, and you're right, Annie, our relationship has been different. But it's important that you understand how intense my life is when I'm working on a film. I wish I could say that I will call you every day, but that just won't happen. I don't want to make a promise that I know I can't keep. Do you understand?" He tightened his grip.

"Yes, I do," I said, looking up at him. "And thank you for being so honest with me. I've always had problems with expectations. Expecting my father to come visit us and waiting and waiting only to be disappointed weekend after weekend. It's no fun."

He kissed the top of my head. "I know, Annie, more than you realize. But you'll have to keep reminding me, okay?"

"I can do that, but if you rely on me and don't take responsibility for this yourself, we'll have a problem. I can't continue to be hurt over and over waiting for your call and then forgive you every time just because you say you're sorry. I need you to think about how that hurts."

"I understand."

"Do you really? Or are you just saying that?" I pulled away from him as I pressed him for his answer.

"No, I really do understand," he said, putting his hand up as though he was asking me to halt. "But you'll have to give me a little slack in the beginning. My work is consuming, and I immerse myself in it. When I take on a new character, there are some weeks when we work long hours, and I try not to let go of the character even when we stop filming. I don't get much sleep then anyway, so it's just as easy to think of myself in character for long stretches of time. And in those times, I probably won't call you."

The door opened and Dr. Wade suddenly appeared. "Millie's waking up, Annie," she said and disappeared just as suddenly.

Casey and I jumped up and hurried to the room. When we entered, Millie was looking around for me. "Annie, are you here?" she asked. Her voice sounded much stronger.

"Yes, honey, I'm right here." I stood by the bed and took her hand. "How're you feeling?"

"Okay, I guess. My shoulder feels funny though, and I can't hear everything the nurses say." She looked puzzled.

"Millie, dear, you have a broken shoulder, so Dr. Wade put this big cast on it. She said she might be able to take it off in a few weeks. And you had a bad cut on your ear, so there's a few stitches in it to fix it. That will be better in a few days, and then we can take the bandages off. You'll be able to hear just fine." I explained her injuries to her slowly and calmly. She stared at me wide-eyed, and I could see that she was beginning to remember what had happened to her. Dr. Wade had left the room. I turned to Casey and asked him to go find her.

"Oh, Annie, it was awful." Millie screwed up her face like a newborn and began to cry. She couldn't move to get closer to me. Instead, she reached out to me with her left hand. I leaned over the bed once again and put my arms around her trying to negotiate around the cast. I put my head on the pillow next to hers, kissed her and told her that she was safe and that I would stay with her. I didn't know what else to do for her.

Dr. Wade entered the room, but she didn't interrupt us right away. She knew Millie needed loving physical contact. In a few moments, she put her hand on my back and said, "Millie, we're all here, dear. Do you want to tell us what happened?"

"It was awful!" Millie wailed. She tried to arch her back as her body contorted to rid itself of the memories, but the heavy cast pinned her to the bed.

I moved aside so the doctor could take Millie's hand. "You don't need to talk about it unless you want to, Millie," she said, brushing Millie's hair away from her face.

Even with her eyelids squeezed shut, Millie could not block out the horror of her ordeal. "I can't help it," she sobbed. "I can see my Daddy's eyes, all wild and mean. He came home from work like that." Her eyes flickered open for a second, then closed again. "Mommy and I were sitting at the table eating our supper and Daddy was mad because we didn't wait for him. I tried to leave the table because he scared me." She began to tremble.

Because of Dr. Wade's need to monitor Millie's vital signs, I had moved to the head of the bed. "I'm right here." I assured her, as I caressed her forehead.

Millie opened her eyes again and tilted her head back. "Oh, Annie, I wish my Daddy wasn't so mad all the time."

"So do I, Millie." I looked at Dr. Wade hoping she would suggest that we end this conversation, but she didn't.

"Millie," the doctor said, "do you remember anything else?"

The doctor explained later that she believed Millie would feel better once she had verbalized everything that had happened. Dr. Wade was sure that Millie blamed herself for her father's actions. In a young child's mind, telling the story was, in truth, a confession. The purging, although agonizing, was a necessary process that would not only help Millie recover, but give the rest of us the information we needed to help her.

"Yes, but it's awful," Millie continued. "Daddy kept yelling at me, telling me that if I were a good girl instead of a selfish brat, everything would be better. I don't know what he meant!"

"He was trying to blame you, Millie, for something that was not your fault," Dr. Wade told her.

"But it *was* my fault," she cried. "I spilled my milk when he sat down at the table because I was so nervous." Now she was crying hysterically. Dr. Wade stepped back so I could comfort the child. I held her and kissed her until she calmed down.

"Millie, honey," I said softly, "spilling your milk is not a reason to hit you. Would you hit someone just because they spilled their milk?"

"No," she whined.

"Well then, your father was wrong, very wrong, to hit you. He was wrong to hit you for any reason at all." I was trying to reassure her, but I felt terribly inadequate.

"But Mommy didn't say he was wrong," Millie wailed.

"Did your mother say anything at all?" I asked.

"No." Her voice was so soft that we could barely hear her. "I think she was afraid of him, too."

"Yes, I believe she was, Millie," Dr. Wade said.

Casey stood near the door, his face ash white, listening to this little girl describe the horrible details of the violence inflicted upon her by her father. When I looked again he was gone.

Millie continued to relive her nightmare with her eyes shut, telling us that her father pulled her out of her chair and hit her several times in the face. This had caused the black eyes. Then he dragged her across the kitchen floor, opened the cellar door, and threw her down the stairs. She remembered falling and then a terrible pain in her right shoulder and on the side of her head. She didn't remember landing in a heap on the cellar floor where the paramedics found her. Evidently, when she hit her head on the way down the stairs, she was knocked unconscious, and mercifully had not heard the commotion upstairs when her mother argued with her father. A neighbor told the police that she had heard their loud, angry voices. Only when she heard Mrs. Carter scream did she call the police.

Dr. Wade took Millie's pulse once again and instructed the nurse to inject a mild sedative into the intravenous tube. Millie continued to cry, but soon she was whimpering and then sleeping. Her hair was matted to one side of her face from sweat. Using a damp washcloth, I wiped the tears from her flushed cheeks and brushed her hair away from her face. Then I put my head down on the bedrail and wept.

"Annie, let's go outside," Dr. Wade said gently, putting her hand under my arm to encourage me to go with her.

When we entered the corridor, I looked for Casey. I found him sitting on a bench a few doors down, his face in his hands, sobbing. A chaplain sat beside him holding a cup of coffee.

When I sat down beside him, he leaned back and looked at me. His cheeks were ruddy with anger. "How could anyone do that to that kid, Annie? God, I felt so useless in there. I wanted to help you and help her, but I couldn't move. It was as if someone had nailed my feet to the floor."

"How are you feeling now?" Dr. Wade asked him.

"Better. This kind gentleman brought me a cup of coffee." The chaplain stood, introduced himself and nodded at Dr. Wade. When Casey assured him that he was feeling better, the chaplain left, telling us he would be in his office if we wanted to talk with him. Dr. Wade suggested that we walk to the waiting area where the seating was more comfortable.

The soft sofa cushions cradled our weary bodies as Dr. Wade spoke to us about Millie's care. "You both need to know that Millie has suffered severe trauma, not only to her body, but to her soul. She believes, because her father brainwashed her throughout her entire life, that she is responsible for his actions. When she learns that her mother is dead, she will take on the guilt for that as well. We need to ask a child psychiatrist to see her and begin working with her."

"By all means, Doctor. Do what you think is best for her," Casey said, looking at me. I just nodded in agreement. "Get the best, please. I'll take care of everything. I feel so helpless. At least I can help in this way."

"Casey, your love means a great deal to Millie," Dr. Wade assured him. "As a trusted male figure, you are very important to her recovery. She must have bonded with the two of you when she was on her vacation. She obviously trusts both of you completely and that's very rare in cases like this."

"She's a special little girl," Casey said.

"Now, Annie, how long can the two of you remain here with her?" Dr. Wade asked.

"I can stay until she's ready to travel. I'm hoping the authorities will allow me to take her back to Maine with me then." I was positive about this.

"I'll have to leave at the end of the week," Casey said flatly. I looked at him with surprise, as he had planned to return to California the next day.

"I thought...," I began, but Casey stopped me.

"I'll stay until the end of the week, and to hell with everything else." He turned to face me and took my hand. "You and Millie are the most important people in my life except for my own children, and they are perfectly okay."

"Good," Dr. Wade interrupted, "but you do realize that we're talking weeks before she'll be able to travel and weeks to process all the legal papers. DHS will insist on trying to contact other relatives to see if any of them will want custody."

I just sighed.

"I'm going to write a letter on your behalf, Annie, and give it to my secretary in the morning. You'll have it tomorrow. I'll also call Dr. Green on PEI and ask him to do the same thing for you. I know two people who are children's advocates. If you agree, I'll ask both of them to come to the hospital this week to interview you and to speak to Millie. I know they'll pick up on the same good vibrations that I have and their recommendations will carry a lot of weight with the court when you get to that step." Dr. Wade had assumed a very business like attitude that seemed strange in contrast to her compassionate bedside manner.

"Your help means a great deal to us, Dr. Wade," I said.

"When I see the trust and love in that child's face every time the two of you are with her, well, I don't mind doing everything I can to help." Dr. Wade's face flushed a bit as she thanked us for what we had done for Millie. "Now listen," she said, "I'm gong to keep Millie sedated until tomorrow morning. Her body needs the rest. There's no need for you to stay with her tonight. Why don't the two of you go to the Mariott just down the street? Come back around eight in the morning, and I'll meet you right here. If anything changes, I'll leave instructions for someone to call you there." With that, Dr. Wade hugged me, shook Casey's hand, and left.

We didn't argue with her. Both of us were exhausted. We checked on Millie, mostly because I wanted to be assured that she was asleep, and told the nurse where we would be staying. She promised to call if Millie's condition changed.

"Do you want to get something to eat, Annie?" Casey asked, as we walked out into the fresh air.

"Let's go get a room and rest for a while." My legs and back ached from stress as well as the awkward position I was forced to take to console Millie.

"Okay, Beautiful," he said, feeling better now that he could take charge and make some specific arrangements.

After we had settled in our room at the hotel, I placed two very difficult calls: one to Linda on PEI to update the information I had given her earlier, and the other to Susan. Linda was relieved to hear from us again, but was terribly upset when I told her the rest of the story. In an attempt to cheer us, she explained that Cal and the band had entertained the neighborhood that afternoon before leaving for Maine.

The call to Susan was more difficult, because she didn't know anything about our trip to New York. When I started to tell her about Millie's injuries, I broke down and couldn't continue. Casey took the phone, explained everything, and assured Susan that he was taking good care of me. He promised that I would call her the next morning. When he hung up, he insisted that I lie down to rest.

While I was resting, Casey called the airport to check with Cal's pilot about our luggage. We had been in such a hurry to get to the hospital, that we left it on the plane. Cal's pilot had already left for Maine, but the airport official assured Casey that the luggage, stored in his office, would be sent over to the hotel. After calling several rental agencies, Casey found an apartment for me to live in while I waited for Millie to heal. Satisfied that he had done everything he could for the moment, he lay down beside me and fell asleep.

Exhausted, we slept soundly for a few hours, but the unfamiliar sounds of closing doors and loud voices in the hallway outside our room woke us around nine. Casey yawned and stretched as he sat on the side of the bed. "Let's call the hospital and check on Millie and then go grab a bite to eat," he suggested.

The resident on call for the night assured us positively that Millie would sleep until the next morning. He also told us that Dr. Wade had made arrangements for a child psychiatrist to see Millie at nine. She wanted all of us there when she told Millie about her mother.

Dinner was a fiasco. Casey tried to help me relax by taking me to a lovely, quiet restaurant on the top floor of the hotel where they served a wonderful late supper of seafood crepes with a light salad and wine, but I couldn't eat any of it. Everything tasted like metal, and all I could do was cry.

Casey ate some of his meal and then suggested that we go back to our room to get a good night's rest. When we opened the door, we found our luggage neatly arranged on a stand beside the bathroom door. Linda's basket had been placed on the bureau, the pink rose wilted and limp from the long day's journey.

When I opened my suitcase, the familiar smell of the cottage danced in the air, reminding me of the peace we had found there. The soft texture of my pajamas caressed my body. Casey held me all night, whispering words of love in my ear whenever I woke, crying for Millie and for all the children who had no one to hold them or protect them.

In the early morning, as the sun poured through the windows, we promised each other that we would love and take care of Millie for the rest of her life. In that commitment, we both knew that Millie was the answer to the question we had been struggling with since we met. Millie was going to be the center of our love, the person who would assure us that we would stay connected throughout time. In that understanding, we knew that we would find a way to share our lives and our love.

Epilogue

Prince Edward Island, Canada   October – 1993

There is a cool breeze blowing across the water from the west, pushing low, rolling waves toward the red shoreline. The sky is as blue as I've ever seen it. Soft clouds float along the horizon. Despite the time of year, the afternoon sun has warmth in it, a warmth that penetrates deep into my soul. Now that we're back on the Island, energy and life have been renewed.

♪♪♪

Millie, Susan and I returned to the Island late last night. True to her word, Linda had closed up the cottage in August. Susan and I fumbled with flashlights until we found the main power switch. We unpacked the car, made up the bed and the sofa, and fell into them like three rag dolls that had lost their stuffing. All of us slept well for the first time in months.

Ed dropped by this morning to make sure the gas and water were working properly and to inquire about Millie. He was surprised to see her with me.

But Millie is with me. The last few months have proven very difficult for all of us. Millie's physical therapy has been quite successful, but her emotional therapy will take much longer. She reacted as Dr. Wade had feared, taking the blame for her mother's death. She didn't speak for three days.

I stayed with her, sleeping in her room for three weeks, until the cast could be removed and until she began to talk and act more like herself. The child psychiatrist that Dr. Wade had recommended worked with her every day. In the third week, she introduced Millie to a group of children who were processing similar issues.

Millie didn't like the group at first, but after a week she settled down and was eager to go to see her new friends each day. She made two good friends there, Allison and Lisa.

When we moved from the hospital to the apartment that Casey had rented for us, Susan came to Albany to spend that first week with us. I slept the clock around the first day. Susan took Millie back to the hospital for both her physical therapy and her group session. I don't know what I would have done without her help.

The Children's Advocate Group interviewed both Casey and me before he left for California and prepared a report for the court. We had not seen it, but Dr. Wade read it and told me not to worry about anything. Three weeks later, DHS gave me temporary custody of Millie while they searched for other members of her family. Before we left for Maine, they had found two maiden aunts in Illinois and were waiting for their reply to our inquiry. I pray every day that the paperwork granting me permanent custody will be processed soon. Once that is approved, I will talk with Millie about adoption. She's not emotionally strong enough now for that conversation.

♪♪♪

Casey stayed with us that first week. Millie's reaction to her mother's death was heartbreaking for all of us. She cried or whimpered almost constantly. We took turns holding her and reading to her.

When the time came for Casey to leave, Dr. Wade insisted that I go to the airport with him, making arrangements for a nurse to stay with Millie while I was gone.

He held me in a bear hug for several minutes, kissed me hard, turned and walked quickly down the entrance ramp to the plane. My heart was breaking as I watched through the large windows in the waiting area until the plane had taken off and become a black speck in the distant sky. I'm not sure how long I stood there, my hands gripping the wooden rail in front of me. I don't remember riding back to the hospital.

When I did return, Dr. Wade had left instructions at the nurses' station asking that I come to her office. I remember the feeling of panic as I walked down the long hall to her door. And I remember the instant relief as the peace of her office embraced me. She sat with me for a very long time while I cried and released the awful stress of the last week. I'll never forget her kindness and friendship.

Casey called me every morning and every night while Millie and I were in the hospital. Once we moved to the apartment, his calls became less frequent. Over the last few weeks, we've heard from him only twice. I miss him terribly. The beautiful cards and flowers that he has sent to both Millie and me have been supportive and loving, but I miss his voice.

Now, here we are back on PEI, the wondrous, safe place where Millie's trust for both Casey and me was born. Over the last eight weeks Millie's physical injuries have healed wonderfully. Her broken bones have mended, and the therapy has helped her regain some of her strength. Her ear healed nicely, leaving just a small scar that is only noticeable when she wears her hair pulled back in pigtails.

Her emotional injuries will take longer to heal, but since we returned to Maine and now to the Island, Millie has begun to act more like the leprechaun I first met earlier in the summer, dancing and singing on the beach in her rainbow shirt and blue shorts. She'll probably never be that same little girl again, but I pray that she will feel that free again.

♪♪♪

"Annie!" Susan's call from inside the cottage startled me. "Annie," she said again, as she pushed the screen door open, "do you want some lunch?"

"Not right now, thanks. I'm just enjoying watching Millie play down there. Look at her," I said smiling.

Millie's yellow windbreaker was the only bright color in the panorama that stretched out before us. She was throwing a stick to a very frisky Irish setter. Every once in a while the wind would bring her delightful squeal up to us. Each time we heard it, Susan and I laughed.

"She's quite a kid, Annie," Susan said, sitting at the picnic table. "Gosh, we're so lucky to have this warm weather."

She was right. Although it was late October, the temperature was unusually comfortable. Earlier this morning, Susan and I had struggled with the Morris chair, tipping it through the door onto the deck. Leaning back into its comfortable cushions, I closed my eyes, almost believing we had been transported back to August. The warmth of the sun soaked into my soul and stirred up memories of Linda's family reunion, Casey's and my ride along the shore road on the antique two-seater, and our lobster dinner with Millie.

"I still can't believe that that dog's name is Casey," Susan laughed, interrupting my daydream.

We had found a two-year-old mixed breed Irish Setter and Golden Retriever at a shelter in Portland. Her original owners had neglected her, but she and Millie fell in love instantly, especially when Millie learned her name was Casey.

"Neither can I, but that dog has done wonders for her," I said, as I looked out across the beach. The yellow windbreaker billowed behind her like a pillowcase full of air as Millie chased the dog, grabbed the stick from its mouth, and threw it again.

"I think they're good for each other," Susan offered.

"Yes, they are. They both have so much love to give. It's definitely a good match." I settled back in the chair and closed my eyes.

"When do you expect to hear that they've granted you permanent custody?" Susan asked me.

"Not until the first of the year," I said with my eyes closed. "I had hoped that we would be able to celebrate over Christmas, but the last letter indicated that there might be a delay."

"Anything that might cause a problem?" Susan asked.

"No. The lawyer's secretary was in a terrible accident and isn't expected to return to work until December. He's lost without her," I explained.

"But you and Millie shouldn't have to suffer because of it," Susan said sharply.

"As long as I know everything is moving in the right direction, I can be patient." The wind changed direction bringing with it the cool air of autumn. I reached for the sweater at my side and draped it over my shoulders.

"Annie, you're the most patient person I know. I don't know how you do it," Susan sighed.

"I do it with a lot of prayer. These last two months have been a living hell. Waiting another month or two for some paperwork to be processed is a piece of cake in comparison. The two aunts that DHS found have both signed agreements to allow me to keep Millie. That was the worst hurdle."

"There isn't anyone else that might come out of the woodwork?" Susan asked, as she passed me a dish of M&M's.

"No. The two aunts have sworn in court that there's no one else who could legally stop the process." Feeling a chill, I pulled the sweater tighter around my shoulders.

"I was surprised that her father agreed so easily," she said.

"I was, too. He cried and apologized in front of the judge, saying he loved his daughter, but he knew she would be better cared for with me. It's a good thing Millie wasn't there to see it. I think he was only trying to make things easier on himself," I said bitterly.

"Annie, he can't do that. He murdered his wife and nearly murdered his daughter. They're not going to let him out for a very long time." Susan's cheeks glowed with anger as she picked through the dish of candy looking for the green pieces. She popped one in her mouth, looked up and changed the subject. "When was the last time you spoke with Casey?" she asked.

"He called last Wednesday. He's been putting together the details for the movie they plan to film near Lake Ontario. Evidently there have been casting problems that have caused major delays. And problems in the movie business, as Casey says, are expensive." I closed my eyes to picture him sitting beside me, gently holding me as we enjoyed the sun and the sounds of the ocean.

"Does he know that we're on the Island?" Susan asked.

"Hmmmm?" I mumbled, still clinging to the mental daydream.

"Does Casey know that we're here?" Susan repeated.

I stood up and went to the railing to check on Millie. "Yes," I said, picking up the binoculars. "I asked him if he could join us, but he said that the recent problems had to take priority. Millie and I will see him in December when we go to Ontario. We're going to spend a week with him there learning all about the movie business. Linda and Barry have asked us all to come to Smith Falls to celebrate Christmas with them."

"Casey is going to be able to go with you to Smith Falls? That's wonderful, Annie!" Susan exclaimed.

"I can't wait! But I've got an awful lot to do when we go home to Maine next week. We really shouldn't have come up here so late in the year, but Dr. Wade thought a week on the Island would be good for both of us. By the looks of Millie down there playing with that dog, she was right."

I sighed as I watched her throw the stick for what seemed the hundredth time. She had a hard time tossing it very far with her right arm, but it was good therapy for her.

"Millie needs a tutor," I continued to ramble. "She's so far behind now in relation to all the other kids that I've decided to wait until after the Christmas holidays to enter her in school. My hope is that with a tutor she'll be able to catch up."

"Isn't that putting an awful lot of stress on her and you, too?" Susan asked.

I set the binoculars on the railing and turned to face Susan. "I don't think so. The school in New York sent her records. She's a bright child with an intelligence quotient that's high for her age. She'll meet a lot of the kids in her grade at Sunday school when we go back to Maine. With the tutor and their help, I think we can get her up to speed by January."

Susan stood and joined me at the railing, putting her arm around my waist. "Annie, I'm so proud of you. Do you realize what you've done for that kid?"

"She's done a lot for me as well, Susan. God has given us to each other. I can't imagine loving her any more or any differently if she were my own flesh and blood."

A movement on the beach caught my eye. Millie was jumping up and down pointing down the beach toward the Lighthouse. I couldn't hear what she was saying, but I looked in that direction. As I turned my head, Millie began to run toward a tall man wearing a red windbreaker who was walking toward her.

I reached for the binoculars to get a better look, but in my heart I knew who he was. And for the first time in a very long time, I felt the peace of being home.

About the Author

Ann Purdy was born in Maine and grew up in Portland. She received a master's degree in divinity from Bangor Theological Seminary. Sing a New Song is her first novel. Ann and her husband live and work in Maine. Both of their family trees are planted securely in Prince Edward Island's red soil.

♪♪♪